In the Days of the Comet

The end of the world..or a new beginning?

At first, the comet was just a tiny speck in the sky—people scarcely noticed it among the countless other specks. But swiftly, without a sound, the comet grew inevitably brighter—brighter than the brightest star. As people continued their lives on earth, the comet came closer, grew bigger, filled the sky. Until finally, one day, a curtain of green mist closed down upon the world, and the earth ceased to be...for a time.

H.G. Wells wrote the science-fiction thriller, *In the Days of the Comet,* in 1906. It is as timely and thought-provoking today as when it first was published.

In the Days of the Comet

H. G. Wells

A WATERMILL CLASSIC

This special and unabridged *Watermill Classic* edition has been completely reset in a size and style designed for easy reading. Format, type, composition, and design of this book are the exclusive property of Watermill Press, Mahwah, New Jersey.

Printed in the United States of America.

ISBN 0-89375-704-7

Contents

In the Days of the Comet

Prologue

The Man Who Wrote in the Tower

I saw a gray-haired man, a figure of hale age, sitting at a desk and writing.

He seemed to be in a room in a tower, very high so that through the tall window on his left one perceived only distances, a remote horizon of sea, a headland and that vague haze and glitter in the sunset that many miles away marks a city. All the appointments of this room were orderly and beautiful, and in some subtle quality, in this small difference and that, new to me and strange. They were in no fashion I could name, and the simple costume the man wore suggested neither period nor country. It might, I thought, be the Happy Future, or Utopia, or the Land of Simple Dreams; an errant mote of memory, Henry James's phrase and story of "The Great Good Place," twinkled across my mind, and passed and left no light.

The man I saw wrote with a thing like a fountain pen, a modern touch that prohibited any historical retrospection, and as he finished each sheet, writing in an easy flowing hand, he added it to a growing pile upon a graceful little table under the window. His last done sheets lay loose, partly covering others that were clipped together into fascicles.

Clearly he was unaware of my presence, and I stood waiting until his pen should come to a pause. Old as he certainly was he wrote with a steady hand...

I discovered that a concave speculum hung slantingly high over his head; a movement in this caught my attention sharply, and I looked up to see, distorted and made fantastic but bright and beautifully colored, the magnified, reflected, evasive rendering of a palace, of a terrace, of the vista of a great roadway with many people, people exaggerated, impossible-looking because of the curvature of the mirror, going to and fro. I turned my head quickly that I might see more clearly through the window behind me, but it was too high for me to survey this nearer scene directly, and after a momentary pause I came back to that distorting mirror again.

But now the writer was leaning back in his chair. He put down his pen and sighed the half-resentful sigh—"ah! you work, you! how you gratify and tire me!"—of a man who has been writing to his satisfaction.

"What is this place?" I asked. "And who are you?"

He looked around with the quick movement of surprise.

"What is this place?" I repeated. "And where am I?"

He regarded me steadfastly for a moment under his wrinkled brows, and then his expression softened to a smile. He pointed to a chair beside the table. "I am writing," he said.

"About this?"

"About the Change."

I sat down. It was a very comfortable chair, and well placed under the light.

"If you would like to read—" he said.

I indicated the manuscript. "This explains?" I asked.

"That explains," he answered.

He drew a fresh sheet of paper toward him as he looked at me.

I glanced from him about his apartment and back to the little table. A fascicle marked very distinctly "1" caught my attention, and I took it up. I smiled in his friendly eyes. "Very well," said I, suddenly at my ease, and he nodded and went on writing. And in a mood between confidence and curiosity, I began to read.

This is the story that happy, active-looking old man in that pleasant place had written.

BOOK I *THE COMET*

Chapter 1

Dust in the Shadows

1

I have set myself to write the story of the Great Change, so far as it has affected my own life and the lives of one or two people closely connected with me, primarily to please myself.

Long ago, in my crude unhappy youth, I conceived the desire of writing a book. To scribble secretly and dream of authorship was one of my chief alleviations, and I read with a sympathetic envy every scrap I could get about the world of literature and the lives of literary people. It is something, even amidst this present happiness, to find leisure and opportunity to take up and partially realize these old and hopeless dreams. But that alone, in a world where so much of vivid and increasing interest presents itself to be done, even by an old man, would not, I think, suffice to set me at this desk. I find some such recapitulation of my past as this will involve, is becoming necessary to my own secure mental continuity. The passage of years brings a man at last to retrospection; at seventy-two one's youth is far more important than it was at forty. And I am out of touch with my youth. The old life seems so cut off from the new, so alien and so unreasonable, that at times I find it bordering upon the incredible. The data have gone, the buildings and places. I stopped dead the other afternoon in my walk across the moor, where once the dismal outskirts of Swathinglea straggled towards Leet, and asked, "Was it here indeed that I crouched among the weeds and refuse and broken crockery and loaded my revolver ready for murder? Did ever such a thing happen in my life? Was such a mood and thought and intention ever possible to me? Rather, has not some queer nightmare spirit out of dreamland slipped a pseudo-memory into the records of my vanished life?" There must be many alive still who have the same perplexities. And I think too that those who are now growing up to take our places in the great enterprise of mankind, will need many such narratives as mine for even the most partial conception of the old world of shadows that came before our day. It chances too that my case is fairly typical of the Change; I was caught midway in a gust of passion; and a curious accident put me for a time in the very nucleus of the new order...

My memory takes me back across the interval of fifty years to a little ill-lit room with a sash window open to a starry sky, and instantly there returns to me the characteristic smell of that room, the penetrating odor of an ill-trimmed lamp, burning cheap paraffin. Lighting by electricity had then been perfected for fifteen years, but still the larger portion of the world used these lamps. All this first scene will go, in my mind at least, to that olfactory accompaniment. That was the evening smell of the room. By day it had a more subtle aroma, a closeness, a peculiar sort of faint pungency that I associate—I know not why—with dust.

Let me describe this room to you in detail. It was perhaps eight feet by seven in area and rather higher than either of these dimensions; the ceiling was of plaster, cracked and bulging in places, gray with the soot of the lamp, and in one place discolored by a system of yellow and olive-green stains caused by the percolation of damp from above. The walls were covered with dun-colored paper, upon which had been printed in oblique reiteration a crimson shape, something of the nature of a curly ostrich feather, or an acanthus flower, that had in its less faded moments a sort of dingy gaiety. There were several big plaster-rimmed wounds in this, caused by Parload's ineffectual attempts to get nails into the wall, whereby there might hang pictures. One nail had hit between two bricks and got home, and from this depended, sustained a little insecurely by frayed and knotted blind cord, Parload's hanging bookshelves, planks painted over with a treacly blue enamel and further decorated by a fringe of pinked American cloth insecurely fixed by tacks. Below this was a little table that behaved with a mulish vindictiveness to any knee that was thrust beneath it suddenly; it was covered with a cloth whose pattern of red and black had been rendered less monotonous by the accidents of Parload's versatile ink bottle, and on it, *leitmotif* of the whole, stood and stank the lamp. This lamp, you must understand, was of some whitish translucent substance that was neither china nor glass; it had a shade of the same substance, a shade that did not protect the eyes of a reader in any measure; and it seemed admirably adapted to bring into pitiless prominence the fact that, after the lamp's trimming, dust and paraffin had been smeared over its exterior with a reckless generosity.

The uneven floor boards of this apartment were covered with scratched enamel of chocolate hue, on which a small island of frayed carpet dimly blossomed in the dust and shadows.

There was a very small grate, made of cast iron in one piece and painted buff, and a still smaller misfit of a cast-iron fender that confessed the gray stone of the hearth. No fire was laid, only a few scraps of torn paper and the bowl of a broken corncob pipe were visible behind the bars, and in the corner and rather thrust away was an angular japanned coal box with a damaged hinge. It was the custom in those days to warm every room separately from a separate fireplace, more prolific of dirt than heat, and the rickety sash window, the small chimney, and the loose-fitting door were expected to organize the ventilation of the room among themselves without any further direction.

Parload's truckle bed hid its gray sheets beneath an old patchwork counterpane on one side of the room, and veiled his boxes and suchlike oddments, and invading the two corners of the window were an old whatnot and the washhand stand, on which were distributed the simple appliances of his toilet.

This washhand stand had been made of deal by someone with an excess of turnery appliances in a hurry, who had tried to distract attention from the rough economies of his workmanship by an arresting ornamentation of blobs and bulbs upon the joints and legs. Apparently the piece had then been placed in the hands of some person of infinite leisure equipped with a pot of ocherous paint, varnish, and a set of flexible combs. This person had first painted the article, then, I fancy, smeared it with varnish, and then sat down to work with the combs to streak and comb the varnish into a weird imitation of the grain of some nightmare timber. The washhand stand so made had evidently had a prolonged career of violent use, had been chipped, kicked, splintered, punched, stained, scorched, hammered, desiccated, damped, and defiled, had met indeed with almost every possible adventure except a conflagration or a scrubbing, until at last it had come to this high refuge of Parload's attic to sustain the simple requirements of Parload's personal cleanliness. There were, in chief, a basin and a jug of water and a slop pail of tin, and, further, a piece of yellow soap in a tray, a toothbrush, a rat-tailed shaving brush, one huckaback towel, and one or two other minor articles. In those days only very prosperous people had more than such an equipage, and it is to be remarked that every drop of water Parload used had to be carried by an unfortunate servant girl—the "slavey," Parload called her—up from the basement to the top of the house and subsequently down again. Already we begin to forget how modern an invention is personal cleanliness. It is a fact that Parload had never stripped for a swim in his life; never had a simultaneous bath all over his body since his childhood. Not one in fifty of us did in the days of which I am telling you.

A chest, also singularly grained and streaked, of two large and two small drawers, held Parload's reserve of garments, and pegs on the door carried his two hats and completed this inventory of a "bed-sitting-room" as I knew it before the Change. But I had forgotten—there was also a chair with a "squab" that apologized inadequately for the defects of its cane seat. I forgot that for the moment because I was sitting on the chair on the occasion that best begins this story.

I have described Parload's room with such particularity because it will help you to understand the key in which my earlier chapters are written, but you must not imagine that this singular equipment or the smell of the lamp engaged my attention at that time to the slightest degree. I took all this grimy unpleasantness as if it were the most natural and proper setting for existence imaginable. It was the world as I knew it. My mind was entirely occupied then by graver and intenser matters, and it is only now in the distant retrospect that I see these details of environment as being remarkable, as significant, as indeed obviously the outward visible manifestations of the old world disorder in our hearts.

2

Parload stood at the open window, opera glass in hand, and sought and found and was uncertain about and lost again, the new comet.

I thought the comet no more than a nuisance then because I wanted to talk of other matters. But Parload was full of it. My head was hot, I was feverish with interlacing annoyances and bitterness, I wanted to open my heart to him—at least I wanted to relieve my heart by some romantic rendering of my troubles—and I gave but little heed to the things he told me. It was the first time I had heard of this new speck among the countless specks of heaven, and I did not care if I never heard of the thing again.

We were two youths much of an age together; Parload was two and twenty, and eight months older than I. He was —I think his proper definition was "engrossing clerk" to a little solicitor in Overcastle, while I was third in the office staff of Rawdon's pot-bank in Clayton. We had met first in the "Parliament" of the Young Men's Christian Association of Swathinglea; we had found we attended simultaneous classes in Overcastle, he in science and I in shorthand, and had started a practice of walking home together, and so our friendship came into being. (Swathinglea, Clayton, and Overcastle were contiguous towns, I should mention, in the great industrial area of the Midlands.) We had shared each other's secret of religious doubt, we had confided to one another a common interest in socialism, he had come twice to supper at my mother's on a Sunday night, and I was free of his apartment. He was then a tall, flaxen-haired, gawky youth, with a disproportionate development of neck and wrist, and capable of vast enthusiasm; he gave two evenings a week to the evening classes of the organized science school in Overcastle, physiography was his favorite "subject," and through this insidious opening of his mind the wonder of outer space had come to take possession of his soul. He had commandeered an old opera glass from his uncle who farmed at Leet over the moors, he had bought a cheap paper planisphere and *Whitaker's Almanack,* and for a time day and moonlight were mere blank interruptions to the one satisfactory reality in his life—stargazing. It was the deeps that had seized him, the immensities, and the mysterious possibilities that might float unlit in that unplumbed abyss. With infinite labor and the help of a very precise article in *The Heavens,* a little monthly magazine that catered for those who were under this obsession, he had at last got his opera glass upon the new visitor to our system from outer space. He gazed in a sort of rapture upon that quivering little smudge of light among the shining pinpoints—and gazed. My troubles had to wait for him.

"Wonderful," he sighed, and then as though his first emphasis did not satisfy him, "wonderful!"

He turned to me. "Wouldn't you like to see?"

I had to look, and then I had to listen, how that this scarce-visible intruder was to be, was presently to be, one of the largest comets this world had ever seen, how that its course must bring it within at most—so many score of millions of miles from the earth, a mere step, Parload seemed to think that; how that the spectroscope was already sounding its chemical secrets, perplexed by the unprecedented band in the green, how it was even now being photographed in the very act of unwinding—in an unusual direction—a sunward tail (which presently it wound up again), and all the while in a sort of undertow I was thinking first of Nettie Stuart and the letter she had just written me, and then of old Rawdon's detestable face as I had seen it that afternoon. Now I planned answers to Nettie and now belated repartees to my employer, and then again "Nettie" was blazing all across the background of my thoughts...

Nettie Stuart was daughter of the head gardener of the rich Mr. Verrall's widow, and she and I had kissed and become sweethearts before we were eighteen years old. My mother and hers were second cousins and old schoolfellows, and though my mother had been widowed untimely by a train accident, and had been reduced to letting lodgings (she was the Clayton curate's landlady), a position esteemed much lower than that of Mrs. Stuart, a kindly custom of occasional visits to the gardener's cottage at Checkshill Towers still kept the friends in touch. Commonly I went with her. And I remember it was in the dusk of one bright evening in July, one of those long golden evenings that do not so much give way to night as admit at last, upon courtesy, the moon and a choice retinue of stars, that Nettie and I, at the pond of goldfish where the yew-bordered walks converged, made our shy beginners' vow. I remember still—something will always stir in me at that memory—the tremulous emotion of that adventure. Nettie was dressed in white, her hair went off in waves of soft darkness from above her dark shining eyes; there was a little necklace of pearls about her sweetly modeled neck, and a little coin of gold that nestled in her throat. I kissed her half-reluctant lips, and for three years of my life thereafter—nay! I almost think for all the rest of her life and mine—I could have died for her sake.

You must understand—and every year it becomes increasingly difficult to understand—how entirely different the world was then from what it is now. It was a dark world; it was full of preventable disorder, preventable diseases, and preventable pain, of harshness and stupid unpremeditated cruelties, but yet, it may be even by virtue of the general darkness, there were moments of a rare and evanescent beauty that seem no longer possible in my experience. The great Change has come forevermore, happiness and beauty are our atmosphere, there is peace on earth and good will to all men. None would dare to dream of returning to the sorrows of the former time, and yet that misery was pierced, ever and again its gray curtain was stabbed through and through by joys of an intensity, by perceptions of a keenness that it seems to me are now altogether gone out of life. Is it the Change, I wonder, that has robbed life of its extremes, or is it perhaps only this, that youth has left me—even the strength of middle years leaves me now—and taken its despairs and raptures, leaving me judgment perhaps, sympathy, memories?

I cannot tell. One would need to be young now and to have been young then as well, to decide that impossible problem.

Perhaps a cool observer even in the old days would have found little beauty in our grouping. I have our two photographs at hand in this bureau as I write, and they show me a gawky youth in ill-fitting ready-made clothing, and Nettie—indeed Nettie is badly dressed, and her attitude is more than a little stiff; but I can see her through the picture, and her living brightness and something of that mystery of charm she had for me, comes back again to my mind. Her face has triumphed over the photographer—or I would long ago have cast this picture away.

The reality of beauty yields itself to no words. I wish that I had the sister art and could draw in my margin something that escapes description. There was a sort of gravity in her eyes. There was something, a matter of the minutest difference, about her upper lip so that her mouth closed sweetly and broke very sweetly to a smile. That grave, sweet smile!

After we had kissed and decided not to tell our parents for a while of the irrevocable choice we had made, the time came for us to part, shyly and before others, and I and my mother went off back across the moonlit park—the bracken thickets rustling with startled deer—to the railway station at Checkshill and so to our dingy basement in Clayton, and I saw no more of Nettie—except that I saw her in my thoughts—for nearly a year. But at our next meeting it was decided that we must correspond, and this we did with much elaboration of secrecy, for Nettie would have no one at home, not even her only sister, know of her attachment. So I had to send my precious documents sealed and under cover by way of a confidential schoolfellow of hers who lived near London...I could write that address down now, though house and street and suburb have gone beyond any man's tracing.

Our correspondence began our estrangement, because for the first time we came into more than sensuous contact and our minds sought expression.

Now you must understand that the world of thought in those days was in the strangest condition, it was choked with obsolete inadequate formulae, it was tortuous to a mazelike degree with secondary contrivances and adaptions, suppressions, conventions, and subterfuges. Base immediacies fouled the truth on every man's lips. I was brought up by my mother in a quaint old-fashioned narrow faith in certain religious formulae, certain rules of conduct, certain conceptions of social and political order, that had no more relevance to the realities and needs of everyday contemporary life than if they were clean linen that had been put away with lavender in a drawer. Indeed, her religion did actually smell of lavender; on Sundays she put away all the things of reality, the garments and even the furnishings of every day, hid her hands, that were gnarled and sometimes chapped with scrubbing, in black, carefully mended gloves, assumed her old black silk dress and bonnet and took me, unnaturally clean and sweet also, to church. There we sang and bowed and heard sonorous prayers and joined in sonorous responses, and rose with a congregational sigh refreshed and relieved when the doxology, with its opening "Now to God the Father, God the Son," bowed out the tame, brief sermon. There was a hell in that religion of my mother's, a red-haired hell of curly flames that had once been very terrible; there was a devil, who was also *ex officio* the British King's enemy, and much denunciation of the wicked lusts of the flesh; we were expected to believe that most of our poor unhappy world was to atone for its muddle and trouble here by suffering exquisite torments for ever after, world without end, Amen. But indeed those curly flames looked rather jolly. The whole thing had been mellowed and faded into a gentle unreality long before my time; if it had much terror even in my childhood I have forgotten it, it was not so terrible as the giant who was killed by the Beanstalk, and I see it all now as a setting for my poor old mother's worn and grimy face, and almost lovingly as a part of her. And Mr. Gabbitas, our plump little lodger, strangely transformed in his vestments and lifting his voice manfully to the quality of those Elizabethan prayers, seemed, I think, to give her a special and peculiar interest with God. She radiated her own tremulous gentleness upon Him, and redeemed Him from all the implications of vindictive theologians; she was in truth, had I but perceived it, the effectual answer to all she would have taught me.

So I see it now, but there is something harsh in the earnest intensity of youth, and having at first taken all these things quite seriously, the fiery hell and God's vindictiveness at any neglect, as though they were as much a matter of fact as Bladden's ironworks and Rawdon's potbank, I presently with an equal seriousness flung them out of my mind again.

Mr. Gabbitas, you see, did sometimes, as the phrase went, "take notice" of me. He had induced me to go on reading after I left school, and with the best intentions in the world and to anticipate the poison of the times, he had lent me Burble's "Skepticism Answered," and drawn my attention to the library of the Institute in Clayton.

The excellent Burble was a great shock to me. It seemed clear from his answers to the skeptic that the case for doctrinal orthodoxy and all that faded and by no means awful hereafter, which I had hitherto accepted as I accepted the sun, was an extremely poor one, and to hammer home that idea the first book I got from the Institute happened to be an American edition of the collected works of Shelley, his gassy prose as well as his atmospheric verse. I was soon ripe for blatant unbelief. And at the Young Men's Christian Association I presently made the acquaintance of Parload, who told me, under promises of the most sinister secrecy, that he was "a Socialist out and out." He lent me several copies of a periodical with the clamant title of *The Clarion,* which was just taking up a crusade against the accepted religion. The adolescent years of any fairly intelligent youth lie open, and will always lie healthily open, to the contagion of philosophical doubts, of scorns and new ideas, and I will confess I had the fever of that phase badly. Doubt, I say, but it was not so much doubt—which is a complex thing—as startled emphatic denial. "Have I believed *this!*" And I was also, you must remember, just beginning love letters to Nettie.

We live now in these days, when the Great Change has been in most things accomplished, in a time when everyone is being educated to a sort of intellectual gentleness, a gentleness that abates nothing from our vigor, and it is hard to understand the stifled and struggling manner in which my generation of common young men did its thinking. To think at all about certain questions was an act of rebellion that set one oscillating between the furtive and the defiant. People begin to find Shelley—for all his melody—noisy and ill conditioned now because his Anarchs have vanished, yet there was a time when novel thought *had* to go to that tune of breaking glass. It becomes a little difficult to imagine the yeasty state of mind, the disposition to shout and say, "Yah!" at constituted authority, to sustain a persistent note of provocation such as we raw youngsters displayed. I began to read with avidity such writing as Carlyle, Browning, and Heine have left for the perplexity of posterity, and not only to read and admire but to imitate. My letters to Nettie, after one or two genuinely intended displays of perfervid tenderness, broke out toward theology, sociology, and the cosmos in turgid and startling expressions. No doubt they puzzled her extremely.

I retain the keenest sympathy and something inexplicably near to envy for my own departed youth, but I should find it difficult to maintain my case against anyone who would condemn me altogether as having been a very silly, posturing, emotional hobbledehoy indeed and quite like my faded photograph. And when I try to recall what exactly must have been the quality and tenor of my more sustained efforts to write memorably to my sweetheart, I confess I shiver...Yet I wish they were not all destroyed.

Her letters to me were simple enough, written in a roundish, unformed hand and badly phrased. Her first two or three showed a shy pleasure in the use of the word "dear," and I remember being first puzzled and then, when I understood, delighted, because she had written "Willie *asthore*" under my name. "Asthore," I gathered, meant "darling." But when the evidences of my fermentation began, her answers were less happy.

I will not weary you with the story of how we quarreled in our silly youthful way, and how I went the next Sunday, all uninvited, to Checkshill, and made it worse, and how afterward I wrote a letter that she thought was "lovely," and mended the matter. Nor will I tell of all our subsequent fluctuations of misunderstanding. Always I was the offender and the final penitent until this last trouble that was now beginning; and in between we had some tender near moments, and I loved her very greatly. There was this misfortune in the business, that in the darkness, and alone, I thought with great intensity of her, of her eyes, of her touch, of her sweet and delightful presence, but when I sat down to write I thought of Shelley and Burns and myself, and other such irrelevant matters. When one is in love, in this fermenting way, it is harder to make love than it is when one does not love at all. And as for Nettie, she loved, I know, not me but those gentle mysteries. It was not my voice should rouse her dreams to passion...So our letters continued to jar. Then suddenly she wrote me one doubting whether she could ever care for anyone who was a Socialist and did not believe in Church, and then hard upon it came another note with unexpected novelties of phrasing. She thought we were not suited to each other, we differed so in tastes and ideas, she had long thought of releasing me from our engagement. In fact, though I really did not apprehend it fully at the first shock, I was dismissed. Her letter had reached me when I came home after old Rawdon's none too civil refusal to raise my wages. On this particular evening of which I write, therefore, I was in a state of feverish adjustment to two new and amazing, two nearly overwhelming facts, that I was neither indispensable to Nettie nor at Rawdon's. And to talk of comets!

Where did I stand?

I had grown so accustomed to think of Nettie as inseparably mine—the whole tradition of "true love" pointed me to that—that for her to face about with these precise small phrases toward abandonment, after we had kissed and whispered and come so close in the little adventurous familiarities of the young, shocked me profoundly. I! I! And Rawdon didn't find me indispensable either. I felt I was suddenly repudiated by the universe and threatened with effacement, that in some positive and emphatic way I must at once assert myself. There was no balm in the religion I had learned, or in the irreligion I had adopted, for wounded self-love.

Should I fling up Rawdon's place at once and then in some extraordinary, swift manner make the fortune of Frobisher's adjacent and closely competitive pot-bank?

The first part of that program, at any rate, would be easy of accomplishment, to go to Rawdon and say, "You will hear from me again," but for the rest, Frobisher might fail me. That, however, was a secondary issue. The predominant affair was with Nettie. I found my mind thick-shot with flying fragments of rhetoric that might be of service in the letter I would write her. Scorn, irony, tenderness—what was it to be?...

"Bother!" said Parload, suddenly.

"What?" said I.

"They're firing up at Bladden's ironworks, and the smoke comes right across my bit of sky."

The interruption came just as I was ripe to discharge my thoughts upon him.

"Parload," said I, "very likely I shall have to leave all this. Old Rawdon won't give me a raise in my wages, and after having asked I don't think I can stand going on upon the old terms anymore. See? So I may have to clear out of Clayton for good and all."

That made Parload put down the opera glass and look at me.

"It's a bad time to change just now," he said after a little pause.

Rawdon had said as much, in a less agreeable tone.

But with Parload I felt always a disposition to the heroic note. "I'm tired," I said, "of humdrum drudgery for other men. One may as well starve one's body out of a place as to starve one's soul in one."

"I don't know about that altogether," began Parload, slowly...

And with that we began one of our interminable conversations, one of those long, wandering, intensely generalizing, diffusely personal talks that will be dear to the hearts of intelligent youths until the world comes to an end. The Change has not abolished that, anyhow.

It would be an incredible feat of memory for me now to recall all that meandering haze of words, indeed I recall scarcely any of it, though its circumstances and atmosphere stand out, a sharp, clear picture in my mind. I posed after my manner and behaved very foolishly no doubt, a wounded, smarting egotist, and Parload played his part of the philosopher preoccupied with the deeps.

We were presently abroad, walking through the warm summer's night and talking all the more freely for that. But one thing that I said I can remember. "I wish at times," said I, with a gesture at the heavens, "that comet of yours or some such thing would indeed strike this world—and wipe us all away, strikes, wars, tumults, loves, jealousies, and all the wretchedness of life!"

"Ah!" said Parload, and the thought seemed to hang about him.

"It could only add to the miseries of life," he said irrelevantly, when presently I was discoursing of other things.

"What would?"

"Collision with a comet. It would only throw things back. It would only make what was left of life more savage than it is at present."

"But why should *anything* be left of life?" said I....

That was our style, you know, and meanwhile we walked together up the narrow street outside his lodging, up the stepway and the lanes toward Clayton Crest and the highroad.

But my memories carry me back so effectually to those days before the Change that I forget that now all these places have been altered beyond recognition, that the narrow street and the stepway and the view from Clayton Crest, and indeed all the world in which I was born and bred and made, had vanished clean away, out of space and out of time, and well-nigh out of the imagination of all those who are younger by a generation than I. You cannot see, as I can see, the dark empty way between the mean houses, the dark empty way lit by a bleary gas-lamp at the corner, you cannot feel the hard checkered pavement under your boots, you cannot mark the dimly lit windows here and there, and the shadows upon the ugly and often patched and crooked blinds of the people cooped within. Nor can you presently pass the beerhouse with its brighter gas and its queer, screening windows, nor get a whiff of foul air and foul language from its door, nor see the crumpled furtive figure—some rascal child—that slinks past us down the steps.

We crossed the longer street, up which a clumsy steam tram, vomiting smoke and sparks, made it clangorous way, and down which one saw the greasy brilliance of shop fronts and the naphtha flares of hawkers' barrows dripping fire into the night. A hazy movement of people swayed along that road, and we heard the voice of an itinerant preacher from a waste place between the houses. You cannot see these things as I can see them, nor can you figure—unless you know the pictures that great artist Hyde has left the world—the effect of the great billboard by which we passed, lit below by a gas-lamp and towering up to a sudden sharp black edge against the pallid sky.

Those billboards! They were the brightest colored things in all that vanished world. Upon them, in successive layers of paste and paper, all the rough enterprises of that time joined in chromatic discord; pill vendors and preachers, theaters and charities, marvelous soaps and astonishing pickles, typewriting machines and sewing machines, mingled in a sort of visualized clamor. And passing that there was a muddy lane of cinders, a lane without a light, that used its many puddles to borrow a star or so from the sky. We splashed along unheeding as we talked.

Then across the allotments, a wilderness of cabbages and evil-looking sheds, past a gaunt abandoned factory, and so to the highroad. The highroad ascended in a curve past a few houses and a beerhouse or so, and round until all the valley in which four industrial towns lay crowded and confluent was overlooked.

I will admit that with the twilight there came a spell of weird magnificence over all that land and brooded on it until dawn. The horrible meanness of its details was veiled, the hutches that were homes, the bristling multitudes of chimneys, the ugly patches of unwilling vegetation amidst the makeshift fences of barrel stave and wire. The rusty scars that framed the opposite ridges where the iron ore was taken and the barren mountains of slag from the blast furnaces were veiled; the reek and boiling smoke and dust from foundry, pot-bank, and furnace, transfigured and assimilated by the night. The dust-laden atmosphere that was gray oppression through the day became at sundown a mystery of deep translucent colors, of blues and purples, of somber and vivid reds, of strange bright clearnesses of green and yellow athwart the darkling sky. Each upstart furnace, when its monarch sun had gone, crowned itself with flames, the dark cinder heaps began to glow with quivering fires, and each pot-bank squatted rebellious in a volcanic coronet of light. The empire of the day broke into a thousand feudal baronies of burning coal. The minor streets across the valley picked themselves out with gas-lamps of faint yellow, that brightened and mingled at all the principal squares and crossings with the greenish pallor of incandescent mantles and the high cold glare of the electric arc. The interlacing railways lifted bright signal boxes over their intersections, and signal stars of red and green in rectangular constellations. The trains became articulated black serpents breathing fire....

Moreover, high overhead, like a thing put out of reach and near forgotten, Parload had rediscovered a realm that was ruled by neither sun nor furnace, the universe of stars.

This was the scene of many a talk we two had held together. And if in the daytime we went right over the crest and looked westward there was farmland, there were parks and great mansions, the spire of a distant cathedral, and sometimes when the weather was near raining, the crests of remote mountains hung clearly in the sky. Beyond the range of sight indeed, out beyond, there was Checkshill; I felt it there always, and in the darkness more than I did by day. Checkshill, and Nettie!

And to us two youngsters as we walked along the cinder path beside the rutted road and argued out our perplexities, it seemed that this ridge gave us compendiously a view of our whole world.

There on the one hand in a crowded darkness, about the ugly factories and work-places, the workers herded together, ill clothed, ill nournished, ill taught, badly and expensively served at every occasion in life, uncertain even of their insufficient livelihood from day to day, the chapels and churches and public houses swelling up amidst their wretched homes like saprophytes amidst a general corruption, and on the other, in space, freedom, and dignity, scarce heeding the few cottages, as overcrowded as they were picturesque, in which the laborers festered, lived the landlords and masters who owned pot-banks and forge and farm and mine. Far away, distant, beautiful, irrelevant, from out of a little cluster of second-hand bookshops, ecclesiastical residences, and the inns and incidentals of a decaying market town, the cathedral of Lowchester pointed a beautiful, unemphatic spire to vague, incredible skies. So it seemed to us that the whole world was planned in those youthful first impressions.

We saw everything simple, as young men will. We had our angry, confident solutions, and whosoever would criticize them was a friend of the robbers. It was a clear case of robbery, we held, visibly so; there in those great houses lurked the Landlord and the Capitalist, with his scoundrel the Lawyer, with his cheat the Priest, and we others were all the victims of their deliberate villainies. No doubt they winked and chuckled over their rare wines, amidst their dazzling, wickedly dressed women, and plotted further grinding for the faces of the poor. And amidst all the squalor on the other hand, amidst brutalities, ignorance, and drunkenness, suffered multitudinously their blameless victim, the Working Man. And we, almost at the first glance, had found all this out; it had merely to be asserted now with sufficient rhetoric and vehemence to change the face of the whole world. The Working Man would arise—in the form of a Labor Party, and with young men like Parload and myself to represent him—and come to his own, and then—?

Then the robbers would get it hot, and everything would be extremely satisfactory.

Unless my memory plays me strange tricks that does no injustice to the creed of thought and action that Parload and I held as the final result of human wisdom. We believed it with heat, and rejected with heat the most obvious qualification of its harshness. At times in our great talks we were full of heady hopes for the near triumph of our doctrine; more often our mood was hot resentment at the wickedness and stupidity that delayed so plain and simple a reconstruction of the order of the world. Then we grew malignant, and thought of barricades and significant violence. I was very bitter, I know, upon this night of which I am now particularly telling, and the only face upon the hydra of Capitalism and Monopoly that I could see at all clearly, smiled exactly as old Rawdon had smiled when he refused to give me more than a paltry twenty shillings a week.

I wanted intensely to salve my self-respect by some revenge upon him, and I felt that if that could be done by slaying the hydra, I might drag its carcass to the feet of Nettie, and settle my other trouble as well. "What do you think of me *now,* Nettie?"

That at any rate comes near enough to the quality of my thinking, then, for you to imagine how I gesticulated and spouted to Parload that night. You figure us as little black figures, unprepossessing in the outline, set in the midst of that desolating night of flaming industrialism, and my little voice with a rhetorical twang protesting, denouncing....

You will consider those notions of my youth poor silly violent stuff; particularly if you are of the younger generation born since the Change you will be of that opinion. Nowadays the whole world thinks clearly, thinks with deliberation, pellucid certainties, you find it impossible to imagine how any other thinking could have been possible. Let me tell you then how you can bring yourself to something like the condition of our former state. In the first place you must get yourself out of health by unwise drinking and eating, and out of condition by neglecting your exercise, then you must contrive to be worried very much and made very anxious and uncomfortable, and then you must work very hard for four or five days and for long hours every day at something too petty to be interesting, too complex to be mechanical, and without any personal significance to you whatever. This done, get straightway into a room that is not ventilated at all, and that is already full of foul air, and there set yourself to think out some very complicated problem. In a very little while you will find yourself in a state of intellectual muddle, annoyed, impatient, snatching at the obvious presently in choosing and rejecting conclusions haphazard. Try to play chess under such conditions and you will play stupidly and lose your temper. Try to do anything that taxes the brain or temper and you will fail.

Now, the whole world before the Change was as sick and feverish as that, it was worried and overworked and perplexed by problems that would not get stated simply, that changed and evaded solution, it was in an atmosphere that had corrupted and thickened past breathing; there was no thorough cool thinking in the world at all. There was nothing in the mind of the world anywhere but half-truths, hasty assumptions, hallucinations, and emotions. Nothing....

I know it seems incredible, that already some of the younger men are beginning to doubt the greatness of the Change our world has undergone, but read—read the newspapers of that time. Every age becomes mitigated and a little ennobled in our minds as it recedes into the past. It is the part of those who like myself have stories of that time to tell, to supply, by a scrupulous spiritual realism, some antidote to that glamour.

4

Always with Parload I was chief talker.

I can look back upon myself with, I believe, an almost perfect detachment; things have so changed that indeed now I am another being, with scarce anything in common with that boastful foolish youngster whose troubles I recall. I see him vulgarly theatrical, egotistical, insincere, indeed I do not like him save with that instinctive material sympathy that is the fruit of incessant intimacy. Because he was myself I may be able to feel and write understandingly about motives that will put him out of sympathy with nearly every reader, but why should I palliate or defend his quality?

Always, I say, I did the talking, and it would have amazed me beyond measure if anyone had told me that mine was not the greater intelligence in these wordy encounters. Parload was a quiet youth, and stiff and restrained in all things, while I had that supreme gift for young men and democracies, the gift of copious expression. Parload I diagnosed in my secret heart as a trifle dull; he posed as pregnant quiet, I thought, and was obsessed by the congenial notion of "scientific caution." I did not remark that while my hands were chiefly useful for gesticulation or holding a pen, Parload's hands could do all sorts of things, and I did not think therefore that fibers must run from those fingers to something in his brain. Nor, though I bragged perpetually of my shorthand, of my literature, of my indispensable share in Rawdon's business, did Parload lay stress on the conics and calculus he "mugged" in the organized science school. Parload is a famous man now, a great figure in a great time, his work upon intersecting radiations has broadened the intellectual horizon of mankind forever, and I, who am at best a hewer of intellectual wood, a drawer of living water, can smile, and he can smile, to think how I patronized and posed and jabbered over him in the darkness of those early days.

That night I was shrill and eloquent beyond measure. Rawdon was, of course, the hub upon which I went round —Rawdon and the Rawdonesque employer and the injustice of "wages slavery" and all the immediate conditions of that industrial blind alley up which it seemed our lives were thrust. But ever and again I glanced at other things. Nettie was always there in the background of my mind, regarding me enigmatically. It was part of my pose to Parload that I had a romantic love affair somewhere away beyond the sphere of our intercourse, and that note gave a Byronic resonance to many of the nonsensical things I produced for his astonishment.

I will not weary you with too detailed an account of the talk of a foolish youth who was also distressed and unhappy, and whose voice was balm for the humiliations that smarted in his eyes. Indeed, now in many particulars I cannot disentangle this harangue of which I tell from many of the things I may have said in other talks to Parload. For example, I forget if it was then or before or afterwards that, as it were by accident, I let out what might be taken as an admission that I was addicted to drugs.

"You shouldn't do that," said Parload, suddenly. "It won't do to poison your brains with that."

My brains, my eloquence, were to be very important assets to our party in the coming revolution....

But one thing does clearly belong to this particular conversation I am recalling. When I started out it was quite settled in the back of my mind that I must not leave Rawdon's. I simply wanted to abuse my employer to Parload. But I talked myself quite out of touch with all the cogent reasons there were for sticking to my place, and I got home that night irrevocably committed to a spirited—not to say a defiant—policy with my employer.

"I can't stand Rawdon's much longer," I said to Parload by way of a flourish.

"There's hard times coming," said Parload.

"Next winter."

"Sooner. The Americans have been overproducing, and they mean to dump. The iron trade is going to have convulsions."

"I don't care. Pot-banks are steady."

"With a corner in borax? No. I've heard—"

"What have you heard?"

"Office secrets. But it's no secret there's trouble coming to potters. There's been borrowing and speculation. The masters don't stick to one business as they used to do. I can tell that much. Half the valley may be 'playing' before two months are out." Parload delivered himself of this unusually long speech in his most pithy and weighty manner.

"Playing" was our local euphemism for a time when there was no work and no money for a man, a time of stagnation and dreary hungry loafing day after day. Such interludes seemed in those days a necessary consequence of industrial organization.

"You'd better stick to Rawdon's," said Parload.

"Ugh," said I, affecting a noble disgust.

"There'll be trouble," said Parload.

"Who cares?" said I. "Let there be trouble—the more the better. This system has got to end, sooner or later. These capitalists with their speculation and corners and trusts make things go from bad to worse. Why should I cower in Rawdon's office, like a frightened dog, while hunger walks the streets? Hunger is the master revolutionary. When he comes we ought to turn out and salute him. Anyway, *I'm* going to do so now."

"That's all very well," began Parload.

"I'm tired of it," I said. "I want to come to grips with all these Rawdons. I think perhaps if I was hungry and savage I could talk to hungry men—"

"There's your mother," said Parload, in his slow judicial way.

That *was* a difficulty.

I got over it by a rhetorical turn. "Why should one sacrifice the future of the world—why should one even sacrifice one's own future—because one's mother is totally destitute of imagination?"

5

It was late when I parted from Parload and came back to my own home.

Our house stood in a highly respectable little square near the Clayton parish church. Mr. Gabbitas, the curate of all work, lodged on our ground floor, and upstairs there was an old lady, Miss Holroyd, who painted flowers on china and maintained her blind sister in an adjacent room; my mother and I lived in the basement and slept in the attics. The front of the house was veiled by a Virginia creeper that defied the Clayton air and clustered in untidy dependent masses over the wooden porch.

As I came up the steps I had a glimpse of Mr. Gabbitas

printing photographs by candlelight in his room. It was the chief delight of his little life to spend his holiday abroad in the company of a queer little snapshot camera, and to return with a great multitude of foggy and sinister negatives that he had made in beautiful and interesting places. These the camera company would develop for him on advantageous terms, and he would spend his evenings the year through in printing from them in order to inflict copies upon his undeserving friends. There was a long frameful of his work in the Clayton National School, for example, inscribed in old English lettering, "Italian Travel Pictures, by the Rev. E.B. Gabbitas." For this it seemed he lived and traveled and had his being. It was his only real joy. By his shaded light I could see his sharp little nose, his little pale eyes behind his glasses, his mouth pursed up with the endeavor of his employment....

"Hireling Liar," I muttered, for was not he also part of the system, part of the scheme of robbery that made wage serfs of Parload and me?—though his share in the proceedings was certainly small.

"Hireling Liar," said I, standing in the darkness, outside even his faint glow of traveled culture....

My mother let me in.

She looked at me, mutely, because she knew there was something wrong and that it was no use for her to ask what.

"Good night, Mummy," said I, and kissed her a little roughly, and lit and took my candle and went off at once up the staircase to bed, not looking back at her.

"I've kept some supper for you, dear."

"Don't want any supper."

"But, dearie—"

"Good night, Mother," and I went up and slammed my door upon her, blew out my candle, and lay down at once upon my bed, lay there a long time before I got up to undress.

There were times when that dumb beseeching of my mother's face irritated me unspeakably. It did so that night.

I felt I had to struggle against it, that I could not exist if I gave way to its pleadings, and it hurt me and divided me to resist it, almost beyond endurance. It was clear to me that I had to think out for myself religious problems, social problems, questions of conduct, questions of expediency, that her poor dear simple beliefs could not help me at all—and she did not understand! Hers was the accepted religion, her only social ideas were blind submissions to the accepted order—to laws, to doctors, to clergymen, lawyers, masters, and all respectable persons in authority over us, and with her to believe was to fear. She knew from a thousand little signs—though still at times I went to church with her—that I was passing out of touch of all these things that ruled her life, into some terrible unknown. From things I said she could infer such clumsy concealments as I made. She felt my socialism, felt my spirit in revolt against the accepted order, felt the impotent resentments that filled me with bitterness against all she held sacred. Yet, you know, it was not her dear gods she sought to defend so much as me! She seemed always to be wanting to say to me, "Dear, I know it's hard—but revolt is harder. Don't make war on it, dear—don't! Don't do anything to offend it. I'm sure it will hurt you if you do—it will hurt you if you do."

She had been cowed into submission, as so many women of that time had been, by the sheer brutality of the accepted thing. The existing order dominated her into a worship of abject observances. It had bent her, aged her, robbed her of eyesight so that at fifty-five she peered through cheap spectacles at my face, and saw it only dimly, filled her with a habit of anxiety, made her hands—Her poor dear hands! Not in the whole world now could you find a woman with hands so grimy, so needle-worn, so misshapen by toil, so chapped and coarsened, so evilly entreated....At any rate, there is this I can say for myself, that my bitterness against the world and fortune was for her sake as well as for my own.

Yet that night I pushed by her harshly. I answered her

curtly, left her concerned and perplexed in the passage, and slammed my door upon her.

And for a long time I lay raging at the hardship and evil of life, at the contempt of Rawdon, and the loveless coolness of Nettie's letter, at my weakness and insignificance, at the things I found intolerable, and the things I could not mend. Over and over went my poor little brain, tired out and unable to stop on my treadmill of troubles. Nettie. Rawdon. My mother. Gabbitas. Nettie....

Suddenly I came upon emotional exhaustion. Some clock was striking midnight. After all, I was young; I had these quick transitions. I remember quite distinctly, I stood up abruptly, undressed very quickly in the dark, and had hardly touched my pillow again before I was asleep.

But how my mother slept that night I do not know.

Oddly enough, I do not blame myself for behaving like this to my mother, though my conscience blames me acutely for my arrogance to Parload. I regret my behavior to my mother before the days of the Change, it is a scar among my memories that will always be a little painful to the end of my days, but I do not see how something of the sort was to be escaped under those former conditions. In that time of muddle and obscurity people were overtaken by needs and toil and hot passions before they had the chance of even a year or so of clear thinking; they settled down to an intense and strenuous application to some partial but immediate duty, and the growth of thought ceased in them. They set and hardened into narrow ways. Few women remained capable of a new idea after five and twenty, few men after thirty-one or two. Discontent with the thing that existed was regarded as immoral, it was certainly an annoyance, and the only protest against it, the only effort against that universal tendency in all human institutions to thicken and clog, to work loosely and badly, to rust and weaken towards catastrophes, came from the young—the crude unmerciful young. It seemed in those days to thoughtful men the harsh law of being—that either we must submit to our elders and be stifled, or disregard them, disobey them, thrust them aside, and make our little step of progress before we too ossified and became obstructive in our turn.

My pushing past my mother, my irresponsive departure to my own silent meditations, was, I now perceive, a figure of the whole hard relationship between parents and son in those days. There appeared no other way; that perpetually recurring tragedy was, it seemed, part of the very nature of the progress of the world. We did not think then that minds might grow ripe without growing rigid, or children honor their parents and still think for themselves. We were angry and hasty because we stifled in the darkness, in a poisoned and vitiated air. That deliberate animation of the intelligence which is now the universal quality, that vigor with consideration, that judgment with confident enterprise which shine through all our world, were things disintegrated and unknown in the corrupting atmosphere of our former state.

[So the first fascicle ended. I put it aside and looked for the second.

"Well?" said the man who wrote.

"This is fiction?"

"It's my story."

"But you— Amidst this beauty— You are not this ill-conditioned, squalidly bred lad of whom I have been reading?"

He smiled. "There intervenes a certain Change," he said. "Have I not hinted at that?"

I hesitated upon a question, then saw the second fascicle at hand, and picked it up.]

Chapter 2

Nettie

1

I cannot now remember [the story resumed] what interval separated that evening on which Parload first showed me the comet—I think I only pretended to see it then—and the Sunday afternoon I spent at Checkshill.

Between the two there was time enough for me to give notice and leave Rawdon's, to seek for some other situation very strenuously in vain, to think and say many hard and violent things to my mother and to Parload, and to pass through some phases of very profound wretchedness. There must have been a passionate correspondence with Nettie, but all the froth and fury of that has faded now out of my memory. All I have clear now is that I wrote one magnificent farewell to her, casting her off forever, and that I got in reply a prim little note to say, that even if there was to be an end to everything, that was no excuse for writing such things as I had done, and then I think I wrote again in a vein I considered satirical. To that she did not reply. That interval was at least three weeks, and probably four, because the comet which had been on the first occasion only a dubious speck in the sky, certainly visible only when it was magnified, was now a great white presence, brighter than Jupiter, and casting a shadow on its own account. It was now actively present in the world of human thought, everyone was looking for its waxing splendor as the sun went down—the papers, the music halls, the billboards, echoed it.

Yes; the comet was already dominant before I went over to make everything clear to Nettie. And Parload had spent two hoarded pounds in buying himself a spectroscope, so that he could see for himself, night after night, that mysterious, that stimulating line—the unknown line in the green. How many times I wonder did I look at the smudgy, quivering symbol of the unknown things that were rushing upon us out of the inhuman void, before I rebelled? But at last I could stand it no longer, and I reproached Parload very bitterly for wasting his time in "astronomical dilettantism."

"Here," said I, "we're on the verge of the biggest lock-out in the history of this countryside; here's distress and hunger coming, here's all the capitalistic competitive system like a wound inflamed, and you spend your time gaping at that damned silly streak of nothing in the sky!"

Parload stared at me. "Yes, I do," he said slowly, as though it was a new idea. "Don't I?...I wonder why."

"*I* want to start meetings of an evening on Howden's Waste."

"You think they'd listen?"

"They'd listen fast enough now."

"They didn't before," said Parload, looking at his pet instrument.

"There was a demonstration of unemployed at Swathinglea on Sunday. They got to stone throwing."

Parload said nothing for a little while and I said several things. He seemed to be considering something.

"But, after all," he said at last, with an awkward movement towards his spectroscope, "that does signify something."

"The comet?"

"Yes."

"What can it signify? You don't want me to believe in astrology. What does it matter what flames in the heavens—when men are starving on earth?"

"It's—it's science."

"Science! What we want now is socialism—not science."

He still seemed reluctant to give up his comet.

"Socialism's all right," he said, "but if that thing up there *was* to hit the earth it might matter."

"Nothing matters but human beings."

"Suppose it killed them all."

"Oh," said I, "that's Rot."

"I wonder," said Parload, dreadfully divided in his allegiance.

He looked at the comet. He seemed on the verge of repeating his growing information about the nearness of the paths of the earth and comet, and all that might ensue from that. So I cut in with something I had got out of a now forgotten writer called Ruskin, a volcano of beautiful language and nonsensical suggestions, who prevailed very greatly with eloquent excitable young men in those days. Something it was about the insignificance of science and the supreme importance of Life. Parload stood listening, half turned towards the sky with the tips of his fingers on his spectroscope. He seemed to come to a sudden decision.

"No. I don't agree with you, Leadford," he said. "You don't understand about science."

Parload rarely argued with that bluntness of opposition. I was so used to entire possession of our talk that his brief contradiction struck me like a blow. "Don't agree with me!" I repeated.

"No," said Parload.

"But how?"

"I believe science is of more importance than socialism," he said. "Socialism's a theory. Science—science is something more."

And that was really all he seemed to be able to say.

We embarked upon one of those queer arguments illiterate young men used always to find so heating. Science or Socialism? It was, of course, like arguing which is right, left-handedness or a taste for onions; it was altogether impossible opposition. But the range of my rhetoric enabled me at last to exasperate Parload, and his mere repudiation of my conclusions sufficed to exasperate me, and we ended in the key of a positive quarrel. "Oh, very well!" said I. "So long as I know where we are!"

I slammed his door as though I dynamited his house, and went raging down the street, but I felt that he was already back at the window worshiping his blessed line in the green, before I got round the corner.

I had to walk for an hour or so, before I was cool enough to go home.

And it was Parload who had first introduced me to socialism!

Recreant!

The most extraordinary things used to run through my head in those days. I will confess that my mind ran persistently that evening upon revolutions after the best French pattern, and I sat on a Committee of Safety and tried backsliders. Parload was there, among the prisoners, backsliderissimus, aware too late of the error of his ways. His hands were tied behind his back ready for the shambles; through the open door one heard the voice of justice, the rude justice of the people. I was sorry, but I had to do my duty.

"If we punish those who would betray us to Kings," said I, with a sorrowful deliberation, "how much the more must we punish those who would give over the State to the pursuit of useless knowledge"; and so with a gloomy satisfaction sent him off to the guillotine.

"Ah, Parload! Parload! If only you'd listened to me earlier, Parload."...

Nonetheless that quarrel made me extremely unhappy.

Parload was my only gossip, and it cost me much to keep away from him and think evil of him with no one to listen to me, evening after evening.

That was a very miserable time for me, even before my last visit to Checkshill. My long unemployed hours hung heavily on my hands. I kept away from home all day, partly to support a fiction that I was sedulously seeking another situation, and partly to escape the persistent question in my mother's eyes. "Why did you quarrel with Mr. Rawdon? Why *did* you? Why do you keep on going about with a sullen face and risk offending *it* more?" I spent most of the morning in the newspaper room of the public library, writing impossible applications for impossible posts—I remember that among other things of the sort I offered my services to a firm of private detectives, a sinister breed of traders upon base jealousies now happily vanished from the world, and wrote apropos of an advertisement for "stevedores" that I did not know what the duties of a stevedore might be, but that I was apt and willing to learn—and in the afternoons and evenings I wandered through the strange lights and shadows of my native valley and hated all created things. Until my wanderings were checked by the discovery that I was wearing out my boots.

The stagnant inconclusive malaria of that time!

I perceive that I was an evil-tempered, ill-disposed youth with a great capacity for hatred, *but*—

There was an excuse for hate.

It was wrong of me to hate individuals, to be rude, harsh, and vindictive to this person or that, but indeed it would have been equally wrong to have taken the manifest offer life made me, without resentment. I see now clearly and calmly, what I then felt obscurely and with an unbalanced intensity, that my conditions were intolerable. My work was tedious and laborious and it took up an unreasonable proportion of my time; I was ill clothed, ill fed, ill housed, ill educated and ill trained; my will was suppressed and cramped to the pitch of torture, I had no reasonable pride in myself and no reasonable chance of putting anything right. It was a life hardly worth living. That a large proportion of the people about me had no better a lot, that many had a worse, does not affect these facts. It was a life in which contentment would have been disgraceful. If some of them were contented or resigned, so much the worse for everyone. No doubt it was hasty and foolish of me to throw up my situation, but everything was so obviously aimless and foolish in our social organization that I do not feel disposed to blame myself even for that, except in so far as it pained my mother and caused her anxiety.

Think of the one comprehensive fact of the lockout!

That year was a bad year, a year of world-wide economic disorganization. Through their want of intelligent direction the great "Trust" of American ironmasters, a gang of energetic, narrow-minded furnace owners, had smelted far more iron than the whole world had any demand for. (In those days there existed no means of estimating any need of that sort beforehand.) They had done this without even consulting the ironmasters of any other country. During their period of activity they had drawn into their employment a great number of workers, and had erected a huge productive plant. It is manifestly just that people who do headlong stupid things of this sort should suffer, but in the old days it was quite possible, it was customary for the real blunderers in such disasters, to shift nearly all the consequences of their incapacity. No one thought it wrong for a light-witted "captain of industry" who had led his workpeople into overproduction, into the disproportionate manufacture, that is to say, of some particular article, to abandon and dismiss them, nor was there anything to prevent the sudden frantic underselling of some trade rival in order to surprise and destroy his trade, secure his customers for one's own destined needs, and shift a portion of one's punishment upon him. This operation of spasmodic underselling was known as "dumping." The American iron-masters were now dumping on the British market. The

British employers were, of course, taking their loss out of their workpeople as much as possible, but in addition they were agitating for some legislation that would prevent—not stupid relative excess in production, but "dumping"—not the disease, but the consequences of the disease. The necessary knowledge to prevent either dumping or its causes, the uncorrelated production of commodities, did not exist, but this hardly weighed with them at all, and in answer to their demands there had arisen a curious party of retaliatory protectionists who combined vague proposals for spasmodic responses to these convulsive attacks from foreign manufacturers, with the very evident intention of achieving financial adventures. The dishonest and reckless elements were indeed so evident in this movement as to add very greatly to the general atmosphere of distrust and insecurity, and in the recoil from the prospect of fiscal power in the hands of the class of men known as the "New Financiers," one heard frightened old-fashioned statesmen asserting with passion that "dumping" didn't occur, or that it was a very charming sort of thing to happen. Nobody would face and handle the rather intricate truth of the business. The whole effect upon the mind of a cool observer was of a covey of unsubstantial jabbering minds drifting over a series of irrational economic cataclysms, prices and employment tumbled about like towers in an earthquake, and amidst the shifting masses were the common workpeople going on with their lives as well as they could, suffering, perplexed, unorganized, and for anything but violent, fruitless protests, impotent. You cannot hope now to understand the infinite want of adjustment in the old order of things. At one time there were people dying of actual starvation in India, while men were burning unsaleable wheat in America. It sounds like the account of a particularly mad dream, does it not? It was a dream, a dream from which no one on earth expected an awakening.

To us youngsters with the positiveness, the rationalism of youth, it seemed that the strikes and lockouts, the overproduction and misery could not possibly result simply from ignorance and want of thought and feeling. We needed more dramatic factors than these mental fogs, these mere atmospheric devils. We fled therefore to that common refuge of the unhappy ignorant, a belief in callous insensate plots—we called them "plots"—against the poor.

You can still see how we figured it in any museum by looking up the caricatures of capital and labor that adorned the German and American socialistic papers of the old time.

2

I had cast Nettie off in an eloquent epistle, had really imagined the affair was over forever—"I've done with women," I said to Parload—and then there was silence for more than a week.

Before that week was over I was wondering with a growing emotion what next would happen between us.

I found myself thinking constantly of Nettie, picturing her—sometimes with stern satisfaction, sometimes with sympathetic remorse—mourning, regretting, realizing the absolute end that had come between us. At the bottom of my heart I no more believed that there was an end between us, than that an end would come to the world. Had we not kissed one another, had we not achieved an atmosphere of whispering nearness, breached our virgin shyness with one another? Of course she was mine, of course I was hers, and separations and final quarrels and harshness and distance were no more than flourishes upon that eternal fact. So at least I felt the thing, however I shaped my thoughts.

Whenever my imagination got to work as that week drew to its close, she came in as a matter of course; I thought of her recurrently all day and dreamed of her at night. On Saturday night I dreamed of her very vividly. Her face was flushed and wet with tears, her hair a little disordered, and when I spoke to her she turned away. In some manner this dream left in my mind a feeling of distress and anxiety. In the morning I had a raging thirst to see her.

That Sunday my mother wanted me to go to church very particularly. She had a double reason for that; she thought that it would certainly exercise a favorable influence upon my search for a situation throughout the next week, and in addition Mr. Gabbitas, with a certain mystery behind his glasses, had promised to see what he could do for me, and she wanted to keep him up to that promise. I half consented, and then my desire for Nettie took hold of me. I told my mother I wasn't going to church, and set off about eleven to walk the seventeen miles to Checkshill.

It greatly intensified the fatigue of that long tramp that the sole of my boot presently split at the toe, and after I had cut the flapping portion off, a nail worked through and began to torment me. However, the boot looked all right after that operation and gave no audible hint of my discomfort. I got some bread and cheese at a little inn on the way, and was in Checkshill park about four. I did not go by the road past the house and so round to the gardens, but cut over the crest beyond the second keeper's cottage, along a path Nettie used to call her own. It was a mere deer track. It led up a miniature valley and through a pretty dell in which we had been accustomed to meet, and so through the hollies and along a narrow path close by the wall of the shrubbery to the gardens.

In my memory that walk through the park before I came upon Nettie stands out very vividly. The long tramp before it is foreshortened to a mere effect of dusty road and painful boot, but the bracken valley and sudden tumult of doubts and unwonted expectations that came to me, stand out now as something significant, as something unforgettable, something essential to the meaning of all that followed. Where should I meet her? What would she say? I had asked these questions before and found an answer. Now they came again with a trail of fresh implications and I had no answer for them at all. As I approached Nettie she ceased to be the mere butt of my egotistical self-projection, the custodian of my sexual pride, and drew together and became over and above this a personality of her own, a personality and a mystery, a sphinx I had evaded only to meet again.

I find a little difficulty in describing the quality of the old-world lovemaking so that it may be understandable now.

We young people had practically no preparation at all for the stir and emotions of adolescence. Towards the young the world maintained a conspiracy of stimulating silence. There came no initiation. There were books, stories of a curiously conventional kind that insisted on certain qualities in every love affair and greatly intensified one's natural desire for them, perfect trust, perfect loyalty, lifelong devotion. Much of the complex essentials of love were altogether hidden. One read these things, got accidental glimpses of this and that, wondered and forgot, and so one grew. Then strange emotions, novel alarming desires, dreams strangely charged with feeling; an inexplicable impulse of self-abandonment began to tickle queerly amongst the familiar purely egotistical and materialistic things of boyhood and girlhood. We were like misguided travelers who had camped in the dry bed of a tropical river. Presently we were knee deep and neck deep in the flood. Our beings were suddenly going out from ourselves seeking other beings—we knew not why. This novel craving for abandonment to someone of the other sex, bore us away. We were ashamed and full of desire. We kept the thing a guilty secret, and were resolved to satisfy it against all the world. In this state it was we drifted in the most accidental way against some other blindly seeking creature, and linked like nascent atoms.

We were obsessed by the books we read, by all the talk about us that once we had linked ourselves we were linked for life. Then afterwards we discovered that other was also an egotism, a thing of ideas and impulses, that failed to correspond with ours.

So it was, I say, with the young of my class and most of the young people in our world. So it came about that I sought Nettie on the Sunday afternoon and suddenly came upon her, light bodied, slenderly feminine, hazel eyed, with her soft sweet young face under the shady brim of her hat of straw, the pretty Venus I had resolved should be wholly and exclusively mine.

There, all unaware of me still, she stood, my essential feminine, the embodiment of the inner thing in life for me—and moreover an unknown other, a person like myself.

She held a little book in her hand, open as if she were walking along and reading it. That chanced to be her pose, but indeed she was standing quite still, looking away towards the gray and lichenous shrubbery wall and, as I think now, listening. Her lips were a little apart, curved to that faint, sweet shadow of a smile.

3

I recall with a vivid precision her queer start when she heard the rustle of my approaching feet, her surprise, her eyes almost of dismay for me. I could recollect, I believe, every significant word she spoke during our meeting, and most of what I said to her. At least, it seems I could, though indeed I may deceive myself. But I will not make the attempt. We were both too ill educated to speak our full meanings, we stamped out our feelings with clumsy stereotyped phrases; you who are better taught would fail to catch our intention. The effect would be inanity. But our first words I may give you, because though they conveyed nothing to me at the time, afterwards they meant much.

"*You*, Willie!" she said.

"I have come," I said—forgetting in the instant all the elaborate things I had intended to say. "I thought I would surprise you—"

"Surprise me?"

"Yes."

She stared at me for a moment. I can see her pretty face now as it looked at me—her impenetrable dear face. She laughed a queer little laugh and her color went for a moment, and then so soon as she had spoken, came back again.

"Surprise me at what?" she said with a rising note.

I was too intent to explain myself to think of what might lie in that.

"I wanted to tell you," I said, "that I didn't mean quite ...the things I put in my letter."

4

When I and Nettie had been sixteen we had been just of an age and contemporaries altogether. Now we were a year and three-quarters older, and she—her metamorphosis was almost complete, and I was still only at the beginning of a man's long adolescence.

In an instant she grasped the situation. The hidden motives of her quick-ripened little mind flashed out their intuitive scheme of action. She treated me with that neat perfection of understanding a young woman has for a boy.

"But how did you come?" she asked.

I told her I had walked.

"Walked!" In an instant she was leading me towards the gardens. I *must* be tired. I must come home with her at once and sit down. Indeed it was near tea-time (the Stuarts had tea at the old-fashioned hour of five). Everyone would be *so* surprised to see me. Fancy walking! Fancy! But she supposed a man thought nothing of seventeen miles. When *could* I have started!

All the while, keeping me at a distance, without even the touch of her hand.

"But, Nettie! I came over to talk to you!"

"My dear boy! Tea first, if you please! And besides—aren't we talking?"

The "dear boy" was a new note, that sounded oddly to me.

She quickened her pace a little.

"I wanted to explain—" I began.

Whatever I wanted to explain I had no chance to do so. I said a few discrepant things that she answered rather by her intonation than her words.

When we were well past the shrubbery, she slackened a little in her urgency, and so we came along the slope under the beeches to the garden. She kept her bright, straightforward-looking girlish eyes on me as we went; it seemed she did so all the time, but now I know, better than I did then, that every now and then she glanced over me and behind me towards the shrubbery. And all the while, behind her quick breathless inconsecutive talk she was thinking.

Her dress marked the end of her transition.

Can I recall it?

Not, I am afraid, in the terms a woman would use. But her bright brown hair, which had once flowed down her back in a jolly pigtail tied with a bit of scarlet ribbon, was now caught up into an intricacy of pretty curves above her little ear and cheek, and the soft long lines of her neck; her white dress had descended to her feet; her slender waist, which had once been a mere geographical expression, an imaginary line like the equator, was now a thing of flexible beauty. A year ago she had been a pretty girl's face sticking out from a little unimportant frock that was carried upon an extremely active and efficient pair of brown-stockinged legs. Now there was coming a strange new body that flowed beneath her clothes with a sinuous insistence. Every movement, and particularly the novel droop of her hand and arm to the unaccustomed skirts she gathered about her, and a graceful forward inclination that had come to her, called softly to my eyes. A very fine scarf—I suppose you would call it a scarf—of green gossamer, that some new-wakened instinct had told her to fling about her shoulders, clung now closely to the young undulations of her body, and now streamed fluttering out for a moment in a breath of wind, and like some shy independent tentacle with a secret to impart, came into momentary contact with my arm.

She caught it back and reproved it.

We went through the green gate in the high garden wall. I held it open for her to pass through, for this was one of my restricted stock of stiff politenesses, and then for a second she was near touching me. So we came to the trim array of flowerbeds near the head gardener's cottage and the vistas of "glass" on our left. We walked between the box edgings and beds of begonias and into the shadow of a yew hedge within twenty yards of that very pond with the goldfish, at whose brim we had plighted our vows, and so we came to the wisteria-smothered porch.

The door was wide open, and she walked in before me. "Guess who has come to see us!" she cried.

Her father answered indistinctly from the parlor, and a chair creaked. I judged he was disturbed in his nap.

"Mother!" she called in her clear young voice. "Puss!"

Puss was her sister.

She told them in a marveling key that I had walked all the way from Clayton, and they gathered about me and echoed her notes of surprise.

"You'd better sit down, Willie," said her father, "now you have got here. How's your mother?"

He looked at me curiously as he spoke.

He was dressed in his Sunday clothes, a sort of brownish tweeds, but the waistcoat was unbuttoned for greater comfort in his slumbers. He was a brown-eyed ruddy man, and I still have now in my mind the bright effect of the red-golden hairs that started out from his cheek to flow down into his beard. He was short but strongly built, and his beard and mustache were the biggest things about him. She had taken all the possibility of beauty he possessed, his clear skin, his bright hazel-brown eyes, and wedded them to a certain quickness she got from her mother. Her mother I remember as a sharp-eyed woman of great activity; she seems to me now to have been perpetually bringing in or taking out meals or doing some such service, and to me—for my mother's sake and my own—she was always welcoming and kind. Puss was a youngster of fourteen perhaps, of whom a hard bright stare, and a pale skin like her mother's, are the chief traces on my memory. All these people were very kind to me, and among them there was a common recognition, sometimes very agreeably finding expression, that I was—"clever." They all stood about me as if they were a little at a loss.

"Sit down!" said her father. "Give him a chair, Puss."

We talked a little stiffly—they were evidently surprised by my sudden apparition, dusty, fatigued, and white-faced; but Nettie did not remain to keep the conversation going.

"There!" she cried suddenly, as if she were vexed. "I declare!" and she darted out of the room.

"Lord! what a girl it is!" said Mrs. Stuart. "I don't know what's come to her."

It was half an hour before Nettie came back. It seemed a long time to me, and yet she had been running, for when she came in again she was out of breath. In the meantime, I had thrown out casually that I had given up my place at Rawdon's. "I can do better than that," I said.

"I left my book in the dell," she said, panting. "Is tea ready?" and that was her apology....

We didn't shake down into comfort even with the coming of the tea things. Tea at the gardener's cottage was a serious meal, with a big cake and little cakes, and preserves and fruit, a fine spread upon a table. You must imagine me, sullen, awkward, and preoccupied, perplexed by the something that was inexplicably unexpected in Nettie, saying little, and glowering across the cake at her, and all the eloquence I had been concentrating for the previous twenty-four hours, miserably lost somewhere in the back of my mind. Nettie's father tried to set me talking; he had a liking for my gift of ready speech, for his own ideas came with difficulty, and it pleased and astonished him to hear me pouring out my views. Indeed, over there I was, I think, even more talkative than with Parload, though to the world at large I was a shy young lout. "You ought to write it out for the newspapers," he used to say. "That's what you ought to do. *I* never heard such nonsense."

Or, "You've got the gift of gab, young man. We ought to ha' made a lawyer of you."

But that afternoon, even in his eyes, I didn't shine. Failing any other stimulus, he reverted to my search for a situation, but even that did not engage me.

5

For a long time I feared I should have to go back to Clayton without another word to Nettie, she seemed insensible to the need I felt for a talk with her, and I was thinking even of a sudden demand for that before them all. It was a transparent maneuver of her mother's who had been watching my face, that sent us out at last together to do something—I forget now what—in one of the greenhouses. Whatever that little mission may have been it was the merest, most barefaced excuse, a door to shut, or a window to close, and I don't think it got done.

Nettie hesitated and obeyed. She led the way through one of the hothouses. It was a low, steamy, brick-floored alley between staging that bore a close crowd of pots and ferns, and behind big branching plants that were spread and nailed overhead so as to make an impervious cover of leaves, and in that close green privacy she stopped and turned on me suddenly like a creature at bay.

"Isn't the maidenhair fern lovely?" she said, and looked at me with eyes that said, *"Now."*

"Nettie," I began, "I was a fool to write to you as I did."

She startled me by the assent that flashed out upon her face. But she said nothing, and stood waiting.

"Nettie," I plunged, "I can't do without you. I—I love you."

"If you loved me," she said trimly, watching the white fingers she plunged among the green branches of a selaginella, "could you write the things you do to me?"

"I don't mean them," I said. "At least not always."

I thought really they were very good letters, and that Nettie was stupid to think otherwise, but I was for the moment clearly aware of the impossibility of conveying that to her.

"You wrote them."

"But then I tramp seventeen miles to say I don't mean them."

"Yes. But perhaps you do."

I think I was at a loss; then I said, not very clearly, "I don't."

"You think you—you love me, Willie. But you don't."

"I do. Nettie! You know I do."

For answer she shook her head.

I made what I thought was a most heroic plunge. "Nettie," I said, "I'd rather have you than—than my own opinions."

The selaginella still engaged her. "You think so now," she said.

I broke out into protestations.

"No," she said shortly. "It's different now."

"But why should two letters make so much difference?" I said.

"It isn't only the letters. But it is different. It's different for good."

She halted a little with that sentence, seeking her expression. She looked up abruptly into my eyes and moved, indeed slightly, but with the intimation that she thought our talk might end.

But I did not mean it to end like that.

"For good?" said I. "No!...Nettie! Nettie! You don't mean that!"

"I do," she said deliberately, still looking at me, and with all her pose conveying her finality. She seemed to brace herself for the outbreak that must follow.

Of course I became wordy. But I did not submerge her. She stood entrenched, firing her contradictions like guns into my scattered discursive attack. I remember that our talk took the absurd form of disputing whether I could be in love with her or not. And there was I, present in evidence, in a deepening and widening distress of soul because she could stand there, defensive, brighter and prettier than ever, and in some inexplicable way cut off from me and inaccessible.

You know, we had never been together before without little enterprises of endearment, without a faintly guilty, quite delightful excitement.

I pleaded, I argued. I tried to show that even my harsh and difficult letters came from my desire to come wholly into contact with her. I made exaggerated fine statements of the longing I felt for her when I was away, of the shock and misery of finding her estranged and cool. She looked at me, feeling the emotion of my speech and impervious to its ideas. I had no doubt—whatever poverty in my words, coolly written down now—that I was eloquent then. I meant most intensely what I said, indeed I was wholly concentrated upon it. I was set upon conveying to her with absolute sincerity my sense of distance, and the greatness of my desire. I toiled toward her painfully and obstinately through a jungle of words.

Her face changed very slowly—by such imperceptible degrees as when at dawn light comes into a clear sky. I could feel that I touched her, that her hardness was in some manner melting, her determination softening toward hesitations. The habit of an old familiarity lurked somewhere within her. But she would not let me reach her.

"No," she cried abruptly, starting into motion.

She laid a hand on my arm. A wonderful new friendliness came into her voice. "It's impossible, Willie. Everything is different now—everything. We made a mistake. We two young sillies made a mistake and everything is different forever. Yes, Yes."

She turned about.

"Nettie!" cried I, and still protesting, pursued her along the narrow alley between the staging toward the hothouse door. I pursued her like an accusation, and she went before me like one who is guilty and ashamed. So I recall it now.

She would not let me talk to her again.

Yet I could see that my talk to her had altogether abolished the clear-cut distance of our meeting in the park. Ever and again I found her hazel eyes upon me. They expressed something novel—a surprise, as though she realized an unwonted relationship, and a sympathetic pity. And still—something defensive.

When we got back to the cottage, I fell talking rather more freely with her father about the nationalization of railways, and my spirits and temper had so far mended at the realization that I could still produce an effect upon Nettie, that I was even playful with Puss. Mrs. Stuart judged from that that things were better with me than they were, and began to beam mightily.

But Nettie remained thoughtful and said very little. She was lost in perplexities I could not fathom, and presently she slipped away from us and went upstairs.

6

I was, of course, too footsore to walk back to Clayton, but I had a shilling and a penny in my pocket for the train between Checkshill and Two-Mile Stone, and that much of the distance I proposed to do in the train. And when I got ready to go, Nettie amazed me by waking up to the most remarkable solicitude for me. I must, she said, go by the road. It was altogether too dark for the short way to the lodge gates.

I pointed out that it was moonlight. "With the comet thrown in," said old Stuart.

"No," she insisted, "you *must* go by the road."

I still disputed.

She was standing near me. "To please *me*," she urged, in a quick undertone, and with a persuasive look that puzzled me. Even in the moment I asked myself why should this please her?

I might have agreed had she not followed that up with, "The hollies by the shrubbery are as dark as pitch. And there's the deerhounds."

"I'm not afraid of the dark," said I. "Nor of the deerhounds, either."

"But those dogs! Supposing one was loose!"

That was a girl's argument, a girl who still had to understand that fear is an overt argument only for her own sex. I thought too of those grisly lank brutes straining at their chains and the chorus they could make of a night when they heard belated footsteps along the edge of the Killing Wood, and the thought banished my wish to please her. Like most imaginative natures I was acutely capable of dreads and retreats, and constantly occupied with their suppression and concealment, and to refuse the shortcut when it might appear that I did it on account of half a dozen almost certainly chained dogs was impossible.

So I set off in spite of her, feeling valiant and glad to be so easily brave, but a little sorry that she should think herself crossed by me.

A thin cloud veiled the moon, and the way under the beeches was dark and indistinct. I was not so preoccupied with my love affairs as to neglect what I will confess was always my custom at night across that wild and lonely park. I made myself a club by fastening a big flint to one end of my twisted handkerchief and tying the other about my wrist, and with this in my pocket, went on comforted.

And it chanced that as I emerged from the hollies by the corner of the shrubbery I was startled to come unexpectedly upon a young man in evening dress smoking a cigar.

I was walking on turf, so that the sound I made was slight. He stood clear in the moonlight, his cigar glowed like a blood-red star, and it did not occur to me at the time that I advanced towards him almost invisibly in an impenetrable shadow.

"Hullo," he cried, with a sort of amiable challenge. "I'm here first!"

I came out into the light. "Who cares if you are?" said I.

I had jumped at once to an interpretation of his words. I knew that there was an intermittent dispute between the House people and the village public about the use of this track, and it is needless to say where my sympathies fell in that dispute.

"Eh?" he cried in surprise.

"Thought I would run away, I suppose," said I, and came close up to him.

All my enormous hatred of his class had flared up at the sight of his costume, at the fancied challenge of his words. I knew him. He was Edward Verrall, son of the man who owned not only this great estate but more than half of Rawdon's pot-bank, and who had interests and possessions, collieries and rents, all over the district of the Four Towns. He was a gallant youngster, people said, and very clever. Young as he was there was talk of Parliament for him; he had been a great success at the university, and he was being sedulously popularized among us. He took with a light confidence, as a matter of course, advantages that I would have faced the rack to get, and I firmly believed myself a better man than he. He was, as he stood there, a concentrated figure of all that filled me with bitterness. One day he had stopped in a motor outside our house, and I remember the thrill of rage with which I had noted the dutiful admiration in my mother's eyes as she peered through her blind at him. "That's young Mr. Verrall," she said. "They say he's very clever."

"They would," I answered. "Damn them and him!"

But that is by the way.

He was clearly astonished to find himself face to face with a man. His note changed.

"Who the devil are *you*?" he asked.

My retort was the cheap expedient of re-echoing, "Who the devil are you?"

"*Well*," he said.

"I'm coming along this path if I like," I said. "See? It's a public path—just as this used to be public land. You've stolen the land—you and yours, and now you want to steal the right of way. You'll ask us to get off the face of the earth next. I shan't oblige. See?"

I was shorter and I suppose a couple of years younger than he, but I had the improvised club in my pocket gripped ready, and I would have fought with him very cheerfully. But he fell a step backward as I came toward him.

"Socialist, I presume?" he said, alert and quiet and with the faintest note of badinage.

"One of many."

"We're all socialists nowadays," he remarked philosophically, "and I haven't the faintest intention of disputing your right of way."

"You'd better not," I said.

"No!"

"No."

He replaced his cigar and there was a brief pause. "Catching a train?" he threw out.

It seemed absurd not to answer. "Yes," I said shortly.

He said it was a pleasant evening for a walk.

I hovered for a moment and there was my path before me, and he stood aside. There seemed nothing to do but go on. "Good night," said he, as that intention took effect.

I growled a surly good night.

I felt like a bombshell of swearing that must presently burst with some violence as I went on my silent way. He had so completely got the best of our encounter.

7

There comes a memory, an odd intermixture of two entirely divergent things, that stands out with the intensest vividness.

As I went across the last open meadow, following the shortcut to Checkshill station, I perceived I had two shadows.

The thing jumped into my mind and stopped its tumid flow for a moment. I remember the intelligent detachment of my sudden interest. I turned sharply, and stood looking at the moon and the great white comet, that the drift of the clouds had now rather suddenly unveiled.

The comet was perhaps twenty degrees from the moon. What a wonderful thing it looked floating there, a greenish-white apparition in the dark blue deeps! It looked brighter than the moon because it was smaller, but the shadow it cast, though clearer cut, was much fainter than the moon's shadow. ...I went on noting these facts, watching my two shadows precede me.

I am totally unable to account for the sequence of my thoughts on this occasion. But suddenly, as if I had come on this new fact round a corner, the comet was out of my mind again, and I was face to face with an absolutely new idea. I wonder sometimes if the two shadows I cast, one with a sort of feminine faintness with regard to the other and not quite so tall, may not have suggested the word or the thought of an assignation to my mind. All that I have clear is that with the certitude of intuition I knew what it was that had brought the youth in evening dress outside the shrubbery. Of course! He had come to meet Nettie!

Once the mental process was started it took no time at all. The day which had been full of perplexities for me, the mysterious invisible thing that had held Nettie and myself apart, the unaccountable strange something in her manner, was revealed and explained.

I knew now why she had looked guilty at my appearance,

what had brought her out that afternoon, why she had hurried me in, the nature of the "book" she had run back to fetch, the reason why she had wanted me to go back by the highroad, and why she had pitied me. It was all in the instant clear to me.

You must imagine me a black little creature, suddenly stricken still—for a moment standing rigid—and then again suddenly becoming active with an impotent gesture, becoming audible with an inarticulate cry, with two little shadows mocking my dismay, and about this figure you must conceive a great wide space of moonlit grass, rimmed by the looming suggestion of distant trees—trees very low and faint and dim, and over it all the domed serenity of that wonderful luminous night.

For a little while this realization stunned my mind. My thoughts came to a pause, staring at my discovery. Meanwhile my feet and my previous direction carried me through the warm darkness to Checkshill station with its little lights, to the ticket-office window, and so to the train.

I remember myself as it were waking up to the thing—I was alone in one of the dingy "third class" compartments of that time—and the sudden nearly frantic insurgence of my rage. I stood up with the cry of an angry animal, and smote my fist with all my strength against the panel of wood before me....

Curiously enough I have completely forgotten my mood after that for a little while, but I know that later, for a minute perhaps, I hung for a time out of the carriage with the door open, contemplating a leap from the train. It was to be a dramatic leap, and then I would go storming back to her, denounce her, overwhelm her; and I hung, urging myself to do it. I don't remember how it was I decided not to do this, at last, but in the end I didn't.

When the train stopped at the next station I had given up all thoughts of going back. I was sitting in the corner of the carriage with my bruised and wounded hand pressed under my arm, and still insensible to its pain, trying to think out clearly a scheme of action—action that should express the monstrous indignation that possessed me.

Chapter 3

The Revolver

1

"That comet is going to hit the earth!"

So said one of the two men who got into the train and settled down.

"Ah!" said the other man.

"They do say that it is made of gas, that comet. We shan't blow up, shall we?" ...

What did it matter to me?

I was thinking of revenge—revenge against the primary conditions of my being. I was thinking of Nettie and her lover. I was firmly resolved he should not have her—though I had to kill them both to prevent it. I did not care what else might happen, if only that end was ensured. All my thwarted passions had turned to rage. I would have accepted eternal torment that night without a second thought, to be certain of revenge. A hundred possibilities of action, a hundred stormy situations, a whirl of violent schemes, chased one another through my shamed, exasperated mind. The sole prospect I could endure was of some gigantic, inexorably cruel vindication of my humiliated self.

And Nettie? I loved Nettie still, but now with the intensest jealousy, with the keen, unmeasuring hatred of wounded pride, and baffled, passionate desire.

2

As I came down the hill from Clayton Crest—for my shilling and a penny only permitted my traveling by train as far as Two-Mile Stone, and thence I had to walk over the hill—I remember very vividly a little man with a shrill voice who was preaching under a gas-lamp against a billboard to a thin crowd of Sunday evening loafers. He was a short man, bald, with a little fair curly beard and hair and watery blue eyes, and he was preaching that the end of the world drew near.

I think that is the first time I heard anyone link the comet with the end of the world. He had got that jumbled up with international politics and prophecies from the Book of Daniel.

I stopped to hear him only for a moment or so. I do not think I should have halted at all but his crowd blocked my path, and the sight of his queer wild expression, the gesture of his upward-pointing finger, held me.

"There is the end of all your Sins and Follies," he bawled. "There! There is the Star of Judgments, the Judgments of the most High God! It is appointed unto all men to die—unto all men to die"—his voice changed to a curious flat chant—"and after death, the Judgment! The Judgment!"

I pushed and threaded my way through the bystanders and went on, and his curious harsh flat voice pursued me. I went on with the thoughts that had occupied me before—where I could buy a revolver, and how I might master its use—and probably I should have forgotten all about him had he not taken a part in the hideous dream that ended the little sleep I had that night. For the most part I lay awake thinking of Nettie and her lover.

Then came three strange days—three days that seem now to have been wholly concentrated upon one business.

This dominant business was the purchase of my revolver. I held myself resolutely to the idea that I must either restore myself by some extraordinary act of vigor and violence in Nettie's eyes or I must kill her. I would not let myself fall away from that. I felt that if I let this matter pass, my last shred of pride and honor would pass with it, that for the rest of my life I should never desire the slightest respect or any woman's love. Pride kept me to my purpose between my gusts of passion.

Yet it was not easy to buy that revolver.

I had a kind of shyness of the moment when I should have to face the shopman, and I was particularly anxious to have a story ready if he should see fit to ask questions why I bought such a thing. I determined to say I was going to Texas, and I thought it might prove useful there. Texas in those days had the reputation of a wild lawless land. As I knew nothing of caliber or impact, I wanted also to be able to ask with a steady face at what distance a man or woman could be killed by the weapon that might be offered me. I was pretty cool-headed in relation to such practical aspects of my affair. I had some little difficulty in finding a gunsmith. In Clayton there were some rook rifles and so forth in a cycle shop, but the only revolvers these people had impressed me as being too small and toylike for my purpose. It was in a pawnshop window in the narrow High Street of Swathinglea that I found my choice, a reasonably clumsy and serious-looking implement ticketed "As used in the American army."

I had drawn out my balance from the savings bank, matter of two pounds and more, to make this purchase, and I found it at last a very easy transaction. The pawnbroker told me where I could get ammunition, and I went home that night with bulging pockets, an armed man.

The purchase of my revolver was, I say, the chief business of those days, but you must not think I was so intent upon it as to be insensible to the stirring things that were happening in the streets through which I went seeking the means to effect my purpose. They were full of murmurings: the whole region of the Four Towns scowled lowering from its narrow doors. The ordinary healthy flow of people going to work, people going about their business, was chilled and checked. Numbers of men stood about the streets in knots and groups, as corpuscles gather and catch in the blood vessels in the opening stages of inflammation. The women looked haggard and worried. The ironworkers had refused the proposed reduction of their wages, and the lockout had begun. They were already at "play." The Conciliation Board was doing its best to keep the coal-miners and masters from a breach, but young Lord Redcar, the greatest of our coal owners and landlord of all Swathinglea and half Clayton, was taking a fine upstanding attiude that made the breach inevitable. He was a handsome young man, a gallant young man; his pride revolted at the idea of being dictated to by a "lot of noisy miners," and he meant, he said, to make a fight for it. The world had treated him sumptuously from his earliest years; the shares in the common stock of five thousand people had gone to pay for his handsome upbringing, and large, romantic, expensive ambitions filled his generously nurtured mind. He had early distinguished himself at Oxford by his scornful attitude towards democracy. There was something that appealed to the imagination in his fine antagonism to the crowd—on the one hand, was the brilliant young nobleman, picturesquely alone; on the other, the ugly, inexpressive multitude, dressed inelegantly in shop-clothes, under-educated, underfed, envious, base, and with a wicked disinclination for work and a wicked appetite for the good things it could so rarely get. For common imaginative purposes one left out the policeman from the design, the stalwart policeman protecting his lordship, and ignored the fact that while Lord Redcar had his hands immediately and legally on the workman's shelter and bread, they could touch him to the skin only by some violent breach of the law.

He lived at Lowchester House, five miles or so beyond Checkshill; but partly to show how little he cared for his antagonists, and partly no doubt to keep himself in touch with the negotiations that were still going on, he was visible almost every day in and about the Four Towns, driving that big motorcar of his that could take him sixty miles an hour. The English passion for fair play one might have thought sufficient to rob this bold procedure of any dangerous possibilities, but he did not go altogether free from insult, and on one occasion at least an intoxicated Irish woman shook her fist at him....

A dark, quiet crowd, that was greater each day, a crowd more than half women, brooded as a cloud will sometimes brood permanently upon a mountain crest, in the marketplace outside the Clayton Town Hall, where the conference was held....

I consider myself justified in regarding Lord Redcar's passing automobile with a special animosity because of the leaks in our roof.

We held our little house on lease; the owner was a mean, saving old man named Pettigrew, who lived in a villa adorned with plaster images of dogs and goats, at Overcastle, and in spite of our specific agreement, he would do no repairs for us at all. He rested secure in my mother's timidity. Once, long ago, she had been behindhand with her rent, with half of her quarter's rent, and he had extended the days of grace a month; her sense that some day she might need the same mercy again made her his abject slave. She was afraid even to ask that he should cause the roof to be mended for fear he might take offense. But one night the rain poured in on her bed and gave her a cold, and stained and soaked her poor old patchwork counterpane. Then she got me to compose an excessively polite letter to old Pettigrew, begging him as a favor to perform his legal obligations. It is part of the general imbecility of those days that such one-sided law as existed was a profound mystery to the common people, its provisions impossible to ascertain, its machinery impossible to set in motion. Instead of the clearly written code, the lucid statements of rules and principles that are now at the service of everyone, the law was the muddled secret of the legal profession. Poor people, overworked people, had constantly to submit to petty wrongs because of the intolerable uncertainty not only of law but of cost, and of the demands upon time and energy, proceedings might make. There was indeed no justice for anyone too poor to command a good solicitor's deference and loyalty; there was nothing but rough police protection and the magistrate's grudging or eccentric advice for the mass of the population. The civil law, in particular, was a mysterious upper-class weapon, and I can imagine no injustice that would have been sufficient to induce my poor old mother to appeal to it.

All this begins to sound incredible. I can only assure you that it was so.

But I, when I learned that old Pettigrew had been down to tell my mother all about his rheumatism, to inspect the roof, and to allege that nothing was needed, gave way to my most frequent emotion in those days, a burning indignation, and took the matter into my own hands. I wrote and asked him, with a withering air of technicality, to have the roof repaired "as per agreement." and added, "if not done in one week from now we shall be obliged to take proceedings." I had not mentioned this high line of conduct to my mother at first, and so when old Pettigrew came down in a state of great agitation with my letter in his hand, she was almost equally agitated.

"How could you write to old Mr. Pettigrew like that?" she asked me.

I said that old Pettigrew was a shameful old rascal, or words to that effect, and I am afraid I behaved in a very undutiful way to her when she said that she had settled everything with him—she wouldn't say how, but I could guess well enough—and that I was to promise her, promise her faithfully, to do nothing more in the matter. I wouldn't promise her.

And—having nothing better to employ me then—I presently went raging to old Pettigrew in order to put the whole thing before him in what I considered the proper light. Old Pettigrew evaded my illumination; he saw me coming up his front steps—I can still see his queer old nose and the crinkled brow over his eye and the little wisp of gray hair that showed over the corner of his window blind—and he instructed his servant to put up the chain when she answered the door, and to tell me that he would not see me. So I had to fall back upon my pen.

Then it was, as I had no idea what were the proper "proceedings" to take, the brilliant idea occurred to me of appealing to Lord Redcar as the ground landlord, and, as it were, our feudal chief, and pointing out to him that his security for his rent was depreciating in old Pettigrew's hands. I added some general observations on leaseholds, the taxation of ground rents, and the private ownership of the soil. And Lord Redcar, whose spirit revolted at democracy, and who cultivated a pert humiliating manner with his inferiors to show as much, earned my distinguished hatred forever by causing his secretary to present his compliments to me, and his request that I would mind my own business and leave him to manage his. At which I was so greatly enraged that I first tore this note into minute innumerable pieces, and then dashed it dramatically all over the floor of my room—from which, to keep my mother from the job, I afterward had to pick it up laboriously on all fours.

I was still meditating a tremendous retort, an indictment of all Lord Redcar's class, their manners, morals, economic and political crimes, when my trouble with Nettie arose to swamp all minor troubles. Yet, not so completely but that I snarled aloud when his lordship's motorcar whizzed by me, as I went about upon my long meandering quest for a weapon. And I discovered after a time that my mother had bruised her knee and was lame. Fearing to irritate me by bringing the thing before me again, she had set herself to move her bed out of the way of the drip without my help, and she had knocked her knee. All her poor furnishings, I discovered, were cowering now close to the peeling bedroom walls; there had come a vast discoloration of the ceiling, and a washing-tub was in occupation of the middle of her chamber....

It is necessary that I should set these things before you, should give the key of inconvenience and uneasiness in which all things were arranged, should suggest the breath of trouble that stirred along the hot summer streets, the anxiety about the strike, the rumors and indignations, the gatherings and meetings, the increasing gravity of the policemen's faces, the combative headlines of the local papers, the knots of picketers who scrutinized anyone who passed near the silent, smokeless forges, but in my mind, you must understand, such impressions came and went irregularly; they made a moving background, changing undertones, to my preoccupation by that darkly shaping purpose to which a revolver was so imperative an essential.

Along the darkling streets, amidst the sullen crowds, the thought of Nettie, my Nettie, and her gentleman lover made ever a vivid inflammatory spot of purpose in my brain.

3

It was three days after this—on Wednesday, that is to say—that the first of those sinister outbreaks occurred that ended in the bloody affair of Peacock Grove and the flooding out of the entire line of the Swathinglea collieries. It was the only one of these disturbances I was destined to see, and at most a mere trivial preliminary of that struggle.

The accounts that have been written of this affair vary very widely. To read them is to realize the extraordinary carelessness of truth that dishonored the press of those latter days. In my bureau I have several files of the daily papers of the old time—I collected them, as a matter of fact—and three or four of about that date I have just this moment taken out and looked through to refresh my impression of what I saw. They lie before me—queer, shriveled, incredible things; the cheap paper has already become brittle and brown and split along the creases, the ink faded or smeared, and I have to handle them with the utmost care when I glance among their raging headlines. As I sit here in this serene place, their quality throughout, their arrangement, their tone, their arguments and exhortations, read as though they came from drugged and drunken men. They give one the effect of faded bawling, of screams and shouts heard faintly in a little gramophone.... It is only on Monday I find, and buried deep below the war news, that these publications contain any intimation that unusual happenings were forward in Clayton and Swathinglea.

What I saw was towards evening. I had been learning to shoot with my new possession. I had walked out with it four or five miles across a patch of moorland and down to a secluded little coppice full of bluebells, halfway along the highroad between Leet and Stafford. Here I had spent the afternoon, experimenting and practicing with careful deliberation and grim persistence. I had brought an old kite-frame of cane with me, that folded and unfolded, and each shot-hole I made I marked and numbered to compare with my other endeavors. At last I was satisfied that I could hit a playing card at thirty paces nine times out of ten; the light was getting too bad for me to see my penciled bull's-eye, and in that state of quiet moodiness that sometimes comes with hunger to passionate men, I returned by the way of Swathinglea towards my home.

The road I followed came down between banks of wretched-looking workingmen's houses, in close-packed rows on either side, and took upon itself the role of Swathinglea High Street, where, at a lamp and a pillar-box, the steam-trams began. So far that dirty hot way had been unusually quiet and empty, but beyond the corner, where the first group of beershops clustered, it became populous.

It was very quiet still, even the children were a little inactive, but there were a lot of people standing dispersedly in little groups, and with a general direction towards the gates of the Bantock Burden coalpit.

The place was being picketed, although at that time the miners were still nominally at work, and the conferences between masters and men still in session at Clayton Town Hall. But one of the men employed at the Bantock Burden pit, Jack Briscoe, was a socialist, and he had distinguished himself by a violent letter upon the crisis to the leading socialistic paper in England, *The Clarion,* in which he had adventured among the motives of Lord Redcar. The publication of this had been followed by instant dismissal. As Lord Redcar wrote a day or so later to the *Times*—I have that *Times,* I have all the London papers of the last month before the Change—

"The man was paid off and kicked out. Any self-respecting employer would do the same." The thing had happened overnight, and the men did not at once take a clear line upon what was, after all, a very intricate and debatable occasion. But they came out in a sort of semi-official strike from all Lord Redcar's collieries beyond the canal that besets Swathinglea. They did so without formal notice, committing a breach of contract by this sudden cessation. But in the long labor struggles of the old days the workers were constantly putting themselves in the wrong and committing illegalities through that overpowering craving for dramatic promptness natural to uneducated minds.

All the men had not come out of the Bantock Burden pit. Something was wrong there, an indecision if nothing else; the mine was still working, and there was a rumor that men from Durham had been held in readiness by Lord Redcar, and were already in the mine. Now, it is absolutely impossible to ascertain certainly how things stood at that time. Newspapers say this and that, but nothing trustworthy remains.

I believe I should have gone striding athwart the dark stage of that stagnant industrial drama without asking a question, if Lord Redcar had not chanced to come upon the scene about the same time as myself and incontinently end its stagnation.

He had promised that if the men wanted a struggle he would put up the best fight they had ever had, and he had been active all that afternoon in meeting the quarrel half-way, and preparing as conspicuously as possible for the scratch force of "black-legs"—as we call them—who were he said and we believed, to replace the strikers in his pits.

I was an eyewitness of the whole of the affair outside the Bantock Burden pit, and—I do not know what happened.

Picture to yourself how the thing came to me.

I was descending a steep, cobbled, excavated road between banked-up footways, perhaps six feet high, upon which, in a monotonous series, opened the living-room doors of rows of dark, low cottages. The perspective of squat blue slate roofs and clustering chimneys drifted downward towards the irregular open space before the colliery—a space covered with coaly, wheel-scarred mud, with a patch of weedy dump to the left and the colliery gates to the right. Beyond, the High Street with shops resumed again in good earnest and went on, and the lines of the steam-tramway that started out from before my feet, and were here shining and acutely visible with reflected skylight and here lost in a shadow, took up for one acute moment the greasy yellow irradiation of a newly lit gas-lamp as they vanished round the bend. Beyond, spread a darkling marsh of homes, an infinitude of little smoking hovels, and emergent, meager churches, public houses, board schools, and other buildings amidst the prevailing chimneys of Swathinglea. To the right, very clear and relatively high, the Bantock Burden pit-mouth was marked by a gaunt lattice bearing a great black wheel, very sharp and distinct in the twilight, and beyond, in an irregular perspective, were others following the lie of the seams. The general effect, as one came down the hill, was of a dark compressed life beneath a very high and wide and luminous evening sky, against which these pit-wheels rose. And ruling the calm spaciousness of that heaven was the great comet, now green-white, and wonderful for all who had eyes to see.

The fading afterglow of the sunset threw up all the contours and skyline to the west, and the comet rose eastward out of the pouring tumult of smoke from Bladden's forges. The moon had still to rise.

By this time the comet had begun to assume the cloudlike form still familiar through the medium of a thousand photographs and sketches. At first it had been an almost telescopic speck; it had brightened to the dimensions of the greatest star in the heavens; it had still grown, hour by hour, in its incredibly swift, its noiseless and inevitable rush upon our earth, until it had equaled and surpassed the moon. Now it was the most splendid thing this sky of earth has ever held. I have never seen a photograph that gave a proper idea of it. Never at any time did it assume the conventional tailed outline comets are supposed to have. Astronomers talked of its double tail, one preceding it and one trailing behind it, but these were foreshortened to nothing, so that it had rather the form of a bellying puff of luminous smoke with an intenser, brighter heart. It rose a hot yellow color, and only began to show its distinctive greenness when it was clear of the mists of the evening.

It compelled my attention for a space. For all my earthly concentration of mind, I could but stare at it for a moment with a vague anticipation that, after all, in some way so strange and glorious an object must have significance, could not possibly be a matter of absolute indifference to the scheme and values of my life.

But how?

I thought of Parload. I thought of the panic and uneasiness that was spreading in this very matter, and the assurances of scientific men that the thing weighed so little—at the utmost a few hundred tons of thinly diffused gas and dust—that even were it to smite this earth fully, nothing could possibly ensue. And, after all, said I, what earthly significance has anyone found in the stars?

Then, as one still descended, the houses and buildings rose up, the presence of those watching groups of people, the tension of the situation; and one forgot the sky.

Preoccupied with myself and with my dark dream about Nettie and my honor, I threaded my course through the stagnating threat of this gathering, and was caught unawares, when suddenly the whole scene flashed into drama....

The attention of everyone swung round with an irresistible magnetism towards the High Street, and caught me as a rush of waters might catch a wisp of hay. Abruptly the whole crowd was sounding one note. It was not a word, it was a sound that mingled threat and protest, something between a prolonged "Ah!" and "Ugh!" Then with a hoarse intensity of anger came a low heavy booing, "Boo! boo—oo!" a note stupidly expressive of animal savagery. "Toot, toot!" said Lord Redcar's automobile in ridiculous repartee. "Toot, toot!" One heard it whizzing and throbbing as the crowd obliged it to slow down.

Everybody seemed in motion towards the colliery gates, I, too, with the others.

I heard a shout. Through the dark figures about me I saw the motorcar stop and move forward again, and had a glimpse of something writhing on the ground....

It was alleged afterwards that Lord Redcar was driving, and that he quite deliberately knocked down a little boy who would not get out of his way. It is asserted with equal confidence that the boy was a man who tried to pass across the front of the motorcar as it came slowly through the crowd, who escaped by a hair's breadth, and then slipped on the tram-rail and fell down. I have both accounts set forth, under screaming headlines, in two of these withered newspapers upon my desk. No one could ever ascertain the truth. Indeed, in such a blind tumult of passion, could there be any truth?

There was a rush forward, the horn of the car sounded, everything swayed violently to the right for perhaps ten yards or so, and there was a report like a pistol-shot.

For a moment everyone seemed running away. A woman, carrying a shawl-wrapped child, blundered into me, and sent me reeling back. Everyone thought of firearms, but, as a matter of fact, something had gone wrong with the motor, what in those old-fashioned contrivances was called a backfire. A thin puff of bluish smoke hung in the air behind the thing. The majority of the people scattered back in a disorderly fashion, and left a clear space about the struggle that centered upon the motorcar.

The man or boy who had fallen was lying on the ground with no one near him, a black lump, an extended arm and two sprawling feet. The motorcar had stopped, and its three occupants were standing up. Six or seven black figures surrounded the car, and appeared to be holding on to it as if to prevent it from starting again; one—it was Mitchell, a well-known labor leader—argued in fierce low tones with Lord Redcar. I could not hear anything they said, I was not near enough. Behind me the colliery gates were open, and there was a sense of help coming to the motorcar from that direction. There was an unoccupied muddy space for fifty yards, perhaps, between car and gate, and then the wheels and head of the pit rose black against the sky. I was one of a rude semicircle of people that hung as yet indeterminate in action about this dispute.

It was natural, I suppose, that my fingers should close upon the revolver in my pocket.

I advanced with the vaguest intentions in the world, and not so quickly but that several men hurried past me to join the little knot holding up the car.

Lord Redcar, in his big furry overcoat, towered up over the group about him; his gestures were free and threatening, and his voice loud. He made a fine figure there, I must admit; he was a big, fair, handsome young man with a fine tenor voice and an instinct for gallant effect. My eyes were drawn to him at first wholly. He seemed a symbol, a triumphant symbol, of all that the theory of aristocracy claims, of all that filled my soul with resentment. His chauffeur sat crouched together, peering at the crowd under his lordship's arm. But Mitchell showed as a sturdy figure also, and his voice was firm and loud.

"You've hurt that lad," said Mitchell, over and over again. "You'll wait here till you see if he's hurt."

"I'll wait here or not as I please," said Redcar; and to the chauffeur, "Here! get down and look at it!"

"You'd better not get down," said Mitchell; and the chauffeur stood bent and hesitating on the step.

The man on the back seat stood up, leaned forward, and spoke to Lord Redcar, and for the first time my attention was drawn to him. It was young Verrall! His handsome face shone clear and fine in the green pallor of the comet.

I ceased to hear the quarrel that was raising the voices of Mitchell and Lord Redcar. This new fact sent them spinning into the background. Young Verrall!

It was my own purpose coming to meet me halfway.

There was to be a fight here, it seemed certain to come to a scuffle, and here we were—

What was I to do? I thought very swiftly. Unless my memory cheats me, I acted with swift decision. My hand tightened on my revolver, and then I remembered it was unloaded. I had thought my course out in an instant. I turned round and pushed my way out of the angry crowd that was now surging back towards the motorcar.

It would be quiet and out of sight, I thought, among the dump heaps across the road, and there I might load unobserved....

A big young man striding forward with his fists clenched, halted for one second at the sight of me.

"What!" said he. "Ain't afraid of them, are you?"

I glanced over my shoulder and back at him, was near showing him my pistol, and the expression changed in his eyes. He hung perplexed at me. Then with a grunt he went on.

I heard the voices growing loud and sharp behind me.

I hesitated, half turned towards the dispute, then set off running towards the heaps. Some instinct told me not to be detected loading. I was cool enough therefore to think of the aftermath of the thing I meant to do.

I looked back once again towards the swaying discussion—or was it a fight now? and then I dropped into the hollow, knelt among the weeds, and loaded with eager trembling fingers. I loaded one chamber, got up and went back a dozen paces, thought of possibilities, vacillated, returned and loaded all the others. I did it slowly because I felt a little clumsy, and at the end came a moment of inspection—had I forgotten anything? And then for a few seconds I crouched before I rose, resisting the first gust of reaction against my impulse. I took thought, and for a moment that great green-white meteor overhead swam back into my conscious mind. For the first time then I linked it clearly with all the fierce violence that had crept into human life. I joined up that with what I meant to do. I was going to shoot young Verrall as it were under the benediction of that green glare.

But about Nettie?

I found it impossible to think out that obvious complication.

I came up over the heap again, and walked slowly back towards the wrangle.

Of course I had to kill him....

Now I would have you believe I did not want to murder young Verrall at all at that particular time. I had not pictured such circumstances as these, I had never thought of him in connection with Lord Redcar and our black industrial world. He was in that distant other world of Checkshill, the world of parks and gardens, the world of sunlit emotions and Nettie. His appearance here was disconcerting. I was taken by surprise. I was too tired and hungry to think clearly, and the hard implication of our antagonism prevailed with me. In the tumult of my past emotions I had thought constantly of conflicts, confrontations, deeds of violence, and now the memory of these things took possession of me as though they were irrevocable resolutions.

There was a sharp exclamation, the shriek of a woman, and the crowd came surging back. The fight had begun.

Lord Redcar, I believe, had jumped down from his car and felled Mitchell, and men were already running out to his assistance from the colliery gates.

I had some difficulty in shoving through the crowd; I can still remember very vividly being jammed at one time between two big men so that my arms were pinned to my sides, but all the other details are gone out of my mind until I found myself almost violently projected forward into the "scrap."

I blundered against the corner of the motorcar, and came round it face to face with young Verrall, who was descending from the back compartment. His face was touched with orange from the automobile's big lamps, which conflicted with the shadows of the comet light, and distorted him oddly. That effect lasted but an instant, but it put me out. Then he came a step forward, and the ruddy lights and queerness vanished.

I don't think he recognized me, but he perceived immediately I meant attacking. He struck out at once at me a haphazard blow, and touched me on the cheek.

Instinctively I let go of the pistol, snatched my right hand out of my pocket and brought it up in a belated parry, and then let out with my left full in his chest.

I sent him staggering, and as he went back I saw recognition mingle with astonishment in his face.

"You know me, you swine," I cried and hit again.

Then I was spinning sideways, half-stunned, with a huge lump of a fist under my jaw. I had an impression of Lord Redcar as a great furry bulk, towering like some Homeric hero above the fray. I went down before him—it made him seem to rush up—and he ignored me further. His big flat voice counseled young Verrall—

"Cut, Teddy! It won't do. The picketa's got i'on bahs...."

Feet swayed about me, and some hobnailed miner kicked my ankle and went stumbling. There were shouts and curses, and then everything had swept past me. I rolled over on my face and beheld the chauffeur, young Verrall, and Lord Redcar—the latter holding up his long skirts of fur, and making a grotesque figure—one behind the other, in full bolt across a coldly comet-lit interval, towards the open gates of the colliery.

I raised myself up on my hands.

Young Verrall!

I had not even drawn my revolver—I had forgotten it. I was covered with coaly mud—knees, elbows, shoulders, back. I had not even drawn my revolver! ...

A feeling of ridiculous impotence overwhelmed me. I struggled painfully to my feet.

I hesitated for a moment towards the gates of the colliery, and then went limping homeward, thwarted, painful, confused, and ashamed. I had not the heart nor desire to help in the wrecking and burning of Lord Redcar's motor.

4

In the night, fever, pain, fatigue—it may be the indigestion of my supper of bread and cheese—roused me at last out of a tormented sleep to face despair. I was a soul lost amidst desolations and shame, dishonored, evilly treated, hopeless. I raged against the God I denied, and cursed him as I lay.

And it was in the nature of my fever, which was indeed only half fatigue and illness, and the rest the disorder of passionate youth, that Nettie, a strangely distorted Nettie, should come through the brief dreams that marked the exhaustions of that vigil, to dominate my misery. I was sensible, with an exaggerated distinctness, of the intensity of her physical charm for me, of her every grace and beauty; she took to herself the whole gamut of desire in me and the whole gamut of pride. She, bodily, was my lost honor. It was not only loss but disgrace to lose her. She stood for life and all that was denied; she mocked me as a creature of failure and defeat. My spirit raised itself towards her, and then the bruise upon my jaw glowed with a dull heat, and I rolled in the mud again before my rivals.

There were times when something near madness took me, and I gnashed my teeth and dug my nails into my hands and ceased to curse and cry out only by reason of the insufficiency of words. At once towards dawn I got out of bed, and sat by my looking glass with my revolver loaded in my hand. I stood up at last and put it carefully in my drawer and locked it—out of reach of any gusty impulse. After that I slept for a little while.

Such nights were nothing rare and strange in that old order of the world. Never a city, never a night the whole year round, but amidst those who slept were those who waked, plumbing the deeps of wrath and misery. Countless thousands there were so ill, so troubled, they agonized near to the very borderline of madness, each one the center of a universe darkened and lost....

The next day I spent in gloomy lethargy.

I had intended to go to Checkshill that day, but my bruised ankle was too swollen for that to be possible. I sat indoors in the ill-lit downstairs kitchen, with my foot bandaged, and mused darkly and read. My dear old mother waited on me, and her brown eyes watched me and wondered at my black silences, my frowning preoccupations. I had not told her how it was my ankle came to be bruised and my clothes muddy. She had brushed my clothes in the morning before I got up.

Ah well! Mothers are not treated in that way now. That I suppose must console me. I wonder how far you will be able to picture that dark, grimy, untidy room, with its bare deal table, its tattered wallpaper, the saucepans and kettle on the narrow, cheap, but by no means economical range, the ashes under the fireplace, the rust-spotted steel fender on which my bandaged feet rested; I wonder how near you can come to seeing the scowling pale-faced hobbledehoy I was, unshaven and collarless, in the Windsor chair, and the little timid, dirty, devoted old woman who hovered about me with love peering out from her puckered eyelids....

When she went out to buy some vegetables in the middle of the morning she got me a halfpenny journal. It was just such a one as these upon my desk, only that the copy I read was damp from the press, and these are so dry and brittle, they crack if I touch them. I have a copy of the actual issue I read that morning; it was a paper called emphatically the *New Paper*, but everybody bought it and everybody called it the "yell." It was full that morning of stupendous news and still more stupendous headlines, so stupendous that for a little while I was roused from my egotistical broodings to wider interests. For it seemed that Germany and England were on the brink of war.

Of all the monstrous irrational phenomena of the former time, war was certainly the most strikingly insane. In reality it was probably far less mischievous than such quieter evil as, for example, the general acquiescence in the private ownership of land, but its evil consequences showed so plainly that even in those days of stifling confusion one marveled at it. On no conceivable grounds was there any sense in modern war. Save for the slaughter and mangling of a multitude of people, the destruction of vast quantities of material, and the waste of innumerable units of energy, it effected nothing. The old war of savage and barbaric nations did at least change humanity, you assumed yourselves to be a superior tribe in physique and discipline, you demonstrated this upon your neighbors, and if successful you took their land and their women and perpetuated and enlarged your superiority. The new war changed nothing but the color of maps, the design of postage stamps, and the relationship of a few accidentally conspicuous individuals. In one of the last of these international epileptic fits, for example, the English, with much dysentery and bad poetry, and a few hundred deaths in battle, conquered the South African Boers at a gross cost of about three thousand pounds per head—they could have bought the whole of that preposterous imitation of a nation for a tenth of that sum—and except for a few substitutions of personalities, this group of partially corrupt officials in the place of that, and so forth, the permanent change was altogether insignificant. (But an excitable young man in Austria committed suicide when at length the Transvaal ceased to be a "nation.") Men went through the seat of that war after it was all over, and found humanity unchanged, except for a general impoverishment, and the convenience of an unlimited supply of empty ration tins and barbed wire and cartridge cases—unchanged and resuming with a slight perplexity all its old habits and misunderstandings, the black still in his slum-like kraal, the white in his ugly ill-managed shanty....

But we in England saw all these things, or did not see them, through the mirage of the *New Paper,* in a light of mania. All my adolescence from fourteen to seventeen went to the music of that monstrous resonating futility, the cheering, the anxieties, the songs and the waving of flags, the wrongs of generous Buller and the glorious heroism of De Wet—who *always* got away; that was the great point about the heroic De Wet—and it never occurred to us that the total population we fought against was less than half the number of those who lived cramped ignoble lives within the compass of the Four Towns.

But before and after that stupid conflict of stupidities, a greater antagonism was coming into being, was slowly and quietly defining itself as a thing inevitable, sinking now a little out of attention only to resume more emphatically, now flashing into some acute definitive expression and now percolating and pervading some new region of thought, and that was the antagonism of Germany and Great Britain.

When I think of that growing proportion of readers who belong entirely to the new order, who are growing up with only the vaguest early memories of the old world, I find the greatest difficulty in writing down the unintelligible confusions that were matter of fact to their fathers.

Here were we British, forty-one millions of people, in a state of almost indescribably aimless, economic, and moral muddle that we had neither the courage, the energy, nor the intelligence to improve, that most of us had hardly the courage to think about, and with our affairs hopelessly entangled with the entirely different confusions of three hundred and fifty million other persons scattered about the globe, and here were the Germans over against us, fifty-six millions, in a state of confusion no whit better than our own, and the noisy little creatures who directed papers and wrote books and gave lectures, and generally in that time of world-dementia pretended to be the national mind, were busy in both countries, with a sort of infernal unanimity, exhorting—and not only exhorting but successfully persuading—the two peoples to divert such small common store of material, moral and intellectual energy as either possessed, into the purely destructive and wasteful business of war. And—I have to tell you these things even if you do not believe them, because they are vital to my story—there was not a man alive who could have told you of any real permanent benefit, of anything whatever to counterbalance the obvious waste and evil, that would result from a war between England and Germany, whether England shattered Germany or was smashed and overwhelmed, or whatever the end might be.

The thing was, in fact, an enormous irrational obsession, it was, in the microcosm of our nation, curiously parallel to the egotistical wrath and jealousy that swayed my individual microcosm. It measured the excess of common emotion over the common intelligence, the legacy of inordinate passion we have received from the brute from which we came. Just as I had become the slave of my own surprise and anger and went hither and thither with a loaded revolver, seeking and intending vague fluctuating crimes, so these two nations went about the earth, hot eared and muddle-headed, with loaded navies and armies terribly ready at hand. Only there was not even a Nettie to justify their stupidity. There was nothing but quiet imaginary thwarting on either side.

And the press was the chief instrument that kept these two huge multitudes of people directed against one another.

The press—those newspapers that are now so strange to us—like the "Empires," the "Nations," the Trusts, and all the other great monstrous shapes of that extraordinary time—was in the nature of an unanticipated accident. It had happened, as weeds happen in abandoned gardens, just as all our world has happened—because there was no clear will in the world to bring about anything better. Towards the end this "press" was almost entirely under the direction of youngish men of that eager, rather unintelligent type, that is never able to detect itself aimless, that pursues nothing with incredible pride and zeal, and if you would really understand this mad era the comet brought to an end, you must keep in mind that every phase in the production of these queer old things was pervaded by a strong aimless energy and happened in a concentrated rush.

Let me describe to you, very briefly, a newspaper day.

Figure first, then, a hastily erected and still more hastily designed building in a dirty, paper-littered back street of old London, and a number of shabbily dressed men coming and going in this with projectile swiftness, and within this factory companies of printers, tensely active with nimble fingers—they were always speeding up the printers—ply their typesetting machines, and cast and arrange masses of metal in a sort of kitchen inferno, above which, in a beehive of little brightly lit rooms, disheveled men sit and scribble. There is a throbbing of telephones and a clicking of telegraph needles, a rushing of messengers, a running to and fro of heated men, clutching proofs and copy. Then begins a clatter roar of machinery catching the infection, going faster and faster, and whizzing and banging—engineers, who have never had time to wash since their birth, flying about with oilcans, while paper runs off its rolls with a shudder of haste. The proprietor you must suppose arriving explosively on a swift motorcar, leaping out before the thing is at a standstill, with letters and documents clutched in his hand, rushing in, resolute to "hustle," getting wonderfully in everybody's way. At the sight of him even the messenger boys who are waiting, get up and scamper to and fro. Sprinkle your vision with collisions, curses, incoherencies. You imagine all the parts of this complex lunatic machine working hysterically toward a crescendo of haste and excitement as the night wears on. At last the only things that seem to travel slowly in all those tearing vibrating premises are the hands of the clock.

Slowly things draw on toward publication, the consummation of all those stresses. Then in the small hours, into the now dark and deserted streets comes a wild whirl of carts and men, the place spurts paper at every door, bales, heaps, torrents of papers, that are snatched and flung about in what looks like a free fight, and off with a rush and clatter east, west, north, and south. The interest passes outwardly; the men from the little rooms are going homeward, the printers disperse yawning, the roaring presses slacken. The paper exists. Distribution follows manufacture, and we follow the bundles.

Our vision becomes a vision of dispersal. You see those bundles hurling into stations, clatching trains by a hair's breadth, speeding on their way, breaking up, smaller bundles of them hurled with a fierce accuracy out upon the platforms that rush by, and then everywhere a division of these smaller bundles into still smaller bundles, into dispersing parcels, into separate papers, and the dawn happens unnoticed amidst a great running and shouting of boys, a shoving through letter slots, openings of windows, spreading out upon bookstalls. For the space of a few hours you must figure the whole country dotted white with rustling papers—placards everywhere vociferating the hurried lie for the day, men and women in trains, men and women eating and reading, men by study-fenders, people sitting up in bed, mothers and sons and daughters waiting for father to finish—a million scattered people reading—reading headlong—or feverishly ready to read. It is just as if some vehement jet had sprayed that white foam of papers over the surface of the land....

And then you know, wonderfully gone—gone utterly, vanished as foam might vanish upon the sand.

Nonsense! The whole affair a noisy paroxysm of nonsense, unreasonable excitement, witless mischief, and waste of strength—signifying nothing....

And one of those white parcels was the paper I held in my hands, as I sat with a bandaged foot on the steel fender in that dark underground kitchen of my mother's, clean roused from my personal troubles by the yelp of the headlines. She sat, sleeves tucked up from her ropy arms, peeling potatoes as I read.

It was like one of a flood of disease germs that have invaded a body, that paper. There I was, one corpuscle in the big amorphous body of the English community, one of forty-one million such corpuscles and, for all my preoccupations, these potent headlines, this paper ferment, caught me and swung me about. And all over the country that day, millions read as I read, and came round into line with me, under the same magnetic spell, came round—how did we say it?—Ah!—"to face the foe."

The comet had been driven into obscurity overleaf. The column headed "Distinguished Scientist says Comet will Strike our Earth. Does it Matter?" went unread. "Germany"—I usually figured this mythical malignant creature as a corseted stiff-mustached Emperor enhanced by heraldic black wings and a large sword—had insulted our flag. That was the message of the *New Paper,* and the monster towered over me, threatening fresh outrages, visibly spitting upon my faultless country's colors. Somebody had hoisted a British flag on the right bank of some tropical river I had never heard of before, and a drunken German officer under ambiguous instructions had torn it down. Then one of the convenient abundant natives of the country, a British subject indisputably, had been shot in the leg. But the facts were by no means clear. Nothing was clear except that we were not going to stand any nonsense from Germany. Whatever had or had not happened we meant to have an apology for, and apparently they did not mean apologizing.

"HAS WAR COME AT LAST?"

That was the headline. One's heart leaped to assent....

There were hours that day when I clean forgot Nettie, in dreaming of battles and victories by land and sea, of shell fire, and entrenchments, and the heaped slaughter of many thousands of men.

But the next morning I started for Checkshill, started, I remember, in a curiously hopeful state of mind, oblivious of comets, strikes, and wars.

5

You must understand that I had no set plan of murder when I walked over to Checkshill. I had no set plan of any sort. There was a great confusion of dramatically conceived intentions in my head, scenes of threatening and denunciation and terror, but I did not mean to kill. The revolver was to turn upon my rival my disadvantage in age and physique....But that was not it really! The revolver!—I took the revolver because I had the revolver and was a foolish young lout. It was a dramatic sort of thing to take. I had, I say, no plan at all.

Ever and again during that second trudge to Checkshill I

was irradiated with a novel unreasonable hope. I had awakened in the morning with the hope, it may have been the last unfaded trail of some obliterated dream, that after all Nettie might relent toward me, that her heart was kind toward me in spite of all that I imagined had happened. I even thought it possible that I might have misinterpreted what I had seen. Perhaps she would explain everything. My revolver was in my pocket for all that.

I limped at the outset, but after the second mile my ankle warmed to forgetfulness, and the rest of the way I walked well. Suppose, after all, I was wrong?

I was still debating that, as I came through the park. By the corner of the paddock near the keeper's cottage, I was reminded by some belated blue hyacinths of a time when I and Nettie had gathered them together. It seemed impossible that we could really have parted ourselves for good and all. A wave of tenderness flowed over me, and still flooded me as I came through the little dell and drew towards the hollies. But there the sweet Nettie of my boy's love faded, and I thought of the new Nettie of desire and the man I had come upon in the moonlight, I thought of the narrow, hot purpose that had grown so strongly out of my springtime freshness, and my mood darkened to night.

I crossed the beech wood and came towards the gardens with a resolute and sorrowful heart. When I reached the green door in the garden wall I was seized for a space with so violent a trembling that I could not grip the latch to lift it, for I no longer had any doubt how this would end. That trembling was succeeded by a feeling of cold, and whiteness, and self-pity. I was astonished to find myself grimacing, to feel my cheeks wet, and thereupon I gave way completely to a wild passion of weeping. I must take just a little time before the thing was done....I turned away from the door and stumbled for a little distance, sobbing loudly, and lay down out of sight among the bracken, and so presently became calm again. I lay there some time. I had half a mind to desist, and then my emotion passed like the shadow of a cloud, and I walked very coolly into the gardens.

Through the open door of one of the glass houses I saw old Stuart. He was leaning against the staging, his hands in his pockets, and so deep in thought he gave no heed to me....

I hesitated and went on towards the cottage, slowly.

Something struck me as unusual about the place, but I could not tell at first what it was. One of the bedroom windows was open, and the customary short blind, with its brass upper rail partly unfastened, drooped obliquely across the vacant space. It looked negligent and odd, for usually everything about the cottage was conspicuously trim.

The door was standing wide open, and everything was still. But giving that usually orderly hall an odd look—it was about half-past two in the afternoon—was a pile of three dirty plates, with used knives and forks upon them, on one of the hall chairs.

I went into the hall, looked into either room, and hesitated.

Then I fell to upon the door-knocker and gave a loud rat-tat-too, and followed this up with an amiable "Hel-lo!"

For a time no one answered me, and I stood listening and expectant, with my fingers about my weapon. Someone moved about upstairs presently, and was still again. The tension of waiting seemed to brace my nerves.

I had my hand on the knocker for the second time, when Puss appeared in the doorway.

For a moment we remained staring at one another without speaking. Her hair was disheveled, her face dirty, tear-stained, and irregularly red. Her expression at the sight of me was pure astonishment. I thought she was about to say something, and then she had darted away out of the house again.

"I say, Puss!" I said. "Puss!"

I followed her out of the door. "Puss! What's the matter? Where's Nettie?"

She vanished round the corner of the house.

I hesitated, perplexed whether I should pursue her. What did it all mean? Then I heard someone upstairs.

"Willie!" cried the voice of Mrs. Stuart. "Is that you?"

"Yes," I answered. "Where's everyone? Where's Nettie? I want to have a talk with her."

She did not answer, but I heard her dress rustle as she moved. I judged she was upon the landing overhead.

I paused at the foot of the stairs, expecting her to appear and come down.

Suddenly came a strange sound, a rush of sounds, words jumbled and hurrying, confused and shapeless, borne along upon a note of throaty distress that at last submerged the words altogether and ended in a wail. Except that it came from a woman's throat it was exactly the babbling sound of a weeping child with a grievance. "I can't," she said, "I can't," and that was all I could distinguish. It was to my young ears the strangest sound conceivable from a kindly motherly little woman, whom I had always thought of chiefly as an unparalleled maker of cakes. It frightened me. I went upstairs at once in a state of infinite alarm, and there she was upon the landing, leaning forward over the top of the chest of drawers beside her open bedroom door, and weeping. I never saw such weeping. One thick strand of black hair had escaped, and hung with a spiral twist down her back; never before had I noticed that she had gray hairs.

As I came up upon the landing her voice rose again. "Oh that I should have to tell you, Willie! Oh that I should have to tell you!" She dropped her head again, and a fresh gust of tears swept all further words away.

I said nothing, I was too astonished; but I drew nearer to her, and waited....

I never saw such weeping; the extraordinary wetness of her dripping handkerchief abides with me to this day.

"That I should have lived to see this day!" she wailed. "I had rather a thousand times she was struck dead at my feet."

I began to understand.

"Mrs. Stuart," I said, clearing my throat, "what has become of Nettie?"

"That I should have lived to see this day!" she said by way of reply.

I waited till her passion abated.

There came a lull. I forgot the weapon in my pocket. I said nothing, and suddenly she stood erect before me, wiping her swollen eyes. "Willie," she gulped, "she's gone!"

"Nettie?"

"Gone!...Run away....Run away from her home. Oh, Willie, Willie! The shame of it! The sin and shame of it!"

She flung herself upon my shoulder, and clung to me, and began again to wish her daughter lying dead at our feet.

"There, there," said I, and all my being was a-tremble. "Where has she gone?" I said as softly as I could.

But for the time she was preoccupied with her own sorrow, and I had to hold her there, and comfort her with the blackness of finality spreading over my soul.

"Where has she gone?" I asked for the fourth time.

"I don't know—we don't know. And oh, Willie, she went out yesterday morning! I said to her, 'Nettie,' I said to her, 'you're mighty fine for a morning call.' 'Fine clo's for a fine day,' she said, and that was her last words to me!—Willie!—the child I suckled at my breast!"

"Yes, yes. But where has she gone?" I said.

She went on with sobs, and now telling her story with a sort of fragmentary hurry: "She went out bright and shining, out of this house forever. She was smiling, Willie—as if she was glad to be going." ("Glad to be going," I echoed with soundless lips.) "'You're mighty fine for the morning,' I says; 'mighty fine.' 'Let the girl be pretty,' says her father, 'while she's young!' And somewhere she'd got a parcel of her things hidden to pick up, and she was going off—out of this house forever!"

She became quiet.

"Let the girl be pretty," she repeated; "let the girl be

pretty while she's young....Oh! how can we go on *living*, Willie?...He doesn't show it, but he's like a stricken beast. He's wounded to the heart. She was always his favorite. He never seemed to care for Puss like he did for her. And she's wounded him—"

"Where has she gone?" I reverted at last to that.

"We don't know. She leaves her own blood, she trusts herself—Oh, Willie, it'll kill me! I wish she and me together were lying in our graves."

"But"—I moistened my lips and spoke slowly—"she may have gone to marry."

"If that was so! I've prayed to God it might be so, Willie. I've prayed that he'd take pity on her—him, I mean, she's with."

I jerked out: "Who's that?"

"In her letter, she said he was a gentleman. She did say he was a gentleman."

"In her letter. Has she written? Can I see her letter?"

"Her father took it."

"But if she writes— When did she write?"

"It came this morning."

"But where did it come from? You can tell—"

"She didn't say. She said she was happy. She said love took one like a storm—"

"Curse that! Where is her letter? Let me see it. And as for this gentleman—"

She stared at me.

"You know who it is."

"Willie!" she protested.

"You know who it is, whether she said or not." Her eyes made a mute unconfident denial.

"Young Verrall?"

She made no answer. "All I could do for you, Willie," she began presently.

"Was it young Verrall?" I insisted.

For a second, perhaps, we faced one another in stark understanding....Then she plumped back to the chest of drawers, and her wet pocket handkerchief, and I knew she sought refuge from my relentless eyes.

My pity for her vanished. She knew it was her mistress's son as well as I! And for some time she had known, she had felt.

I hovered over her for a moment, sick with amazed disgust. I suddenly bethought me of old Stuart, out in the greenhouse, and turned and went downstairs. As I did so, I looked up to see Mrs. Stuart moving droopingly and lamely back into her own room.

6

Old Stuart was pitiful.

I found him still inert in the greenhouse where I had first seen him. He did not move as I drew near him; he glanced at me, and then stared hard again at the flowerpots before him.

"Eh, Willie," he said, "this is a black day for all of us."

"What are you going to do?" I asked.

"The missus takes on so," he said. "I came out here."

"What do you mean to do?"

"What *is* a man to do in such a case?"

"Do!" I cried, "why— Do!"

"He ought to marry her," he said.

"By God, yes!" I cried. "He must do that anyhow."

"He ought to. It's—it's cruel. But what am *I* to do? Suppose he won't? Likely he won't. What then?"

He drooped with an intensified despair.

"Here's this cottage," he said, pursuing some contracted argument. "We've lived here all our lives, you might say. ...Clear out. At my age....One can't die in a slum."

I stood before him for a space, speculating what thoughts might fill the gaps between those broken words. I found his lethargy, and the dimly shaped mental attitudes his words indicated, abominable. I said abruptly, "You have her letter?"

He dived into his breast pocket, became motionless for ten seconds, then woke up again and produced her letter. He drew it clumsily from its envelope, and handed it to me silently.

"Why!" he cried, looking at me for the first time, "What's come to your chin, Willie?"

"It's nothing," I said. "It's a bruise;" and I opened the letter.

It was written on greenish tinted fancy notepaper, and with all and more than Nettie's usual triteness and inadequacy of expression. Her handwriting bore no traces of emotion; it was round and upright and clear as though it had been done in a writing lesson. Always her letters were like masks upon her image; they fell like curtains before the changing charm of her face; one altogether forgot the sound of her light clear voice, confronted by a perplexing stereotyped thing that had mysteriously got a hold upon one's heart and pride. How did that letter run?—

> MY DEAR MOTHER,
>
> Do not be distressed at my going away. I have gone somewhere safe, and with someone who cares for me very much. I am sorry for your sakes, but it seems that it had to be. Love is a very difficult thing, and takes hold of one in ways one does not expect. Do not think I am ashamed about this, I glory in my love, and you must not trouble too much about me. I am very, very happy (deeply underlined).
>
> Fondest love to Father and Puss.
>
> Your loving
>
> Nettie.

That queer little document! I can see it now for the childish simple thing it was, but at the time I read it in a suppressed anguish of rage. It plunged me into a pit of hopeless shame; there seemed to remain no pride for me in life until I had revenge. I stood staring at those rounded upstanding letters, not trusting myself to speak or move. At last I stole a glance at Stuart.

He held the envelope in his hand, and stared down at the postmark between his horny thumbnails.

"You can't even tell where she is," he said, turning the thing round in a hopeless manner, and then desisting. "It's hard on us, Willie. Here she is; she hadn't anything to complain of; a sort of pet for all of us. Not even made to do her share of the 'ousework. And she goes off and leaves us like a bird that's learned to fly. Can't *trust* us, that's what takes me. Puts 'erself— But there! What's to happen to her?"

"What's to happen to him?"

He shook his head to show that problem was beyond him.

"You'll go after her," I said in an even voice; "you'll make him marry her?"

"Where am I to go?" he asked helplessly, and held out the envelope with a gesture; "and what could I do? Even if I knew—How could I leave the gardens?"

"Great God!" I cried, "not leave these gardens! It's your Honor, man! If she was my daughter—if she was my daughter—I'd tear the world to pieces!" . . . I choked. "You mean to stand it?"

"What can I do?"

"Make him marry her! Horsewhip him! Horsewhip him, I say!—I'd strangle him!"

He scratched slowly at his hairy cheek, opened his mouth, and shook his head. Then, with an intolerable note of sluggish gentle wisdom, he said, "People of our sort, Willie, can't do things like that."

I came near to raving. I had a wild impulse to strike him in the face. Once in my boyhood I happened upon a bird terribly mangled by some cat, and killed it in a frenzy of horror and pity. I had a gust of that same emotion now, as this shameful mutilated soul fluttered in the dust, before me. Then, you know, I dismissed him from the case.

"May I look?" I asked.

He held out the envelope reluctantly.

"There it is," he said, and pointing with his garden-rough forefinger, "I.A.P.A.M.P. What can you make of that?"

I took the thing in my hands. The adhesive stamp customary in those days was defaced by a circular post-mark, which bore the name of the office of departure and the date. The impact in this particular case had been light or made without sufficient ink, and half the letters of the name had left no impression. I could distinguish—

IAP AMP

and very faintly below D.S.O.

I guessed the name in an instant flash of intuition. It was Shaphambury. The very gaps shaped that to my mind. Perhaps in a sort of semi-visibility other letters were there, at least hinting themselves. It was a place somewhere on the east coast, I knew, either in Norfolk or Suffolk.

"Why!" cried I—and stopped.

What was the good of telling him?

Old Stuart had glanced up sharply, I am inclined to think almost fearfully, into my face. "You—you haven't got it?" he said.

Shaphambury—I should remember that.

"You don't think you got it?" he said.

I handed the envelope back to him.

"For a moment I thought it might be Hampton," I said.

"Hampton," he repeated. "Hampton. How could you make Hampton?" He turned the envelope about. "H.A.M. —why, Willie, you're a worse hand at the job than me!"

He replaced the letter in the envelope and stood erect to put this back in his breast pocket.

I did not mean to take any risks in this affair. I drew a stump of pencil from my waistcoat pocket, turned a little away from him and wrote "Shaphambury" very quickly on my frayed and rather grimy shirt cuff.

"Well," said I, with an air of having done nothing remarkable.

I turned to him with some unimportant observation—I have forgotten what.

I never finished whatever vague remark I commenced.

I looked up to see a third person waiting at the greenhouse door.

7

It was old Mrs. Verrall.

I wonder if I can convey the effect of her to you. She was a little old lady with extraordinarily flaxen hair, her weak aquiline features were pursed up into an assumption of dignity, and she was richly dressed. I would like to underline that "richly dressed," or have the words printed in florid Old English or Gothic lettering. No one on earth is now quite so richly dressed as she was, no one old or young indulges in so quiet and yet so profound a sumptuosity. But you must not imagine any extravagance of outline or any beauty or richness of color. The predominant colors were black and fur browns, and the effect of richness was due entirely to the extreme costliness of the materials employed. She affected silk brocades with rich and elaborate patterns, priceless black lace over creamy or purple satin, intricate trimmings through which threads and bands of velvet wriggled, and in the winter rare furs. Her gloves fitted exquisitely, and ostentatiously simple chains of fine gold and pearls, and a great number of bracelets, laced about her little person. One was forced to feel that the slightest article she wore cost more than all the wardrobe of a dozen girls like Nettie; her bonnet affected the simplicity that is beyond rubies. Richness, that is the first quality about this old lady that I would like to convey to you, and the second is cleanliness. You felt that old Mrs. Verrall was exquisitely clean. If you had boiled my poor dear old mother in soda for a month you couldn't have got her so clean as Mrs. Verrall constantly and manifestly was. And pervading all her presence shone her third great quality, her manifest confidence in the respectful subordination of the world.

She was pale and a little out of breath that day, but without any loss of her ultimate confidence, and it was clear to me that she had come to interview Stuart upon the outbreak of passion that had bridged the gulf between their families.

And here again I find myself writing in an unknown language, so far as my younger readers are concerned. You who know only the world that followed the Great Change will find much that I am telling inconceivable. Upon these points I cannot appeal, as I have appealed for other confirmations, to the old newspapers; these were the things that no one wrote about because everyone understood and everyone had taken up an attitude. There were in England and America, and indeed throughout the world, two great informal divisions of human beings—the Secure and the Insecure. There was not and never had been in either country a nobility—it was and remains a common error that the British peers were noble—neither in law nor custom were there noble families, and we altogether lacked the edification one found in Russia, for example, of a poor nobility. A peerage was an hereditary possession that, like the family land, concerned only the eldest sons of the house; it radiated no luster of *noblesse oblige.* The rest of the world were in law and practice common—and all America was common. But through the private ownership of land that had resulted from the neglect of feudal obligations in Britain and the utter want of political foresight in the Americas, large masses of property had become artificially stable in the hands of a small minority, to whom it was necessary to mortgage all new public and private enterprises, and who were held together not by any tradition of service and nobility but by the natural sympathy of common interests and a common large scale of living. It was a class without any very definite boundaries; vigorous individualities, by methods for the most part violent and questionable, were constantly thrusting themselves from insecurity to security, and the sons and daughters of secure people, by marrying insecurity or by wild extravagance or flagrant vice, would sink into the life of anxiety and insufficiency which was the ordinary life of man. The rest of the population was landless and, except by working directly or indirectly for the Secure, had no legal right to exist. And such was the shallowness and insufficiency of our thought, such the stifled egotism of all our feelings before the Last Days, that very few indeed of the Secure could be found to doubt that this was the natural and only conceivable order of the world.

It is the life of the Insecure under the old order that I am displaying, and I hope that I am conveying something of its hopeless bitterness to you, but you must not imagine that the Secure lived lives of paradisiacal happiness. The pit of insecurity below them made itself felt, even though it was not comprehended. Life about them was ugly; the sight of ugly and mean houses, of ill-dressed people, the vulgar appeals of the dealers in popular commodities, were not to be escaped. There was below the threshold of their minds an uneasiness; they not only did not think clearly about social economy but they displayed an instinctive disinclination to think. Their security was not so perfect that they had not a dread of falling towards the pit, they were always lashing themselves by new ropes, their cultivation of "connections," of interests, their desire to confirm and improve their positions, was a constant ignoble preoccupation. You must read Thackeray to get the full flavor of their lives. Then the bacterium was apt to disregard class distinctions, and they were never really happy in their servants. Read their surviving books. Each generation bewails the decay of that "fidelity" of servants no generation ever saw. A world that is squalid in one corner is squalid altogether, but that they never understood. They believed there was not enough of anything to go round, they believed that this was the intention of God and an incurable condition of life, and they held passionately and with a sense of right to their disproportionate share. They maintained a common intercourse as "Society" of all who were practically secure, and their choice of that word is exhaustively eloquent of the quality of their philosophy. But, if you can master these alien ideas upon which the old system rested, just in the same measure will you understand the horror these people had for marriages with the Insecure. In the case of their girls and women it was extraordinarily rare, and in the case of either sex it was regarded as a disastrous social crime. Anything was better than that.

You are probably aware of the hideous fate that was only too probably the lot, during those last dark days, of every girl of the insecure classes who loved and gave way to the impulse of self-abandonment without marriage, and so you will understand the peculiar situation of Nettie with young Verrall. One or the other had to suffer. And as they were both in a state of great emotional exaltation and capable of strange generosities toward each other, it was an open question and naturally a source of great anxiety to a mother in Mrs. Verrall's position, whether the sufferer might not be her son—whether, as the outcome of that glowing irresponsible commerce, Nettie might not return prospective mistress of Checkshill Towers. The chances were greatly against that conclusion, but such things did occur.

These laws and customs sound, I know, like a record of some nasty-minded lunatic's inventions. They were invincible facts in that vanished world into which, by some accident, I had been born, and it was the dream of any better state of things that was scouted as lunacy. Just think of it! This girl I loved with all my soul, for whom I was ready to sacrifice my life, was not good enough to marry young Verrall. And I had only to look at his even, handsome, characterless face to perceive a creature weaker and no better than myself. She was to be his pleasure until he chose to cast her aside, and the poison of our social system had so saturated her nature—his evening dress, his freedom and his money had seemed so fine to her and I so clothed in squalor—that to that prospect she had consented. And to resent the social conventions that created their situation was called "class envy," and gently born preachers reproached us for the mildest resentment against an injustice no living man would now either endure or consent to profit by.

What was the sense of saying "peace" when there was no peace? If there was one hope in the disorders of that old world it lay in revolt and conflict to the death.

But if you can really grasp the shameful grotesqueness of the old life, you will begin to appreciate the interpretation of old Mrs. Verrall's appearance that leaped up at once in my mind.

She had come to compromise the disaster!

And the Stuarts *would* compromise! I saw that only too well.

An enormous disgust at the prospect of the imminent encounter between Stuart and his mistress made me behave in a violent and irrational way. I wanted to escape seeing that, seeing even Stuart's first gesture in that, at any cost.

"I'm off," said I, and turned my back on him without any further farewell.

My line of retreat lay by the old lady, and so I advanced toward her.

I saw her expression change, her mouth fell a little way open, her forehead wrinkled, and her eyes grew round. She found me a queer customer even at the first sight, and there was something in the manner of my advance that took away her breath.

She stood at the top of the three or four steps that descended to the level of the hothouse floor. She receded a pace or two, with a certain offended dignity at the determination of my rush.

I gave her no sort of salutation.

Well, as a matter of fact, I did give her a sort of salutation. There is no occasion for me to begin apologizing now for the thing I said to her—I strip these things before you—if only I can get them stark enough you will understand and forgive. I was filled with a brutal and overpowering desire to insult her.

And so I addressed this poor little expensive old woman in the following terms, converting her by a violent metonymy into a comprehensive plural. "You infernal land thieves!" I said pointblank into her face. *"Have you come to offer them money?"*

And without waiting to test her powers of repartee I passed rudely beyond her and vanished, striding with my fists clenched, out of her world again....

I have tried since to imagine how the thing must have looked to her. So far as her particular universe went I had not existed at all, or I had existed only as a dim black thing, an insignificant speck, far away across her park in irrelevant, unimportant transit, until this moment when she came, sedately troubled, into her own secure gardens and sought for Stuart among the greenhouses. Then abruptly I flashed into being down that green-walled, brick-floored vista as a black-visaged, ill-clad young man, who first stared and then advanced scowling toward her. Once in existence I developed rapidly. I grew larger in perspective and became more and more important and sinister every moment. I came up the steps with inconceivable hostility and disrespect in my bearing, towered over her, becoming for an instant at least a sort of second French Revolution, and delivered myself with the intensest concentration of those wicked and incomprehensible words. Just for a second I threatened annihilation. Happily that was my climax.

And then I had gone by, and the Universe was very much as it had always been except for the swirl in it, and the faint sense of insecurity my episode left in its wake.

The thing that never entered my head in those days was that a large proportion of the rich were rich in absolute good faith. I thought they saw things exactly as I saw them, and wickedly denied. But indeed old Mrs. Verrall was no more capable of doubting the perfection of her family's right to dominate a wide countryside, than she was of examining the Thirty-nine Articles or dealing with any other of the adamantine pillars upon which her universe rested in security.

No doubt I startled and frightened her tremendously. But she could not understand.

None of her sort of people ever did seem to understand such livid flashes of hate, as ever and again lit the crowded darkness below their feet. The thing leaped out of the black for a moment and vanished, like a threatening figure by a desolate roadside lit for a moment by one's belated carriage-lamp and then swallowed up by the night. They counted it with nightmares, and did their best to forget what was evidently as insignificant as it was disturbing.

Chapter 4

War

1

From that moment when I insulted old Mrs. Verrall I became representative, I was a man who stood for all the disinherited of the world. I had no hope of pride or pleasure left in me, I was raging rebellion against God and mankind. There were no more vague intentions swaying me this way and that; I was perfectly clear now upon what I meant to do. I would make my protest and die.

I would make my protest and die. I was going to kill Nettie—Nettie who had smiled and promised and given herself to another, and who stood now for all the conceivable delightfulnesses, the lost imaginations of the youthful heart, the unattainable joys in life; and Verrall who stood for all who profited by the incurable injustice of our social order. I would kill them both. And that being done I would blow my brains out and see what vengeance followed my blank refusal to live.

So indeed I was resolved. I raged monstrously. And above me, abolishing the stars, triumphant over the yellow waning moon that followed it below, the giant meteor towered up towards the zenith.

"Let me only kill!" I cried. "Let me only kill!"

So I shouted in my frenzy. I was in a fever that defied hunger and fatigue; for a long time I had prowled over the heath towards Lowchester talking to myself, and now that night had fully come I was tramping homeward, walking the long seventeen miles without a thought of rest. And I had eaten nothing since the morning.

I suppose I must count myself mad, but I can recall my ravings.

There were times when I walked weeping through that brightness that was neither night nor day. There were times when I reasoned in a topsy-turvy fashion with what I called the Spirit of All Things. But always I spoke to that white glory in the sky.

"Why am I here only to suffer ignominies?" I asked. "Why have you made me with pride that cannot be satisfied, with desires that turn and rend me? Is it a jest, this world—a joke you play on your guests? I—even I—have a better humor than that!

"Why not learn from me a certain decency of mercy? Why not undo? Have I ever tormented—day by day, some wretched worm—making filth for it to trail through, filth that disgusts it, starving it, bruising it, mocking it? Why should you? Your jokes are clumsy. Try—try some milder fun up there; do you hear? Something that doesn't hurt so infernally.

"You say this is your purpose—your purpose with me. You are making something with me—birth pangs of a soul. Ah! How can I believe you? You forget I have eyes for other things. Let my own case go, but what of that frog beneath the cartwheel, God?—and the bird the cat had torn?"

And after such blasphemies I would fling out a ridiculous little debating society hand. "Answer me that!"

A week ago it had been moonlight, white and black and hard across the spaces of the park, but now the light was livid and full of the quality of haze. An extraordinarily low white mist, not three feet above the ground, drifted broodingly across the grass, and the trees rose ghostly out of that phantom sea. Great and shadowy and strange was the world that night, no one seemed abroad; I and my little cracked voice drifted solitary through the silent mysteries. Sometimes I argued as I have told, sometimes I tumbled along in moody vacuity, sometimes my torment was vivid and acute.

Abruptly out of apathy would come a boiling paroxysm of fury, when I thought of Nettie mocking me and laughing, and of her and Verrall clasped in one another's arms.

"I will not have it so!" I screamed. "I will not have it so!"

And in one of these raving fits I drew my revolver from my pocket and fired into the quiet night. Three times I fired it.

The bullets tore through the air, and startled trees told one another in diminishing echoes the thing I had done, and then, with a slow finality, the vast and patient night healed again to calm. My shots, my curses and blasphemies, my prayers—for anon I prayed—that Silence took them all.

It was—how can I express it?—a stifled outcry tranquilized, lost, amid the serene assumptions, the overwhelming empire of that brightness. The noise of my shots, the impact upon things had for the instant been enormous, then it had passed away. I found myself standing with the revolver held up, astonished, my emotions penetrated by something I could not understand. Then I looked up over my shoulder at the great star, and remained staring at it.

"Who are *you?*" I said at last.

I was like a man in a solitary desert who has suddenly heard a voice....

That, too, passed.

As I came over Clayton Crest I recalled that I missed the multitude that now night after night walked out to stare at the comet, and the little preacher in the waste beyond the billboards, who warned sinners to repent before the Judgment, was not in his usual place.

It was long past midnight, and everyone had gone home. But I did not think of this at first, and the solitude perplexed me and left a memory behind. The gas-lamps were all extinguished because of the brightness of the comet, and that too was unfamiliar. The little news agent in the still High Street had shut up and gone to bed, but one belated board had been put out late and forgotten, and it still bore its placard.

The word upon it—there was but one word upon it in staring letters—was: "WAR."

You figure that empty mean street, emptily echoing to my footsteps—no soul awake and audible but me. Then my halt at the placard. And amidst that sleeping stillness, smeared hastily upon the board, a little askew and crumpled, but quite distinct beneath that cool meteoric glare, preposterous and appalling, the measureless evil of that word—

"WAR!"

2

I awoke in that state of equanimity that so often follows an emotional drenching.

It was late, and my mother was beside my bed. She had some breakfast for me on a battered tray.

"Don't get up yet, dear," she said. "You've been sleeping. It was three o'clock when you got home last night. You must have been tired out.

"Your poor face," she went on, "was as white as a sheet and your eyes shining.... It frightened me to let you in. And you stumbled on the stairs."

My eyes went quietly to my coat pocket, where something still bulged. She probably had not noticed. "I went to Checkshill," I said. "You know—perhaps—?"

"I got a letter last evening, dear," and as she bent near me to put the tray upon my knees, she kissed my hair softly. For a moment we both remained still, resting on that, her cheek just touching my head.

I took the tray from her to end the pause.

"Don't touch my clothes, Mummy," I said sharply, as she moved towards them. "I'm still equal to a clothes brush."

And then, as she turned away, I astonished her by saying, "You dear mother, you! A little—I understand. Only—now—dear mother; oh! let me be! Let me be!"

And, with the docility of a good servant, she went from me. Dear heart of submission that the world and I had used so ill!

It seemed to me that morning that I could never give way to a gust of passion again. A sorrowful firmness of the mind possessed me. My purpose seemed now as inflexible as iron; there was neither love nor hate nor fear left in me—only I pitied my mother greatly for all that was still to come. I ate my breakfast slowly, and thought where I could find out about Shaphambury, and how I might hope to get there. I had not five shillings in the world.

I dressed methodically, choosing the least frayed of my collars, and shaving much more carefully than was my wont; then I went down to the Public Library to consult a map.

Shaphambury was on the coast of Essex, a long and complicated journey from Clayton. I went to the railway station and made some memoranda from the timetables. The porters I asked were not very clear about Shaphambury, but the booking-office clerk was helpful, and we puzzled out all I wanted to know. Then I came out into the coaly street again. At the least I ought to have two pounds.

I went back to the Public Library and into the newspaper room to think over this problem.

A fact intruded itself upon me. People seemed in an altogether exceptional stir about the morning journals, there was something unusual in the air of the room, more people and more talking than usual, and for a moment I was puzzled. Then I bethought me: "This war with Germany, of course!" A naval battle was supposed to be in progress in the North Sea. Let them! I returned to the consideration of my own affairs.

Parload?

Could I go and make it up with him, and then borrow? I weighed the chances of that. Then I thought of selling or pawning something, but that seemed difficult. My winter overcoat had not cost a pound when it was new, my watch was not likely to fetch many shillings. Still, both these things might be factors. I thought with a certain repugnance of the little store my mother was probably making for the rent. She was very secretive about that, and it was locked in an old tea caddy in her bedroom. I knew it would be almost impossible to get any of that money from her willingly, and though I told myself that in this issue of passion and death no detail mattered, I could not get rid of tormenting scruples whenever I thought of that tea caddy. Was there no other course? Perhaps after every other source had been tapped I might supplement them with a few shillings frankly begged from her. "These others," I said to myself, thinking without passion for once of the sons of the Secure, "would find it difficult to run their romances on a pawnshop basis. However, we must manage it."

I felt the day was passing on, but I did not get excited about that. "Slow is swiftest," Parload used to say, and I meant to get everything thought out completely, to take a long aim and then to act as a bullet flies.

I hesitated at a pawnshop on my way home to my midday meal, but I determined not to pledge my watch until I could bring my overcoat also.

I ate silently, revolving plans.

3

After our midday dinner—it was a potato pie, mostly potato with some scraps of cabbage and bacon—I put on my overcoat and got it out of the house while my mother was in the scullery at the back.

A scullery in the old world was, in the case of such houses as ours, a damp, unsavory, mainly subterranean region behind the dark living-room kitchen, that was rendered more than typically dirty in our case by the fact that into it the coal-cellar, a yawning pit of black uncleanness, opened, and diffused small crunchable particles about the uneven brick floor. It was the region of "washing-up," that greasy, damp function that followed every meal; its atmosphere had ever a cooling steaminess and the memory of boiled cabbage, and the sooty black stains where saucepan or kettle had been put down for a minute, scraps of potato peel caught by the strainer of the escape-pipe, and rags of a quite indescribable horribleness of acquisition, called "dish-clouts," rise in my memory at the name. The altar of this place was the "sink," a tank of stone, revolting to a refined touch, grease-filmed and unpleasant to see, and above this was a tap for cold water, so arranged that when the water descended it splashed and wetted whoever had turned it on. This tap was our water supply. And in such a place you must fancy a little old woman, rather incompetent and very gentle, a soul of unselfishness and sacrifice, in dirty clothes, all come from their original colors to a common dusty dark gray, in worn, ill-fitting boots, with hands distorted by ill use, and untidy graying hair—my mother. In the winter her hands would be "chapped," and she would have a cough. And while she washes up I go out, to sell my overcoat and watch in order that I may desert her.

I gave way to queer hesitations in pawning my two negotiable articles. A weakly indisposition to pawn in Clayton, where the pawnbroker knew me, carried me to the door of the place in Lynch Street, Swathinglea, where I had bought my revolver. Then came an idea that I was giving too many facts about myself to one man, and I came back to Clayton after all. I forget how much money I got, but I remember that it was rather less than the sum I had made out to be the single fare to Shaphambury. Still deliberate, I was back to the Public Library to find out whether it was possible, by walking for ten or twelve miles anywhere, to shorten the journey. My boots were in a dreadful state, the sole of the left one also was now peeling off, and I could not help perceiving that all my plans might be wrecked if at this crisis I went on shoe leather in which I could only shuffle. So long as I went softly they would serve, but not for hard walking. I went to the shoemaker in Hacker Street, but he would not promise any repairs for me under forty-eight hours.

I got back home about five minutes to three, resolved to start by the five train for Birmingham in any case, but still dissatisfied about my money. I thought of pawning a book or something of that sort, but I could think of nothing of obvious value in the house. My mother's silver—two gravy spoons and a saltcellar—had been pawned for some weeks, since, in fact, the June quarter day. But my mind was full of hypothetical opportunities.

As I came up the steps to our door, I remarked that Mr. Gabbitas looked at me suddenly round his dull red curtains with a sort of alarmed resolution in his eye and vanished, and as I walked along the passage he opened his door upon me suddenly and intercepted me.

You are figuring me, I hope, as a dark and sullen lout in shabby, cheap, old-world clothes that are shiny at all the wearing surfaces, and with a discolored red tie and frayed linen. My left hand keeps in my pocket as though there is something it prefers to keep a grip upon there. Mr. Gabbitas was shorter than I, and the first note he struck in the impression he made upon anyone was of something bright and birdlike. I think he wanted to be birdlike, he possessed the possibility of an avian charm, but, as a matter of fact, there was nothing of the glowing vitality of the bird in his being. And a bird is never out of breath and with an open mouth. He was in the clerical dress of that time, that costume that seems now almost the strangest of all our old-world clothing, and he presented it in its cheapest form—black of a poor texture, ill-fitting, strangely cut. Its long skirts accentuated the tubbiness of his body, the shortness of his legs. The white tie below his all-round collar, beneath his innocent large-spectacled face, was a little grubby, and between his not very clean teeth he held a briar pipe. His complexion was whitish, and although he was only thirty-three or four perhaps, his sandy hair was already thinning from the top of his head.

To your eye, now, he would seem the strangest figure, in the utter disregard of all physical beauty or dignity about him. You would find him extraordinarily odd, but in the old days he met not only with acceptance but respect. He was alive until within a year or so ago, but his later appearance changed. As I saw him that afternoon he was a very slovenly, ungainly little human being indeed; not only was his clothing altogether ugly and queer, but had you stripped the man stark, you would certainly have seen in the bulging paunch that comes from flabby muscles and flabbily controlled appetites, and in the rounded shoulders and flawed and yellowish skin, the same failure of any effort toward clean beauty. You had an instinctive sense that so he had been from the beginning. You felt he was not only drifting through life, eating what came in his way, believing what came in his way, doing without any vigor what came in his way, but that *into* life also he had drifted. You could not believe him the child of pride and high resolve, or of any splendid passion of love. He had just *happened.*...But we all happened then. Why am I taking this tone over this poor little curate in particular?

"Hello!" he said, with an assumption of friendly ease. "Haven't seen you for weeks! Come in and have a gossip."

An invitation from the drawing-room lodger was in the

nature of a command. I would have liked very greatly to have refused it, never was an invitation more inopportune, but I had not the wit to think of an excuse. "All right," I said awkwardly, and he held the door open for me.

"I'd be very glad if your would," he amplified. "One doesn't get much opportunity of intelligent talk in this parish."

What the devil was he up to, was my secret preoccupation. He fussed about me with a nervous hospitality, talking in jumpy fragments, rubbing his hands together, and taking peeps at me over and round his glasses. As I sat down in his leather-covered armchair, I had an odd memory of the one in the Clayton dentist's operating room —I know not why.

"They're going to give us trouble in the North Sea, it seems," he remarked with a sort of innocent zest. "I'm glad they mean fighting."

There was an air of culture about his room that always cowed me, and that made me constrained even on this occasion. The table under the window was littered with photographic material and the later albums of his continental souvenirs, and on the American cloth-trimmed shelves that filled the recesses on either side of the fireplace were what I used to think in those days a quite incredible number of books—perhaps eight hundred altogether, including the reverend gentleman's photograph albums and college and school textbooks. This suggestion of learning was enforced by the little wooden shield bearing a college coat-of-arms that hung over the looking glass, and by a photograph of Mr. Gabbitas in cap and gown in an Oxford frame that adorned the opposite wall. And in the middle of that wall stood his writing desk, which I knew to have pigeonholes when it was open, and which made him seem not merely cultured but literary. At that he wrote sermons, composing them himself!

"Yes," he said, taking possession of the hearthrug, "the war had to come sooner or later. If we smash their fleet for them now; well, there's an end to the matter!"

He stood on his toes and then bumped down on his heels, and looked blandly through his spectacles at a watercolor by his sister—the subject was a bunch of violets—above the sideboard which was his pantry and tea chest and cellar. "Yes," he said as he did so.

I coughed, and wondered how I might presently get away.

He invited me to smoke—that queer old practice!—and then when I declined, began talking in a confidential tone of this "dreadful business" of the strikes. "The war won't improve *that* outlook," he said, and was grave for a moment.

He spoke of the want of thought for their wives and children shown by the colliers in striking merely for the sake of the union, and this stirred me to controversy, and distracted me a little from my resolution to escape.

"I don't quite agree with that," I said, clearing my throat. "If the men didn't strike for the union now, if they let that be broken up, where would they be when the pinch of reductions did come?"

To which he replied that they couldn't expect to get top-price wages when the masters were selling bottom-price coal. I replied, "That isn't it. The masters don't treat them fairly. They have to protect themselves."

To which Mr. Gabbitas answered, "Well, I don't know. I've been in the Four Towns some time, and I must say I don't think the balance of injustice falls on the masters' side."

"It falls on the men," I agreed, willfully misunderstanding him.

And so we worked our way toward an argument. "Confound this argument!" I thought; but I had no skill in self-extraction, and my irritation crept into my voice. Three little spots of color came into the cheeks and nose of Mr. Gabbitas, but his voice showed nothing of his ruffled temper.

"You see," I said, "I'm a socialist. I don't think this world was made for a small minority to dance on the faces of everyone else."

"My dear fellow," said the Rev. Gabbitas, "*I'm* a socialist too. Who isn't? But that doesn't lead me to class hatred."

"You haven't felt the heel of this confounded system. *I* have."

"Ah!" said he; and catching him on that note came a rap at the front door, and, as he hung suspended, the sound of my mother letting someone in and a timid rap.

"*Now*," thought I, and stood up, resolutely, but he would not let me. "No, no, no!" said he. "It's only for the Dorcas money."

He put his hand against my chest with an effect of physical compulsion, and cried, "Come in!"

"Our talk's just getting interesting," he protested; and there entered Miss Ramell, an elderly little lady who was mighty in Church help in Clayton.

He greeted her—she took no notice of me—and went to his bureau, and I remained standing by my chair but unable to get out of the room. "I'm not interrupting?" asked Miss Ramell.

"Not in the least," he said, drew out the carriers and opened his desk. I could not help seeing what he did.

I was so fretted by my impotence to leave him that at the moment it did not connect at all with the research of the morning that he was taking out money. I listened sullenly to his talk with Miss Ramell, and saw only, as they say in Wales, with the front of my eyes, the small flat drawer that had, it seemed, quite a number of sovereigns scattered over its floor. "They're so unreasonable," complained Miss Ramell. Who could be otherwise in a social organization that bordered on insanity?

I turned away from them, put my foot on the fender, stuck my elbow on the plush-fringed mantelboard, and studied the photographs, pipes, and ashtrays that adorned it. What was it I had to think out before I went to the station?

Of course! My mind made a queer little reluctant leap—

it felt like being forced to leap over a bottomless chasm—and alighted upon the sovereigns that were just disappearing again as Mr. Gabbitas shut his drawer.

"I won't interrupt your talk further," said Miss Ramell, receding doorward.

Mr. Gabbitas played round her politely, and opened the door for her and conducted her into the passage, and for a moment or so I had the fullest sense of proximity to those—it seemed to me there must be ten or twelve—sovereigns....

The front door closed and he returned. My chance of escape had gone.

4

"I *must* be going," I said, with a curiously reinforced desire to get away out of that room.

"My dear chap!" he insisted, "I can't think of it. Surely—there's nothing to call you away." Then with an evident desire to shift the venue of our talk, he asked "You never told me what you thought of Burble's little book."

I was now, beneath my dull display of submission, furiously angry with him. It occurred to me to ask myself why I should defer and qualify my opinions to him. Why should I pretend a feeling of intellectual and social inferiority toward him. He asked what I thought of Burble. I resolved to tell him—if necessary with arrogance. Then perhaps he would release me. I did not sit down again, but stood by the corner of the fireplace.

"That was the little book you lent me last summer?" I said.

"He reasons closely, eh?" he said, and indicated the armchair with a flat hand, and beamed persuasively.

I remained standing. "I didn't think much of his reasoning powers," I said.

"He was one of the cleverest bishops London ever had."

"That may be. But he was dodging about in a jolly feeble case," said I.

"You mean?"

"That he's wrong. I don't think he proves his case. I don't think Christianity is true. He knows himself for the pretender he is. His reasoning's—Rot."

Mr. Gabbitas went, I think, a shade paler than his wont, and propitiation vanished from his manner. His eyes and mouth were round, his face seemed to get round, his eyebrows curved at my remarks.

"I'm sorry you think that," he said at last with a catch in his breath.

He did not repeat his suggestion that I should sit. He made a step or two toward the window and turned. "I suppose you will admit—" he began, with a faintly irritating note of intellectual condescension....

I will not tell you of his arguments or mine. You will find if you care to look for them, in out-of-the-way corners of our book museums, the shriveled cheap publications—the publications of the Rationalist Press Association, for example—on which my arguments were based. Lying in that curious limbo with them, mixed up with them and indistinguishable, are the endless "Replies" of orthodoxy, like the mixed dead in some hard-fought trench. All those disputes of our fathers, and they were sometimes furious disputes, have gone now beyond the range of comprehension. You younger people, I know, read them with impatient perplexity. You cannot understand how sane creatures could imagine they had joined issue at all in most of these controversies. All the old methods of systematic thinking, the queer absurdities of the Aristotelian logic, have followed magic numbers and mystical numbers, and the Rumpelstiltskin magic of names now into the blackness of the unthinkable. You can no more understand our theological passions than you can understand the fancies that made all ancient peoples speak of their gods only by circumlocutions, that made savages pine away and die because they had been photographed, or an Elizabethan farmer turn back from a day's expedition because he had met three crows. Even I, who have been through it all, recall our controversies now with something near incredulity.

Faith we can understand today, all men live by faith, but in the old time everyone confused quite hopelessly Faith and a forced, incredible Belief in certain pseudo-concrete statements. I am inclined to say that neither believers nor unbelievers had power. They could not trust unless they had something to see and touch and say, like their barbarous ancestors who could not make a bargain without exchange of tokens. If they no longer worshiped sticks and stones, or eked out their needs with pilgrimages and images, they still held fiercely to audible images, to printed words and formulae.

But why revive the echoes of the ancient logomachies?

Suffice it that we lost our tempers very readily in pursuit of God and Truth, and said exquisitely foolish things on either side. And on the whole—from the impartial perspective of my three and seventy years—I adjudicate that if my dialectic was bad, that of the Rev. Gabbitas was altogether worse.

Little pink spots came into his cheeks, a squealing note into his voice. We interrupted each other more and more rudely. We invented facts and appealed to authorities whose names I mispronounced; and, finding Gabbitas shy of the higher criticism and the Germans, I used the names of Karl Marx and Engels as Bible exegetes with no little effect. A silly wrangle! a preposterous wrangle!—you must imagine our talk becoming louder, with a developing quarrelsome note—my mother no doubt hovering on the staircase and listening in alarm as who should say, "My dear, don't offend it! Oh, don't offend it! Mr. Gabbitas enjoys its friendship. Try to think whatever Mr. Gabbitas says"—though we still kept in touch with a pretense of mutual deference. The ethical superiority of Christianity to all other religions came to the fore—I know not how. We dealt with the matter in bold, imaginative generalizations, because of the insufficiency of our historical knowledge. I was moved to denounce Christianity as the ethic of slaves, and declare myself a disciple of a German writer of no little vogue in those days, named Nietzsche.

For a disciple I must confess I was particularly ill acquainted with the works of the master. Indeed, all I knew of him had come to me through a two-column article in *The Clarion* for the previous week....But the Rev. Gabbitas did not read *The Clarion*.

I am, I know, putting a strain upon your credulity when I tell you that I now have little doubt that the Rev. Gabbitas was absolutely ignorant even of the name of Nietzsche, although that writer presented a separate and distinct attitude of attack upon the faith that was in the reverend gentleman's keeping.

"I'm a disciple of Nietzsche," said I, with an air of extensive explanation.

He shied away so awkwardly at the name that I repeated it at once.

"But do you know what Nietzsche says?" I pressed him viciously.

"He has certainly been adequately answered," said he, still trying to carry it off.

"Who by?" I rapped out hotly. "Tell me that!" and became mercilessly expectant.

5

A happy accident relieved Mr. Gabbitas from the embarrassment of that challenge, and carried me another step along my course of personal disaster.

It came on the heels of my question in the form of a clatter of horses without, and the grind and cessation of wheels. I glimpsed a straw-hatted coachman and a pair of grays. It seemed an incredibly magnificent carriage for Clayton.

"Eh!" said the Rev. Gabbitas, going to the window. "Why, it's old Mrs. Verrall! It's old Mrs. Verrall. Really! What *can* she want with me?"

He turned to me, and the flush of controversy had passed and his face shone like the sun. It was not every day, I perceived, that Mrs. Verrall came to see him.

"I get so many interruptions," he said, almost grinning. "You must excuse me a minute! Then—then I'll tell you about that fellow. But don't go. I pray you don't go. I can assure you...*most* interesting."

He went out of the room waving vague prohibitory gestures.

"I *must* go," I cried after him.

"No, no, no!" in the passage. "I've got your answer," I think it was he added, and "quite mistaken"; and I saw him running down the steps to talk to the old lady.

I swore. I made three steps to the window, and this brought me within a yard of that accursed drawer.

I glanced at it, and then at that old woman who was so absolutely powerful, and instantly her son and Nettie's face were flaming in my brain. The Stuarts had, no doubt, already accepted accomplished facts. And I too—

What was I doing here?

What was I doing here while judgment escaped me?

I woke up. I was injected with energy. I took one reassuring look at the curate's obsequious back, at the old lady's projected nose and quivering hand, and then with swift, clean movements I had the little drawer open, four sovereigns in my pocket, and the drawer shut again. Then again at the window—they were still talking.

That was all right. He might not look in that drawer for hours. I glanced at his clock. Twenty minutes still before the Birmingham train. Time to buy a pair of boots and get away. But how was I to get to the station?

I went out boldly into the passage, and took my hat and stick....Walk past him?

Yes. That was all right! He could not argue with me while so important a person engaged him....I came boldly down the steps.

"I want a list made, Mr. Gabbitas, of all the really

deserving cases,'' old Mrs. Verrall was saying.

It is curious, but it did not occur to me that here was a mother whose son I was going to kill. I did not see her in that aspect at all. Instead, I was possessed by a realization of the blazing imbecility of a social system that gave this palsied old woman the power to give or withhold the urgent necessities of life from hundreds of her fellow creatures just according to her poor, foolish old fancies of desert.

''We could make a *provisional* list of that sort,'' he was saying, and glanced round with a preoccupied expression at me.

''I *must* go,'' I said at his flash of inquiry, and added, ''I'll be back in twenty minutes,'' and went on my way. He turned again to his patroness as though he forgot me on the instant. Perhaps after all he was not sorry.

I felt extraordinarily cool and capable, exhilarated, if anything, by this prompt, effectual theft. After all, my great determination would achieve itself. I was no longer oppressed by a sense of obstacles, I felt I could grasp accidents and turn them to my advantage. I would go now down Hacker Street to the little shoemaker's—get a sound, good pair of boots—ten minutes—and then to the railway station—five minutes more—and off! I felt as efficient and nonmoral as if I was Nietzsche's Over-man already come. It did not occur to me that the curate's clock might have a considerable margin of error.

6

I missed the train.

Partly that was because the curate's clock was slow, and partly it was due to the commercial obstinacy of the shoemaker, who would try on another pair after I had declared my time was up. I bought the final pair however, gave him a wrong address for the return of the old ones, and only ceased to feel like the Nietzschean Over-man, when I saw the train running out of the station.

Even then I did not lose my head. It occurred to me almost at once that, in the event of a prompt pursuit, there would be a great advantage in not taking a train from Clayton; that, indeed, to have done so would have been an error from which only luck had saved me. As it was, I had already been very indiscreet in my inquiries about Shaphambury; for once on the scent the clerk could not fail to remember me. Now the chances were against his coming into the case. I did not go into the station therefore at all, I made no demonstration of having missed the train, but walked quietly past, down the road, crossed the iron footbridge, and took the way back circuitously by White's brickfields and the allotments to the way over Clayton Crest to Two-Mile Stone, where I calculated I should have an ample margin for the 6:13 train.

I was not very greatly excited or alarmed then. Suppose, I reasoned, that by some accident the curate goes to that drawer at once: will he be certain to miss four out of ten or eleven sovereigns? If he does, will he at once think I have taken them? If he does, will he act at once or wait for my return? If he acts at once, will he talk to my mother or call in the police? Then there are a dozen roads and even railways out of the Clayton region, how is he to know which I have taken? Suppose he goes straight at once to the right station, they will not remember my departure for the simple reason that I didn't depart. But they may remember about Shaphambury? It was unlikely.

I resolved not to go directly to Shaphambury from Birmingham, but to go thence to Monkshampton, thence to Wyvern, and then come down on Shaphambury from the north. That might involve a night at some intermediate stopping place but it would effectually conceal me from any but the most persistent pursuit. And this was not a case of murder yet, but only the theft of four sovereigns.

I had argued away all anxiety before I reached Clayton Crest.

At the Crest I looked back. What a world it was! And

suddenly it came to me that I was looking at this world for the last time. If I overtook the fugitives and succeeded, I should die with them—or hang. I stopped and looked back more attentively at that wide ugly valley.

It was my native valley, and I was going out of it, I thought never to return, and yet in that last prospect, the group of towns that had borne me and dwarfed and crippled and made me, seemed, in some indefinable manner, strange. I was, perhaps, more used to seeing it from this comprehensive viewpoint when it was veiled and softened by night; now it came out in all its weekday reek, under a clear afternoon sun. That may account a little for its unfamiliarity. And perhaps, too, there was something in the emotions through which I had been passing for a week and more, to intensify my insight, to enable me to pierce the unusual, to question the accepted. But it came to me then, I am sure, for the first time, how promiscuous, how higgledy-piggledy was the whole of that jumble of mines and homes, collieries and pot-banks, railway yards, canals, schools, forges and blast furnaces, churches, chapels, allotment hovels, a vast irregular agglomeration of ugly smoking accidents in which men lived as happy as frogs in a dustbin. Each thing jostled and damaged the other things about it, each thing ignored the other things about it; the smoke of the furnace defiled the pot-bank clay, the clatter of the railway deafened the worshipers in church, the public house thrust corruption at the school doors, the dismal homes squeezed miserably amidst the monstrosities of industrialism, with an effect of groping imbecility. Humanity choked amidst its products, and all its energy went in increasing its disorder, like a blind stricken thing that struggles and sinks in a morass.

I did not think these things clearly that afternoon. Much less did I ask how I, with my murderous purpose, stood to them all. I write down that realization of disorder and suffocation here and now as though I had thought it, but indeed then I only felt it, felt it transitorily as I looked back, and then stood with the thing escaping from my mind.

I should never see that countryside again.

I came back to that. At any rate I wasn't sorry. The chances were I should die in sweet air, under a clean sky.

From distant Swathinglea came a little sound, the minute undulation of a remote crowd, and then rapidly three shots.

That held me perplexed for a space.... Well, anyhow I was leaving it all! Thank God I was leaving it all! Then, as I turned to go on, I thought of my mother.

It seemed an evil world in which to leave one's mother. My thoughts focused upon her very vividly for a moment. Down there, under that afternoon light, she was going to and fro, unaware as yet that she had lost me, bent and poking about in the darkling underground kitchen, perhaps carrying a lamp into the scullery to trim, or sitting patiently, staring into the fire, waiting tea for me. A great pity for her, a great remorse at the blacker troubles that lowered over her innocent head, came to me. Why, after all, was I doing this thing?

Why?

I stopped again dead, with the hill crest rising between me and home. I had more than half a mind to return to her.

Then I thought of the curate's sovereigns. If he has missed them already, what should I return to? And, even if I returned, how could I put them back?

And what of the night after I renounced my revenge? What of the time when young Verrall came back? And Nettie?

No! The thing had to be done.

But at least I might have kissed my mother before I came away, left her some message, reassured her at least for a little while. All night she would listen and wait for me....

Should I send her a telegram from Two-Mile Stone?

It was no good now; too late, too late. To do that would be to tell the course I had taken, to bring pursuit upon me, swift and sure, if pursuit there was to be. No. My mother must suffer!

I went on grimly toward Two-Mile Stone, but now as if some greater will than mine directed my footsteps thither.

I reached Birmingham before darkness came, and just caught the last train for Monkshampton, where I had planned to pass the night.

Chapter 5

The Pursuit of the Two Lovers

1

As the train carried me on from Birmingham to Monkshampton, it carried me not only into a country where I had never been before, but out of the commonplace daylight and the touch and quality of ordinary things, into the strange unprecedented night that was ruled by the giant meteor of the last days.

There was at that time a curious accentuation of the common alternation of night and day. They became separated with a widening difference of value in regard to all mundane affairs. During the day, the comet was an item in the newspapers, it was jostled by a thousand more living interests, it was as nothing in the skirts of the war storm that was now upon us. It was an astronomical phenomenon, somewhere away over China, millions of miles away in the deeps. We forgot it. But directly the sun sank one turned ever and again toward the east, and the meteor resumed its sway over us.

One waited for its rising, and yet each night it came as a

surprise. Always it rose brighter than one had dared to think, always larger and with some wonderful change in its outline, and now with a strange, less luminous, greener disk upon it that grew with its growth, the umbra of the earth. It shone also with its own light, so that this shadow was not hard or black, but it shone phosphorescently and with a diminishing intensity where the stimulus of the sun's rays was withdrawn. As it ascended toward the zenith, as the last trailing daylight went after the abdicating sun, its greenish-white illumination banished the realities of day, diffused a bright ghostliness over all things. It changed the starless sky about it to an extraordinary deep blue, the profoundest color in the world, such as I have never seen before or since. I remember, too, that as I peered from the train that was rattling me along to Monkshampton, I perceived and was puzzled by a coppery red light that mingled with all the shadows that were cast by it.

It turned our ugly English industrial towns to phantom cities. Everywhere the local authorities discontinued street lighting—one could read small print in the glare—and so at Monkshampton I went about through pale, white, unfamiliar streets, whose electric globes had shadows on the path. Lit windows here and there burnt ruddy orange, like holes cut in some dream curtain that hung before a furnace. A policeman with noiseless feet showed me an inn woven of moonshine, a green-faced man opened to us, and there I abode the night. And the next morning it opened with a mighty clatter, and was a dirty little beerhouse that stank of beer, and there was a fat and grimy landlord with red spots upon his neck, and much noisy traffic going by on the cobbles outside.

I came out, after I had paid my bill, into a street that echoed to the bawlings of two newsvendors and to the noisy yappings of a dog they had raised to emulation. They were shouting: "Great British disaster in the North Sea. A battleship lost with all hands!"

I bought a paper, went on to the railway station reading

such details as were given of this triumph of the old civilization, of the blowing up of this great iron ship, full of guns and explosives and the most costly and beautiful machinery of which that time was capable, together with nine hundred able-bodied men, all of them above the average, by a contact mine towed by a German submarine. I read myself into a fever of warlike emotions. Not only did I forget the meteor, but for a time I forgot even the purpose that took me on to the railway station, bought my ticket, and was now carrying me onward to Shaphambury.

So the hot day came to its own again, and people forgot the night.

Each night, there shone upon us more and more insistently, beauty, wonder, the promise of the deeps, and we were hushed, and marveled for a space. And at the first gray sounds of dawn again, at the shooting of bolts and the noise of milk-carts, we forgot, and the dusty habitual day came yawning and stretching back again. The strains of coal smoke crept across the heavens, and we rose to the soiled disorderly routine of life.

"Thus life has always been," we said; "thus it will always be."

The glory of those nights was almost universally regarded as spectacular merely. It signified nothing to us. So far as western Europe went, it was only a small and ignorant section of the lower classes who regarded the comet as a portent of the end of the world. Abroad, where there were peasantries, it was different, but in England the peasantry had already disappeared. Everyone read. The newspaper, in the quiet days before our swift quarrel with Germany rushed to its climax, had absolutely dispelled all possibilities of a panic in this matter. The very tramps upon the high-roads, the children in the nursery, had learned that at the utmost the whole of that shining cloud could weigh but a few score tons. This fact had been shown quite conclusively by the enormous deflections that had at last swung it round squarely at our world. It had passed near three of the smallest asteroids without producing the minutest perceptible deflection in their course; while, on its own part, it had described a course through nearly three degrees. When it struck our earth there was to be a magnificent spectacle, no doubt, for those who were on the right side of our planet to see, but beyond that nothing. It was doubtful whether we were on the right side. The meteor would loom larger and larger in the sky, but with the umbra of our earth eating its heart of brightness out, and at last it would be the whole sky, a sky of luminous green clouds, with a white brightness about the horizon, west and east. Then a pause—a pause of not very exactly definite duration—and then, no doubt, a great blaze of shooting stars. They might be of some unwonted color because of the unknown element that line in the green revealed. For a little while the zenith would spout shooting stars. Some, it was hoped, would reach the earth and be available for analysis.

That, science said, would be all. The green clouds would whirl and vanish, and there might be thunderstorms. But through the attenuated wisps of comet shine, the old sky, the old stars, would reappear, and all would be as it had been before. And since this was to happen between one and eleven in the morning of the approaching Tuesday—I slept at Monkshampton on Saturday night—it would be only partially visible, if visible at all, on our side of the earth. Perhaps, if it came late, one would see no more than a shooting star low down in the sky. All this we had with the utmost assurances of science. Still it did not prevent the last nights being the most beautiful and memorable of human experiences.

The nights had become very warm, and when next day I had ranged Shaphambury in vain, I was greatly tormented, as that unparalleled glory of the night returned, to think that under its splendid benediction young Verrall and Nettie made love to one another.

I walked backward and forward, backward and forward, along the sea front, peering into the faces of the young couples who promenaded, with my hand in my pocket ready, and a curious ache in my heart that had no kindred with rage. Until at last all the promenaders had gone home to bed, and I was alone with the star.

My train from Wyvern to Shaphambury that morning was a whole hour late; they said it was on account of the movement of troops to meet a possible raid from the Elbe.

2

Shaphambury seemed an odd place to me even then. But something was quickening in me at that time to feel the oddness of many accepted things. Now in the retrospect I see it as intensely queer. The whole place was strange to my untraveled eyes; the sea even was strange. Only twice in my life had I been at the seaside before, and then I had gone by excursion to places on the Welsh coast whose great cliffs of rock and mountain backgrounds made the effect of the horizon very different from what it is upon the East Anglian seaboard. Here what they call a cliff was a crumbling bank of whitey-brown earth not fifty feet high.

So soon as I arrived I made a systematic exploration of Shaphambury. To this day I retain the clearest memories of the plan I shaped out then, and how my inquiries were incommoded by the overpowering desire of everyone to talk of the chances of a German raid, before the Channel Fleet got round to us. I slept at a small public house in a Shaphambury back street on Sunday night. I did not get on to Shaphambury from Wyvern until two in the afternoon, because of the infrequency of Sunday trains, and I got no clue whatever until late in the afternon of Monday. As the little local train bumped into sight of the place round the curve of a swelling hill, one saw a series of undulating grassy spaces, amidst which a number of conspicuous notice-boards appealed to the eye and cut up the distant sea horizon. Most of these referred to comestibles or to remedies to follow the comestibles; and they were colored with a view to be memorable rather than beautiful, to "stand out" amidst the gentle grayish tones of the east coast scenery. The greater number, I may remark, of the advertisements that were so conspicuous a factor in the life of those days, and which rendered our vast tree-pulp newspapers possible, referred to foods, drinks, tobacco, and the drugs that promised a restoration of the equanimity these other articles had destroyed. Wherever one went one was reminded in glaring letters that, after all, man was little better than a worm, that eyeless, earless thing that burrows and lives uncomplainingly amidst nutritious dirt, "an alimentary canal with the subservient appendages thereto." But in addition to such boards there were also the big black and white boards of various grandiloquently named "estates." The individualistic enterprise of that time had led to the plotting out of nearly all the country round the seaside towns into roads and building plots—all but a small portion of the south and east coast was in this condition, and had the promises of those schemes been realized the entire population of the island might have been accommodated upon the sea frontiers. Nothing of the sort happened, of course; the whole of this uglification of the coastline was done to stimulate a little foolish gambling in plots, and one saw everywhere agents' boards in every state of freshness and decay, ill-made exploitation roads overgrown with grass, and here and there, at a corner, a label, "Trafalgar Avenue," or "Sea View Road." Here and there, too, some small investor, some shopman with "savings," had delivered his soul to the local builders and built himself a house, and there it stood, ill-designed, mean-looking, isolated, ill-placed on a cheaply fenced plot, athwart which his domestic washing fluttered in the breeze amidst a bleak desolation of enterprise. Then presently our railway crossed a highroad, and a row of mean yellow brick houses—workmen's cottages, and the filthy black sheds that made the "allotments" of that time a universal eyesore, marked our approach to the more central areas of—I quote the local guidebook—"one of the most delightful resorts in the East Anglian poppyland." Then more mean houses, the gaunt ungainliness of the electric force station—it had a huge chimney, because no one understood how to make combustion of coal complete—and then we were in the railway station, and barely three-qauarters of a mile from the center of this haunt of health and pleasure.

I inspected the town thoroughly before I made my inquiries. The road began badly with a row of cheap, pretentious, insolvent-looking shops, a public house, and a cabstand, but, after an interval of little red villas that were partly hidden amidst shrubbery gardens, broke into a confusedly bright but not unpleasing High Street, shuttered that afternoon and sabbatically still. Somewhere in the background a church bell jangled, and children in bright, new-looking clothes were going to Sunday school. Thence through a square of stuccoed lodging houses, that seemed a finer and cleaner version of my native square, I came to a garden of asphalt and trees and shrubs—the Sea Front. I sat down on a cast-iron seat, and surveyed first of all the broad stretches of muddy, sandy beach, with its queer wheeled bathing machines, painted with the advertisements of somebody's pills—and then at the house fronts that stared out upon these visceral counsels. Boarding houses, private hotels, and lodging houses in terraces clustered closely right and left of me, and then came to an end; in one direction scaffolding marked a building enterprise in progress, in the other, after a waste interval, rose a monstrous bulging red shape, a huge hotel, that dwarfed all other things. Northward were low pale cliffs with white denticulations of tents, where the local volunteers, all under arms, lay encamped, and southward, a spreading waste of sandy dunes, with occasional bushes and clumps of stunted pine and an advertisement board or so. A hard blue sky hung over all this prospect, the sunshine cast inky shadows, and eastward was a whitish sea. It was Sunday, and the midday meal still held people indoors....

A queer world! thought I even then—to you now it must seem impossibly queer—and after an interval I forced myself back to my own affair.

How was I to ask? What was I to ask for?

I puzzled for a long time over that—at first I was a little tired and indolent—and then presently I had a flow of ideas.

My solution was fairly ingenious. I invented the following story. I happened to be taking a holiday in Shaphambury, and I was making use of the opportunity to seek the owner of a valuable feather boa, which had been left behind in the hotel of my uncle at Wyvern by a young lady, traveling with a young gentleman—no doubt a youthful married couple. They had reached Shaphambury sometime on Thursday. I went over the story many times, and gave my imaginary uncle and his hotel plausible names. At any rate this yarn would serve as a complete justification for all the questions I might wish to ask.

I settled that, but I still sat for a time, wanting the energy to begin. Then I turned toward the big hotel. Its gorgeous magnificence seemed to my inexpert judgment to indicate the very place a rich young man of good family would select.

Huge draft-proof doors were swung round for me by an ironically polite underporter in a magnificent green uniform, who looked at my clothes as he listened to my question and then with a German accent referred me to a gorgeous head porter, who directed me to a princely young man behind a counter of brass and polish, like a bank—like several banks. This young man, while he answered me, kept his eye on my collar and tie—and I knew that they were abominable.

"I want to find a lady and gentleman who came to Shaphambury on Thursday," I said.

"Friends of yours?" he asked with a terrible fineness of irony.

I made out at last that here at any rate the young people had not been. They might have lunched there, but they had had no room. But I went out—door opened again for me obsequiously—in a state of social discomfiture, and did not attack any other establishment that afternoon.

My resolution had come to a sort of ebb. More people were promenading, and their Sunday smartness abashed me. I forgot my purpose in an acute sense of myself. I felt that the bulge of my pocket caused by the revolver was conspicuous, and I was ashamed. I went along the sea front away from the town, and presently lay down among pebbles and sea poppies. This mood of reaction prevailed with me all that afternoon. In the evening, about sundown, I went to the station and asked questions of the outporters there. But outporters, I found, were a class of men who remembered luggage rather than people, and I had no sort of idea what luggage young Verrall and Nettie were likely to have with them.

Then I fell into conversation with a salacious wooden-legged old man with a silver ring, who swept the steps that went down to the beach from the parade. He knew much about young couples, but only in general terms, and nothing of the particular young couple I sought. He reminded me in the most disagreeable way of the sensuous aspects of life, and I was not sorry when presently a gunboat appeared in the offing signaling the coastguard and the camp, and cut short his observations upon holidays, beaches, and morals.

I went, and now I was past my ebb, and sat in a seat upon the parade, and watched the brightening of those rising clouds of chilly fire that made the ruddy west seem tame. My midday lassitude was going, my blood was running warmer again. And as the twilight and that filmy brightness replaced the dusty sunlight and robbed this unfamiliar place of all its matter-of-fact queerness, its sense of aimless materialism, romance returned to me, and passion, and my thoughts of honor and revenge. I remember that change of mood as occurring very vividly on this occasion, but I fancy that less distinctly I had felt this before many times. In the old times, night and the starlight had an effect of intimate reality the daytime did not possess. The daytime—as one saw it in towns and populous places—had hold of one, no doubt, but only as an uproar might; it was distracting, conflicting, insistent. Darkness veiled the more salient aspects of those agglomerations of human absurdity, and one could exist—one could imagine.

I had a queer illusion that night, that Nettie and her lover were close at hand, that suddenly I should come on them. I have already told how I went through the dusk seeking them in every couple that drew near. And I dropped asleep at last in an unfamiliar bedroom hung with gaudily decorated texts, cursing myself for having wasted a day.

3

I sought them in vain the next morning, but after midday I came in quick succession on a perplexing multitude of clues. After failing to find any young couple that corresponded to young Verrall and Nettie, I presently discovered an unsatisfactory quartet of couples.

Any of these four couples might have been the one I sought; with regard to none of them was there conviction. They had all arrived either on Wednesday or Thursday. Two couples were still in occupation of their rooms, but neither of these were at home. Late in the afternoon I reduced my list by eliminating a young man in drab, with side whiskers and long cuffs, accompanied by a lady, of thirty or more, of consciously ladylike type. I was disgusted at the sight of them; the other two young people had gone for a long walk, and though I watched their boarding house until the fiery cloud shone out above, sharing and mingling in an unusually splendid sunset, I missed them. Then I discovered them dining at a separate table in the bow window, with red-shaded candles between them, peering out ever and again at this splendor that was neither night nor day. The girl in her pink evening dress looked very light and pretty to me—pretty enough to enrage me—she had well-shaped arms and white, well-modeled shoulders, and the turn of her cheek and the fair hair about her ears were full of subtle delights; but she was not Nettie, and the happy man with her was that odd degenerate type of old aristocracy produced with such odd frequency, chinless, large bony nose, small fair head, languid expression, and a neck that had demanded and received a veritable sleeve of collar. I stood outside in the meteor's livid light, hating them and cursing them for having delayed me so long. I stood until it was evident they remarked me, a black shape of envy, silhouetted against the glare.

That finished Shaphambury. The question I now had to debate was which of the remaining couples I had to pursue.

I walked back to the parade trying to reason my next step out, and muttering to myself, because there was something in that luminous wonderfulness that touched one's brain, and made one feel a little lightheaded.

One couple had gone to London; the other had gone to the Bungalow village at Bone Cliff. Where, I wondered, was Bone Cliff?

I came upon my wooden-legged man at the top of his steps.

"Hullo," said I.

He pointed seaward with his pipe, his silver ring shone in the sky light.

"Rum," he said.

"What is?" I asked.

"Searchlights! Smoke! Ships going north! If it wasn't for this blasted Milky Way gone green up there, we might see."

He was too intent to heed my questions for a time. Then he vouchsafed over his shoulder—

"Know Bungalow village?—rather. Artis' and such. Nice goings on! Mixed bathing—something scandalous. Yes."

"But where is it?" I said, suddenly exasperated.

"There!" he said. "What's that flicker? A gunflash—or I'm a lost soul!"

"You'd hear," I said, "long before it was near enough to see a flash."

He didn't answer. Only by making it clear I would distract him until he told me what I wanted to know could I get him to turn from his absorbed contemplation of that phantom dance between the sea rim and the shine. Indeed I gripped his arm and shook him. Then he turned upon me cursing.

"Seven miles," he said, "along this road. And now go to 'ell with yer!"

I answered with some foul insult by way of thanks, and so we parted, and I set off towards the Bungalow village.

I found a policeman, standing stargazing, a little way beyond the end of the parade, and verified the wooden-legged man's directions.

"It's a lonely road, you know," he called after me....

I had an odd intuition that now at last I was on the right track. I left the dark masses of Shaphambury behind me, and pushed out into the dim pallor of that night, with the quiet assurance of a traveler who nears his end.

The incidents of that long tramp I do not recall in any orderly succession, the one progressive thing is my memory of a growing fatigue. The sea was for the most part smooth and shining like a mirror, a great expanse of reflecting silver, barred by slow broad undulations, but at one time a little breeze breathed like a faint sigh and ruffled their long bodies into faint scaly ripples that never completely died out again. The way was sometimes sandy, thick with silvery colorless sand, and sometimes chalky and lumpy, with lumps that had shining facets; a black scrub was scattered, sometimes in thickets, sometimes in single bunches, among the somnolent hummocks of sand. At one place came grass, and ghostly great sheep looming up among the gray. After a time black pinewoods intervened, and made sustained darknesses along the road, woods that frayed out at the edges to weirdly warped and stunted trees. Then isolated pine witches would appear, and make their rigid gestures at me as I passed. Grotesquely incongruous amidst these forms, I presently came on estate boards, appealing, "Houses can be built to suit purchaser," to the silence, to the shadows, and the glare.

Once I remember the persistent barking of a dog from somewhere inland of me, and several times I took out and examined my revolver very carefully. I must, of course, have been full of my intention when I did that, I must have been thinking of Nettie and revenge, but I cannot now recall those emotions at all. Only I see again very distinctly the greenish gleams that ran over lock and barrel as I turned the weapon in my hand.

Then there was the sky, the wonderful, luminous, starless, moonless sky, and the empty blue deeps of the edge of it, between the meteor and the sea. And once—strange phantoms!—I saw far out upon the shine, and very small and distant, three long black warships, without masts, or sails, or smoke, or any lights, dark, deadly, furtive things, traveling very swiftly and keeping an equal distance. And when I looked again they were very small, and then the shine had swallowed them up.

Then once a flash and what I thought was a gun, until I looked up and saw a fading trail of greenish light still hanging in the sky. And after that there was a shiver and whispering in the air, a stronger throbbing in one's arteries, a sense of refreshment, a renewal of purpose....

Somewhere upon my way the road forked, but I do not remember whether that was near Shaphambury or near the end of my walk. The hesitation between two rutted unmade roads alone remains clear in my mind.

At last I grew weary. I came to piled heaps of decaying seaweed and cart tracks running this way and that, and then I had missed the road and was stumbling among sand hummocks quite close to the sea. I came out on the edge of the dimly glittering sandy beach, and something phosphorescent drew me to the water's edge. I bent down and peered at the little luminous specks that floated in the ripples.

Presently with a sigh I stood erect, and contemplated the lonely peace of that last wonderful night. The meteor had now trailed its shining nets across the whole space of the sky and was beginning to set; in the east the blue was coming to its own again; the sea was an intense edge of blackness, and now, escaped from that great shine, and faint and still tremulously valiant, one weak elusive star could just be seen, hovering on the verge of the invisible.

How beautiful it was! how still and beautiful! Peace! peace!—the peace that passeth understanding, robed in light descending!...

My heart swelled, and suddenly I was weeping.

There was something new and strange in my blood. It came to me that indeed I did not want to kill.

I did not want to kill. I did not want to be the servant of my passions anymore. A great desire had come to me to escape from life, from the daylight which is heat and conflict and desire, into that cool night of eternity—and rest. I had played—I had done.

I stood upon the edge of the great ocean, and I was filled with an inarticulate spirit of prayer, and I desired greatly—peace from myself.

And presently, there in the east, would come again the red discoloring curtain over these mysteries, the finite world again, the gray and growing harsh certainties of dawn. My resolve I knew would take up with me again. This was a rest for me, an interlude, but tomorrow I should be William Leadford once more, ill-nourished, ill-dressed, ill-equipped and clumsy, a thief and shamed, a wound upon the face of life, a source of trouble and sorrow even to the mother I loved; no hope in life left for me now but revenge before my death.

Why this paltry thing, revenge? It entered into my thoughts that I might end the matter now and let these others go.

To wade out into the sea, into this warm lapping that mingled the natures of water and light, to stand there breast-high, to thrust my revolver barrel into my mouth—?

Why not?

I swung about with an effort. I walked slowly up the beach thinking....

I turned and looked back at the sea. No! Something within me said, "No!"

I must think.

It was troublesome to go further because the hummocks and the tangled bushes began. I sat down amidst a black cluster of shrubs, and rested, chin on hand. I drew my revolver from my pocket and looked at it, and held it in my hand. Life? Or Death?...

I seemed to be probing the very deeps of being, but indeed imperceptibly I fell asleep, and sat dreaming.

4

Two people were bathing in the sea.

I had awakened. It was still that white and wonderful night, and the blue band of clear sky was no wider than before. These people must have come into sight as I fell asleep, and awakened me almost at once. They waded breast-deep in the water, emerging, coming shoreward, a woman, with her hair coiled about her head, and in pursuit of her a man, graceful figures of black and silver, with a bright green surge flowing off from them, a pattering of flashing wavelets about them. He smote the water and splashed it toward her, she retaliated, and then they were knee-deep, and then for an instant their feet broke the long silver margin of the sea.

Each wore a tightly fitting bathing dress that hid nothing of the shining, dripping beauty of their youthful forms.

She glanced over her shoulder and found him nearer than she thought, started, gesticulated, gave a little cry that pierced me to the heart, and fled up the beach obliquely toward me, running like the wind, and passed me, vanished amidst the black distorted bushes, and was gone—she and her pursuer, in a moment, over the ridge of sand.

I heard him shout between exhaustion and laughter....

And suddenly I was a thing of bestial fury, standing up with hands held up and clenched, rigid in gesture of impotent threatening, against the sky....

For this striving, swift thing of light and beauty was Nettie—and this was the man for whom I had been betrayed!

And, it blazed upon me, I might have died there by the sheer ebbing of my will—unavenged!

In another moment I was running and stumbling, revolver in hand, in quiet unsuspected pursuit of them, through the soft and noiseless sand.

5

I came up over the little ridge and discovered the Bungalow village I had been seeking, nestling in a crescent lap of dunes. A door slammed, the two runners had vanished, and I halted staring.

There was a group of three bungalows nearer to me than the others. Into one of these three they had gone, and I was too late to see which. All had doors and windows carelessly open, and none showed a light.

This place, upon which I had at last happened, was a fruit of the reaction of artistic-minded and carelessly living people against the costly and uncomfortable social stiffness of the more formal seaside resorts of that time. It was, you must understand, the custom of the steam-railway companies to sell their carriages after they had been obsolete for a sufficient length of years, and some genius had hit upon the possibility of turning these into little habitable cabins for the summer holiday. The thing had become a fashion with a certain Bohemian-spirited class; they added cabin to cabin, and these little improvised homes, gaily painted and with broad verandas and supplementary lean-to's added to their accommodation, made the brightest contrast conceivable to the dull rigidities of the decorous resorts. Of course there were many discomforts in such camping that had to be faced cheerfully, and so this broad sandy beach was sacred to high spirits and the young. Art muslin and banjos, Chinese lanterns and frying, are leading "notes," I find, in the impression of those who once knew such places well. But so far as I was concerned this odd settlement of pleasure-squatters was a mystery as well as a surprise, enhanced rather than mitigated by an imaginative suggestion or so I had received from the wooden-legged man at Shaphambury. I saw the thing as no gathering of light hearts and gay idleness, but grimly—after the manner of poor men poisoned by the suppression of all their cravings after joy. To the poor man, to the grimy workers, beauty and cleanness were absolutely denied; out of a life of greasy dirt, of muddied desires, they watched their happier fellows with a bitter envy and foul, tormenting suspicions. Fancy a world in which the common people held love to be a sort of beastliness, own sister to being drunk!...

There was in the old time always something cruel at the bottom of this business of sexual love. At least that is the impression I have brought with me across the gulf of the great Change. To succeed in love seemed such triumph as no other success could give, but to fail was as if one was tainted....

I felt no sense of singularity that this thread of savagery should run through these emotions of mine and become now the whole strand of these emotions. I believed, and I think I was right in believing, that the love of all true lovers was a sort of defiance then, that they closed a system in each other's arms and mocked the world without. You loved against the world, and these two loved at me. They had their business with one another, under the threat of a watchful fierceness. A sword, a sharp sword, the keenest edge in life, lay among their roses.

Whatever may be true of this for others, for me and my imagination, at any rate, it was altogether true. I was never for dalliance, I was never a jesting lover. I wanted fiercely; I made love impatiently. Perhaps I had written irrelevant love letters for that very reason; because with this stark theme I could not play....

The thought of Nettie's shining form, of her shrinking bold abandon to her easy conqueror, gave me now a body of rage that was nearly too strong for my heart and nerves and the tense powers of my merely physical being. I came down among the pale sand heaps slowly toward that queer village of careless sensuality, and now within my puny body I was coldly sharpset for pain and death, a darkly gleaming hate, a sword of evil, drawn.

6

I halted, and stood planning what I had to do.

Should I go to bungalow after bungalow until one of the two I sought answered to my rap? But suppose some servant intervened!

Should I wait where I was—perhaps until morning—watching? And meanwhile—

All the nearer bungalows were very still now. If I walked softly to them, from open windows, from something seen or overheard, I might get a clue to guide me. Should I advance circuitously, creeping upon them, or should I walk straight to the door? It was bright enough for her to recognize me clearly at a distance of many paces.

The difficulty to my mind lay in this, that if I involved other people by questions, I might at last confront my betrayers with these others close about me, ready to snatch my weapon and seize my hands. Besides, what names might they bear here?

"Boom!" the sound crept upon my senses, and then again it came.

I turned impatiently as one turns upon an impertinence, and beheld a great ironclad not four miles out, steaming fast across the dappled silver, and from its funnels sparks, intensely red, poured out into the night. As I turned, came the hot flash of its guns, firing seaward, and answering this, red flashes and a streaming smoke in the line between sea and sky. So I remembered it, and I remember myself staring at it—in a state of stupid arrest. It was an irrelevance. What had these things to do with me?

With a shuddering hiss, a rocket from a headland beyond the village leaped up and burst hot gold against the glare, and the sound of the third and fourth guns reached me.

The windows of the dark bungalows, one after another, leaped out, squares of ruddy brightness that flared and flickered and became steadily bright. Dark heads appeared looking seaward, a door opened, and sent out a brief lane of yellow to mingle and be lost in the comet's brightness. That brought me back to the business in hand.

"Boom! boom!" and when I looked again at the great ironclad, a little torchlike spurt of flame wavered behind her funnels. I could hear the throb and clangor of her straining engines....

I became aware of the voices of people calling to one another in the village. A white-robed, hooded figure, some man in a bathing wrap, absurdly suggestive of an Arab in his burnoose, came out from one of the nearer bungalows, and stood clear and still and shadowless in the glare.

He put his hands to shade his seaward eyes, and shouted to people within.

The people within—*my* people! My fingers tightened on my revolver. What was this war nonsense to me? I would go round among the hummocks with the idea of approaching the three bungalows inconspicuously from the flank. This fight at sea might serve my purpose—except for that, it had no interest for me at all. Boom! boom! The huge voluminous concussions rushed past me, beat at my heart and passed. In a moment Nettie would come out to see.

First one and then two other wrappered figures came out of the bungalows to join the first. His arm pointed seaward, and his voice, a full tenor, rose in explanation. I could hear some of the words. "It's a German!" he said. "She's caught."

Some one disputed that, and there followed a little indistinct babble of argument. I went on slowly in the circuit I had marked out, watching these people as I went.

They shouted together with such a common intensity of direction that I halted and looked seaward. I saw the tall fountain flung by a shot that had just missed the great warship. A second rose still nearer us, a third, and a fourth, and then a great uprush of dust, a whirling cloud, leaped out of the headland whence the rocket had come, and spread with a slow deliberation right and left. Hard on that an enormous crash, and the man with the full voice leaped and cried, "Hit!"

Let me see! Of course, I had to go round beyond the bungalows, and then come up towards the group from behind.

A high-pitched woman's voice called, "Honeymooners! honeymooners! Come out and see!"

Something gleamed in the shadow of the nearer bungalow, and a man's voice answered from within. What he said I did not catch, but suddenly I heard Nettie calling very distinctly, "We've been bathing."

The man who had first come out shouted, "Don't you hear the guns? They're fighting—not five miles from shore."

"Eh?" answered the bungalow, and a window opened.

"Out there!"

I did not hear the reply, because of the faint rustle of my own movements. Clearly these people were all too much occupied by the battle to look in my direction, and so I walked now straight toward the darkness that held Nettie and the black desire of my heart.

"Look!" cried someone, and pointed skyward.

I glanced up, and behold! The sky was streaked with bright green trails. They radiated from a point halfway between the western horizon and the zenith, and within the shining clouds of the meteor a streaming movement had begun, so that it seemed to be pouring both westwardly and back toward the east, with a crackling sound, as though the whole heaven was stippled over with phantom pistol-shots. It seemed to me then as if the meteor was coming to help me, descending with those thousand pistols like a curtain to fend off this unmeaning foolishness of the sea.

"Boom!" went a gun on the big ironclad, and "boom!' and the guns of the pursuing cruisers flashed in reply.

To glance up at that streaky, stirring light scum of the sky made one's head swim. I stood for a moment dazed, and more than a little giddy. I had a curious instant of purely speculative thought. Suppose, after all, the fanatics were right, and the world *was* coming to an end! What a score that would be for Parload!

Then it came into my head that all these things were happening to consecrate my revenge! The war below, the heavens above, were the thunderous garment of my deed. I heard Nettie's voice cry out not fifty yards away, and my passion surged again. I was to return to her amid these terrors bearing unanticipated death. I was to possess her, with a bullet, amidst thunderings and fear. At the thought I lifted up my voice to a shout that went unheard, and advanced now recklessly, revolver displayed in my hand.

It was fifty yards, forty yards, thirty yards—the little group of people, still heedless of me, was larger and more important now, the green-shot sky and the fighting ships remoter. Someone darted out from the bungalow, with an interrupted question, and stopped, suddenly aware of me. It was Nettie, with some coquettish dark wrap about her, and the green glare shining on her sweet face and white throat. I could see her expression, stricken with dismay and terror, at my advance, as though something had seized her by the heart and held her still—a target for my shots.

"Boom!" came the ironclad's gunshot like a command. "Bang!" the bullet leaped from my hand. Do you know, I did not want to shoot her then. Indeed I did not want to shoot her then! Bang! and I had fired again, still striding on, and—each time it seemed I had missed.

She moved a step or so toward me, still staring, and then someone intervened, and near beside her I saw young Verrall.

A heavy stranger, the man in the hooded bathgown, a fat, foreign-looking man, came out of nowhere like a shield before them. He seemed a preposterous interruption. His face was full of astonishment and terror. He rushed across my path with arms extended and open hands, as one might try to stop a runaway horse. He shouted some nonsense. He seemed to want to dissuade me, as though dissuasion had anything to do with it now.

"Not you, you fool!" I said hoarsely. "Not you!" But he hid Nettie nevertheless.

By an enormous effort I resisted a mechanical impulse to shoot through his fat body. Anyhow, I knew I mustn't shoot him. For a moment I was in doubt, then I became very active, turned aside abruptly and dodged his pawing arm to the left, and so found two others irresolutely in my way. I fired a third shot in the air, just over their heads, and ran at them. They hastened left and right; I pulled up and faced about within a yard of a foxy-faced young man coming sideways, who seemed about to grapple me. At my resolute halt he fell back a pace, ducked, and threw up a defensive arm, and then I perceived the course was clear, and ahead of me, young Verrall and Nettie—he was holding her arm to help her—running away. "Of course!" said I.

I fired a fourth ineffectual shot, and then in an access of fury at my misses, started out to run them down and shoot them barrel to backbone. "These people!" I said, dismissing all these interferences...."A yard," I panted, speaking aloud to myself, "a yard! Till then, take care, you mustn't—mustn't shoot again."

Someone pursued me, perhaps several people—I do not know, we left them all behind....

We ran. For a space I was altogether intent upon the swift monotony of flight and pursuit. The sands were changed to a whirl of green moonshine, the air was thunder. A luminous green haze rolled about us. What did such things matter? We ran. Did I gain or lose? that was the question. They ran through a gap in a broken fence that sprang up abruptly out of nothingness, and turned to the right. I noted we were in a road. But this green mist! One seemed to plow through it. They were fading into it, and at that thought I made a spurt that won a dozen feet or more.

She staggered. He gripped her arm, and dragged her forward. They doubled to the left. We were off the road again and on turf. It felt like turf. I tripped and fell at a ditch that was somehow full of smoke, and was up again, but now they were phantoms half gone into the livid swirls about me....

Still I ran.

On, on! I groaned with the violence of my effort. I staggered again and swore. I felt the concussions of great guns tear past me through the murk.

They were gone! Everything was going, but I kept on running. Once more I stumbled. There was something about my feet that impeded me, tall grass or heather, but I could not see what it was, only this smoke that eddied about my knees. There was a noise and spinning in my brain, a vain resistance to a dark green curtain that was falling, falling, falling, fold upon fold. Everything grew darker and darker.

I made one last frantic effort, and raised my revolver, fired my penultimate shot at a venture, and fell headlong to the ground. And behold! the green curtain was a black one, and the earth and I and all things ceased to be.

BOOK 2 *THE GREEN VAPORS*

Chapter 1

The Change

1

I seemed to awaken out of a refreshing sleep.

I did not awaken with a start, but opened my eyes, and lay very comfortably looking at a line of extraordinarily scarlet poppies that glowed against a glowing sky. It was the sky of a magnificent sunrise, and an archipelago of gold-beached purple islands floated in a sea of golden green. The poppies too, swan-necked buds, blazing corollas, translucent stout seed-vessels, stoutly upheld, had a luminous quality, seemed wrought only from some more solid kind of light.

I stared unwonderingly at these things for a time, and then there rose upon my consciousness, intermingling with these, the bristling golden green heads of growing barley.

A remote faint question, where I might be, drifted and vanished again in my mind. Everything was very still.

Everything was as still as death.

I felt very light, full of the sense of physical well-being. I perceived I was lying on my side in a little trampled space in a weedy, flowering barley field, that was in some inexplicable way saturated with light and beauty. I sat up, and remained for a long time filled with the delight and charm of the delicate little convolvulus that twined among the barley stems, the pimpernel that laced the ground below.

Then the question returned. What was this place? How had I come to be sleeping here?

I could not remember.

It perplexed me that somehow my body felt strange to me. It was unfamiliar—I could not tell how—and the barley, and the beautiful weeds, and the slowly developing glory of the dawn behind; all those things partook of the same unfamiliarity. I felt as though I was a thing in some very luminous painted window, as though this dawn broke through me. I felt I was part of some exquisite picture painted in light and joy.

A faint breeze bent and rustled the barley heads, and jogged my mind forward.

Who was I? That was a good way of beginning.

I held up my left hand and arm before me, a grubby hand, a frayed cuff; but with a quality of painted unreality, transfigured as a beggar might have been by Botticelli. I looked for a time steadfastly at a beautiful pearl sleeve-link.

I remembered Willie Leadford, who had owned that arm and hand, as though he had been someone else.

Of course! My history—its rough outline rather than the immediate past—began to shape itself in my memory, very small, very bright and inaccessible, like a thing watched through a miscroscope. Clayton and Swathinglea returned to my mind; the slums and darkness, Dureresque, minute and in their rich dark colors pleasing, and through them I went towards my destiny. I sat hands on knees recalling that queer passionate career that had ended with my futile shot into the growing darkness of the End. The thought of that shot awoke my emotions again.

There was something in it now, something absurd, that made me smile pityingly.

Poor little angry, miserable creature! Poor little angry, miserable world!

I sighed for pity, not only pity for myself, but for all the hot hearts, the tormented brains, the straining, striving things of hope and pain, who had found their peace at last beneath the pouring mist and suffocation of the comet. Because certainly that world was over and done. They were all so weak and unhappy, and I was now so strong and so serene. For I felt sure I was dead; no one living could have this perfect assurance of good, this strong and confident peace. I had made an end of the fever called living. I was dead, and it was all right, and these—?

I felt an inconsistency.

These, then, must be the barley fields of God!—the still and silent barley fields of God, full of unfading poppy flowers whose seeds bear peace.

2

It was queer to find barley fields in heaven, but no doubt there were many surprises in store for me.

How still everything was! Peace! The peace that passeth understanding. After all it had come to me! But, indeed, everything was very still! No bird sang. Surely I was alone in the world! No birds sang. Yes, and all the distant sounds of life had ceased, the lowing of cattle, the barking of dogs....

Something that was like fear beatified came into my heart. It was all right, I knew; but to be alone! I stood up and met the hot summons of the rising sun, hurrying towards me, as it were, with glad tidings, over the spikes of the barley....

Blinded, I made a step. My foot struck something hard, and I looked down to discover my revolver, a blue-black thing, like a dead snake at my feet.

For a moment that puzzled me.

Then I clean forgot about it. The wonder of the quiet took possession of my soul. Dawn, and no birds singing!

How beautiful was the world! How beautiful, but how still! I walked slowly through the barley towards a line of elder bushes, wayfaring tree and bramble that made the hedge of the field. I noted as I passed along a dead shrew mouse, as it seemed to me, among the grasses; then a still toad. I was surprised that this did not leap aside from my footfalls, and I stooped and picked it up. Its body was limp like life, but it made no struggle, the brightness of its eye was veiled, it did not move in my hand.

It seems to me now that I stood holding that lifeless little creature for some time. Then very softly I stooped down and replaced it. I was trembling—trembling with a nameless emotion. I looked with quickened eyes closely among the barley stems, and behold, now everywhere I saw beetles, flies, and little creatures that did not move, lying as they fell when the vapors overcame them; they seemed no more than painted things. Some were novel creatures to me. I was very unfamiliar with natural things. "My God!" I cried; "but is it only I—?"

And then at my next movement something squealed sharply. I turned about, but I could not see it, only I saw a little stir in a rut and heard the diminishing rustle of the unseen creature's flight. And at that I turned to my toad again, and its eye moved and it stirred. And presently, with infirm and hesitating gestures, it stretched its limbs and began to crawl away from me.

But wonder, that gentle sister of fear, had me now. I saw a little way ahead a brown and crimson butterfly perched upon a cornflower. I thought at first it was the breeze that stirred it, and then I saw its wings were quivering. And even as I watched it, it started into life, and spread itself, and fluttered into the air.

I watched it fly, a turn this way, a turn that, until suddenly it seemed to vanish. And now, life was returning to this thing and that on every side of me, with slow stretchings and bendings, with twitterings, with a little start and stir....

I came slowly, stepping very carefully because of these drugged, feebly awakening things, through the barley to the hedge. It was a very glorious hedge, so that it held my eyes. It flowed along and interlaced like splendid music. It was rich with lupin, honeysuckle, campions, and ragged robin; bed straw, hops, and wild clematis twined and hung among its branches, and all along its ditch border the starry stitchwort lifted its childish faces, and chorused in lines and masses. Never had I seen such a symphony of notelike flowers and tendrils and leaves. And suddenly in its depths, I heard a chirrup and the whirr of startled wings.

Nothing was dead, but everything had changed to beauty! And I stood for a time with clean and happy eyes looking at the intricate delicacy before me and marveling how richly God has made his worlds....

"Tweedle-Tweezle," a lark had shot the stillness with his shining thread of song; one lark, and then presently another, invisibly in the air, making out of that blue quiet a woven cloth of gold....

The earth recreated—only by the reiteration of such phrases may I hope to give the intense freshness of that dawn. For a time I was altogether taken up with the beautiful details of being, as regardless of my old life of jealous passion and impatient sorrow as though I was Adam new made. I could tell you now with infinite particularity of the shut flowers that opened as I looked, of tendrils and grass blades, of a blue titmouse I picked up very tenderly—never before had I remarked the great delicacy of feathers—that presently disclosed its bright black eye and judged me, and perched, swaying fearlessly, upon my finger, and spread unhurried wings and flew away, and of a great ebullition of tadpoles in the ditch; like all the things that lived beneath the water, they had passed unaltered through the Change. Amid such incidents, I lived those first great moments, losing for a time in the wonder of each little part the mighty wonder of the whole.

A litle path ran between hedge and barley, and along this,

leisurely and content and glad, looking at this beautiful thing and that, moving a step and stopping, then moving on again, I came presently to a stile, and deep below it, and overgrown, was a lane.

And on the worn oak of the stile was a round label, and on the label these words, "Swindells' G 90 Pills."

I sat myself astraddle on the stile, not fully grasping all the implications of these words. But they perplexed me even more than the revolver and my dirty cuff.

About me now the birds lifted up their little hearts and sang, ever more birds and more.

I read the label over and over again, and joined it to the fact that I still wore my former clothes, and that my revolver had been lying at my feet. One conclusion stared out at me. This was no new planet, no glorious hereafter such as I had supposed. This beautiful wonderland was the world, the same old world of my rage and death! But at least it was like meeting a familiar house-slut, washed and dignified, dressed in a queen's robes, worshipful and fine....

It might be the old world indeed, but something new lay upon all things, a glowing certitude of health and happiness. It might be the old world, but the dust and fury of the old life was certainly done. At least I had no doubt of that.

I recalled the last phases of my former life, that darkling climax of pursuit and anger and universal darkness and the whirling green vapors of extinction. The comet had struck the earth and made an end to all things; of that too I was assured.

But afterward?...

And now?

The imaginations of my boyhood came back as speculative possibilities. In those days I had believed firmly in the necessary advent of a last day, a great coming out of the sky, trumpetings and fear, the Resurrection, and the Judgment. My roving fancy now suggested to me that this Judgment must have come and passed. That it had passed and in some manner missed me. I was left alone here, in a swept and garnished world (except, of course, for this label of Swindells') to begin again perhaps....

No doubt Swindells has got his deserts.

My mind ran for a time on Swindells, on the imbecile pushfulness of that extinct creature, dealing in rubbish, covering the countryside with lies in order to get—what had he sought?—a silly, ugly, great house, a temper-destroying motorcar, a number of disrespectful, abject servants; thwarted intrigues for a party-fund baronetcy as the crest of his life, perhaps. You cannot imagine the littleness of those former times; their naive, queer absurdities! And for the first time in my existence I thought of these things without bitterness. In the former days I had seen wickedness, I had seen tragedy, but now I saw only the extraordinary foolishness of the old life. The ludicrous side of human wealth and importance turned itself upon me, a shining novelty, poured down upon me like the sunrise, and engulfed me in laughter. Swindells! Swindells, damned! My vision of Judgment became a delightful burlesque. I saw the chuckling Angel sayer with his face veiled, and the corporeal presence of Swindells upheld amidst the laughter of the spheres. "Here's a thing, and a very pretty thing, and what's to be done with this very pretty thing?" I saw a soul being drawn from a rotund, substantial-looking body like a whelk from its shell....

I laughed loudly and long. And behold! even as I laughed the keen point of things accomplished stabbed my mirth, and I was weeping, weeping aloud, convulsed with weeping, and the tears were pouring down my face.

3

Everywhere the awakening came with the sunrise. We awakened to the gladness of the morning; we walked dazzled in a light that was joy. Everywhere that was so. It was always morning. It was morning because, until the direct rays of the sun touched it, the changing nitrogen of our atmosphere did not pass into its permanent phase, and the sleepers lay as they had fallen. In its intermediate state the air hung inert, incapable of producing either revival or stupefaction, no longer green, but not yet changed to the gas that now lives in us....

To everyone, I think, came some parallel to the mental states I have already sought to describe—a wonder, an impression of joyful novelty. There was also very commonly a certain confusion of the intelligence, a difficulty in self-recognition. I remember clearly as I sat on my stile that presently I had the clearest doubts of my own identity and fell into the oddest metaphysical questionings. "If this be I," I said, "then how is it I am no longer madly seeking Nettie? Nettie is now the remotest thing—and all my wrongs. Why have I suddenly passed out of all that passion? Why does not the thought of Verrall quicken my pulses?"...

I was only one of many millions who that morning had the same doubts. I suppose one knows one's self for one's self when one returns from sleep or insensibility by the familiarity of one's bodily sensations, and that morning all our most intimate bodily sensations were changed. The intimate chemical processes of life were changed, its nervous metaboly. For the fluctuating, uncertain, passion-darkened thought and feeling of the old time became steady, full-bodied, wholesome processes. Touch was different, sight was different, sound and all the senses were subtler; had it not been that our thought was steadier and fuller, I believe great multitudes of men would have gone mad. But, as it was, we understood. The dominant impression I would convey in this account of the Change is one of enormous release, of a vast substantial exaltation. There was an effect, as it were, of lightheadedness that was also clear-headedness, and the alteration in one's bodily sensations, instead of producing the mental obfuscation, the loss of identity that was a common mental trouble under former conditions, gave simply a new detachment from the tumid passions and entanglements of the personal life.

In this story of my bitter, restricted youth that I have been telling you, I have sought constantly to convey the narrowness, the intensity, the confusion, muddle, and dusty heat of the old world. It was quite clear to me, within an hour of my awakening, that all that was, in some mysterious way, over and done. That, too, was the common experience. Men stood up; they took the new air into their lungs—a deep long breath, and the past fell from them; they could forgive, they could disregard, they could attempt.... And it was no new thing, no miracle that sets aside the former order of the world. It was a change in material conditions, a change in the atmosphere, that at one bound had released them. Some of them it had released to death....Indeed, man himself had changed not at all. We knew before the Change, the meanest knew, by glowing moments in ourselves and others, by histories and music and beautiful things, by heroic instances and splendid stories, how fine mankind could be, how fine almost any human being could upon occasion be; but the poison in the air, its poverty in all the nobler elements which made such moments rare and remarkable—all that has changed. The air was changed, and the Spirit of Man that had drowsed and slumbered and dreamed dull and evil things, awakened, and stood with wonder-clean eyes, refreshed, looking again on life.

4

The miracle of the awakening came to me in solitude, the laughter, and then the tears. Only after some time did I come upon another man. Until I heard his voice calling I did not seem to feel there were any other people in the world. All that seemed past, with all the stresses that were past. I had come out of the individual pit in which my shy egotism had lurked, I had overflowed to all humanity, I had seemed to be all humanity; I had laughed at Swindells as I could have laughed at myself, and this shout that came to me seemed like the coming of an unexpected thought in my own mind. But when it was repeated I answered.

"I am hurt," said the voice, and I descended into the lane forthwith, and so came upon Melmount sitting near the ditch with his back to me.

Some of the incidental sensory impressions of that morning bit so deeply into my mind that I verily believe, when at last I face the greater mysteries that lie beyond this life, when the things of this life fade from me as the mists of the morning fade before the sun, these irrelevant petty details will be the last to leave me, will be the last wisps visible of that attenuating veil. I believe, for instance, I could match the fur upon the collar of his great motoring coat now, could paint the dull red tinge of his big cheek with his fair eyelashes just catching the light and showing beyond. His hat was off, his dome-shaped head, with its smooth hair between red and extreme fairness, was bent forward in scrutiny of his twisted foot. His back seemed enormous. And there was something about the mere massive sight of him that filled me with liking.

"What's wrong?" said I.

"I say," he said, in his full deliberate tones, straining round to see me and showing a profile, a well-modeled nose, a sensitive, clumsy, big lip, known to every caricaturist in the world, "I'm in a fix. I fell and wrenched my ankle. Where are you?"

I walked round him and stood looking at his face. I perceived he had his gaiter and sock and boot off, the motor gauntlets had been cast aside, and he was kneading the injured part in an exploratory manner with his thick thumbs.

"By Jove!" I said, "you're Melmount!"

"Melmount!" He thought. "That's my name," he said, without looking up.... "But it doesn't affect my ankle."

We remained silent for a few moments except for a grunt of pain from him.

"Do you know?" I asked, "what has happened to things?"

He seemed to complete his diagnosis. "It's not broken," he said.

"Do you know," I repeated, "what has happened to everything?"

"No," he said, looking up at me incuriously for the first time.

"There's some difference—"

"There's a difference." He smiled, a smile of unexpected pleasantness, and an interest was coming into his eyes. "I've been a little preoccupied with my own internal sensations. I remark an extraordinary brightness about things. Is that it?"

"That's part of it. And a queer feeling, a clear-headedness—"

He surveyed me and meditated gravely. "I woke up," he said, feeling his way in his memory.

"And I."

"I lost my way—I forget quite how. There was a curious green fog." He stared at his foot, remembering. "Something to do with a comet. I was by a hedge in the darkness. Tried to run.... Then I must have pitched into this lane. Look!" He pointed with his head. "There's a wooden rail new broken there. I must have stumbled over that out of the field above." He scrutinized this and concluded, "Yes...."

"It was dark," I said, "and a sort of green gas came out of nothing everywhere. That is the last *I* remember."

"And then you woke up? So did I.... In a state of great bewilderment. Certainly there's something odd in the air. I was—I was rushing along a road in a motorcar, very much excited and preoccupied. I got down—" He held out a triumphant finger. "Ironclads!"

"*Now* I've got it! We'd strung our fleet from here to Texel. We'd got right across them and the Elbe mined.

We'd lost the *Lord Warden*. By Jove, yes. The *Lord Warden!* A battleship that cost two million pounds—and that fool Rigby said it didn't matter! Eleven hundred men went down.... I remember now. We were sweeping up the North Sea like a net, with the North Atlantic fleet waiting at the Faroes for 'em—and not one of 'em had three days' coal! Now, was that a dream? No! I told a lot of people as much—a meeting was it?—to reassure them. They were warlike but extremely frightened. Queer people—paunchy and bald like gnomes, most of them. Where? Of course! We had it all over—a big dinner—oysters!—Colchester. I'd been there, just to show all this raid scare was nonsense. And I was coming back here.... But it doesn't seem as though that was—recent. I suppose it was. Yes, of course!—it was. I got out of my car at the bottom of the rise with the idea of walking along the cliff path, because everyone said one of their battleships was being chased along the shore. That's clear! I heard their guns—"

He reflected. "Queer I should have forgotten! Did *you* hear any guns?"

I said I had heard them.

"Was it last night?"

"Late last night. One or two in the morning."

He leaned back on his hand and looked at me, smiling frankly. "Even now," he said, "it's odd, but the whole of that seems like a silly dream. Do you think there *was* a *Lord Warden?* Do you really believe we sank all that machinery—for fun? It was a dream. And yet—it happened."

By all the standards of the former time it would have been remarkable that I talked quite easily and freely with so great a man. "Yes," I said; "that's it. One feels one has awakened—from something more than that green gas. As though the other things also—weren't quite real."

He knitted his brows and felt the calf of his leg thoughtfully. "I made a speech at Colchester," he said.

I thought he was going to add something more about that, but there lingered a habit of reticence in the man that held him for the moment. "It is a very curious thing," he broke away; "that this pain should be, on the whole, more interesting than disagreeable."

"You are in pain?"

"My ankle is! It's either broken or badly sprained—I think sprained; it's very painful to move, but personally I'm not in pain. That sort of general sickness that comes with local injury—not a trace of it!..." He mused and remarked, "I was speaking at Colchester, and saying things about the war. I begin to see it better. The reporters—scribble, scribble. Max Sutaine, 1885. Hubbub. Compliments about the oysters. Mm-mm....What was it? About the war? A war that must needs be long and bloody, taking toll from castle and cottage, taking toll!...Rhetorical gusto! Was I drunk last night?"

His eyebrows puckered. He had drawn up his right knee, his elbow rested thereon and his chin on his fist. The deep-set gray eyes beneath his thatch of eyebrow stared at unknown things. "My God!" he murmured, "My God!" with a note of disgust. He made a big brooding figure in the sunlight, he had an effect of more than physical largeness; he made me feel that it became me to wait upon his thinking. I had never met a man of this sort before; I did not know such men existed....

It is a curious thing, that I cannot now recall any ideas whatever that I had before the Change about the personalities of statesmen, but I doubt if ever in those days I thought of them at all as tangible individual human beings, conceivably of some intellectual complexity. I believe that my impression was a straightforward blend of caricature and newspaper leader. I certainly had no respect for them. And now without servility or any insincerity whatever, as if it were a first-fruit of the Change, I found myself in the presence of a human being towards whom I perceived myself inferior and subordinate, before whom I stood without servility or any insincerity whatever, in an attitude of respect and attention. My inflamed, my rancid egotism

—or was it after all only the chances of life?—had never once permitted that before the Change.

He emerged from his thoughts, still with a faint perplexity in his manner. "That speech I made last night," he said, "was damned mischievous nonsense, you know. Nothing can alter that. Nothing.... No!... Little fat gnomes in evening dress—gobbling oysers. Gulp!"

It was a most natural part of the wonder of that morning that he should adopt this incredible note of frankness, and that it should abate nothing from my respect for him.

"Yes," he said, "you are right. It's all indisputable fact, and I can't believe it was anything but a dream."

5

That memory stands out against the dark past of the world with extraordinary clearness and brightness. The air, I remember, was full of the calling and piping and singing of birds. I have a curious persuasion too that there was a distant happy clamor of pealing bells, but that I am half-convinced is a mistake. Nevertheless, there was something in the fresh bite of things, in the dewy newness of sensation that set bells rejoicing in one's brain. And that big, fair, pensive man sitting on the ground had beauty even in his clumsy pose, as though indeed some Great Master of strength and humor had made him.

And—it is so hard now to convey these things—he spoke to me, a stranger, without reservations, carelessly, as men now speak to men. Before those days, not only did we think badly, but what we thought, a thousand shortsighted considerations, dignity, objective discipline, discretion, a hundred kindred aspects of shabbiness of soul, made us muffle before we told it to our fellow men.

"It's all returning now," he said, and told me half soliloquizingly what was in his mind.

I wish I could give every word he said to me; he struck out

image after image to my nascent intelligence, with swift broken fragments of speech. If I had a precise full memory of that morning I should give it you, verbatim, minutely. But here, save for the little sharp things that stand out, I find only blurred general impressions. Throughout I have to make up again his half-forgotten sentences and speeches, and be content with giving you the general effect. But I can see and hear him now as he said, "The dream got worst at the end. The war—a perfectly horrible business! Horrible! And it was just like a nightmare, you couldn't do anything to escape from it—everyone was driven!"

His sense of indiscretion was gone.

He opened the war out to me—as everyone sees it now. Only that morning it was astonishing. He sat there on the ground, absurdly forgetful of his bare and swollen foot, treating me as the humblest accessory and as altogether an equal, talking out to himself the great obsessions of his mind. "We could have prevented it! Any of us who chose to speak out could have prevented it. A little decent frankness. What was there to prevent us being frank with one another? Their emperor—his position was a pile of ridiculous assumptions, no doubt, but at bottom—he was a sane man." He touched off the emperor in a few pithy words, the German press, the German people, and our own. He put it as we should put it all now, but with a certain heat as of a man half-guilty and wholly resentful. "Their damned little buttoned-up professors!" he cried, incidentally. "Were there ever such men? And ours! Some of us might have taken a firmer line.... If a lot of us had taken a firmer line and squashed that nonsense early...."

He lapsed into inaudible whisperings, into silence....

I stood regarding him, understanding him, learning marvelously from him. It is a fact that for the best part of the morning of the Change I forgot Nettie and Verrall as completely as though they were no more than characters in some novel that I had put aside to finish at my leisure, in order that I might talk to this man.

"Eh, well," he said, waking startingly from his thoughts. "Here we are awakened! The thing can't go on now; all this must end. How it ever began—! My dear boy, how did all those things ever begin? I feel like a new Adam.... Do you think this has happened—generally? Or shall we find all these gnomes and things?... Who cares?"

He made as if to rise, and remembered his ankle. He suggested I should help him as far as his bungalow. There seemed nothing strange to either of us that he should requisition my services or that I should cheerfully obey. I helped him bandage his ankle, and we set out, I his crutch, the two of us making up a sort of limping quadruped, along the winding lane toward the cliffs and the sea.

6

His bungalow beyond the golf links was, perhaps, a mile and a quarter from the lane. We went down to the beach margin and along the pallid wave-smoothed sands, and we got along by making a swaying, hopping, tripod dance forward until I began to give under him, and then, as soon as we could, sitting down. His ankle was, in fact, broken, and he could not put it to the ground without exquisite pain. So that it took us nearly two hours to get to the house, and it would have taken longer if his butler-valet had not come out to assist me. They had found motorcar and chauffeur smashed and still at the bend of the road near the house, and had been on that side looking for Melmount, or they would have seen us before.

For most of that time we were sitting now on turf, now on a chalk boulder, now on a timber groin, and talking one to the other, with the frankness proper to the intercourse of men of good intent, without reservations or aggressions, in the common, open fashion of contemporary intercourse today, but which then, nevertheless, was the rarest and strangest thing in the world. He for the most part talked, but at some shape of a question I told him—as plainly as I could tell of passions that had for a time become incomprehensible to me—of my murderous pursuit of Nettie and her lover, and how the green vapors overcame me. He watched me with grave eyes and nodded understandingly, and afterwards he asked me brief penetrating questions about my education, my upbringing, my work. There was a deliberation in his manner, brief full pauses, that had in them no element of delay.

"Yes," he said, "yes—of course. What a fool I have been!" and said no more until we had made another of our tripod struggles along the beach. At first I did not see the connection of my story with that self-accusation.

"Suppose," he said, panting on the groin, "there had been such a thing as a statesman!..."

He turned to me. "If one had decided all this muddle shall end! If one had taken it, as an artist takes his clay, as a man who builds takes site and stone, and made—" He flung out his big broad hand at the glories of sky and sea, and drew a deep breath, "something to fit that setting."

He added in explanation, "Then there wouldn't have been such stories as yours at all, you know....

"Tell me more about it," he said, "tell me all about yourself. I feel all these things have passed away, all these things are to be changed forever.... You won't be what you have been from this time forth. All the things you have done—don't matter now. To us, at any rate, they don't matter at all. We have met, who were separated in that darkness behind us. Tell me.

"Yes," he said; and I told my story straight and as frankly as I have told it to you. "And there, where those little skerries of weed rock run out to the ebb, beyond the headland, is Bungalow village. What did you do with your pistol?"

"I left it lying there—among the barley."

He glanced at me from under his light eyelashes. "If others feel like you and I," he said, "there'll be a lot of pistols left among the barley today...."

So we talked, I and that great, strong man, with the love of brothers so plain between us it needed not a word. Our souls went out to one another in stark good faith; never before had I had anything but a guarded watchfulness for any fellow man. Still I see him, upon that wild desolate beach of the ebb tide, I see him leaning against the shelly buttress of a groin, looking down at the poor drowned sailor whose body we presently found. For we found a newly drowned man who had just chanced to miss this great dawn in which we rejoiced. We found him lying in a pool of water, among brown weeds in the dark shadow of the timberings. You must not overrate the horrors of the former days; in those days it was scarcely more common to see death in England than it would be today. This dead man was a sailor from the *Rother Adler*, the great German battleship that—had we but known it—lay not four miles away along the coast amidst plowed-up mountains of chalk ooze, a torn and battered mass of machinery, wholly submerged at high water, and holding in its interstices nine hundred drowned brave men, all strong and skillful, all once capable of doing fine things....

I remember that poor boy very vividly. He had been drowned during the anesthesia of the green gas, his fair young face was quiet and calm, but the skin of his chest had been crinkled by scalding water and his right arm was bent queerly back. Even to this needless death and all its tale of cruelty, beauty and dignity had come. Everything flowed together to significance as we stood there. I, the ill-clad, cheaply equipped proletarian, and Melmount in his great fur-trimmed coat—he was hot with walking but he had not thought to remove it—leaning upon the clumsy groins and pitying this poor victim of the war he had helped to make. "Poor lad!" he said, "poor lad! A child we blunderers sent to death! Do look at the quiet beauty of that face, that body—to be flung aside like this!"

(I remember that near this dead man's hand a stranded starfish writhed its slowly feeling limbs, struggling back toward the sea. It left grooved traces in the sand.)

"There must be no more of this," panted Melmount, leaning on my shoulder, "no more of this...."

But most I recall Melmount as he talked a little later, sitting upon a great chalk boulder with the sunlight on his big, perspiration-dewed face. He made his resolves. "We must end war," he said, in that full whisper of his; "it is stupidity. With so many people able to read and think— even as it is—there is no need of anything of the sort. Gods! What have we rulers been at?...Drowsing like people in a stifling room, too dull and sleepy and too base toward each other for anyone to get up and open the window. What haven't we been at?"

A great powerful figure he sits there still in my memory, perplexed and astonished at himself and all things. "We must change all this," he repeated, and threw out his broad hands in a powerful gesture against the sea and sky. "We have done so weakly—Heaven alone knows why!" I can see him now, queer giant that he looked on that dawnlit beach of splendor, the sea birds flying about us and that crumpled death hard by, no bad symbol in his clumsiness and needless heat of the unawakened powers of the former time. I remember it as an integral part of that picture that far away across the sandy stretches one of those white estate boards I have described, stuck up a little askew amidst the yellow-green turf upon the crest of the low cliffs.

He talked with a sort of wonder of the former things. "Has it ever dawned upon you to imagine the pettiness— the pettiness!—of every soul concerned in a declaration of war?" he asked. He went on, as though speech was necessary to make it credible, to describe Laycock, who first gave the horror words at the cabinet council, "an undersized Oxford prig with a tenoring voice and a garbage of Greek—the sort of little fool who is brought up on the admiration of his elder sisters....

"All the time almost," he said, "I was watching him— thinking what an ass he was to be trusted with men's lives....I might have done better to have thought that of myself. I was doing nothing to prevent it all! The damned little imbecile was up to his neck in the drama of the thing, he liked to trumpet it out, he goggled round at us. 'Then it is war!' he said. Richover shrugged his shoulders. I made some slight protest and gave in. Afterward I dreamed of him.

"What a lot we were! All a little scared at ourselves—all, as it were, instrumental...

"And it's fools like that lead to things like this!" He jerked his head at that dead man near by us.

"It will be interesting to know what has happened to the world...This green vapor—queer stuff. But I know what has happened to me. It's Conversion. I've always known...But this is being a fool. Talk! I'm going to stop it."

He motioned to rise with his clumsy outstretched hands.

"Stop what?" said I, stepping forward instinctively to help him.

"War," he said in his great whisper, putting his big hand on my shoulder but making no further attempt to arise, "I'm going to put an end to war—to any sort of war! And all these things that must end. The world is beautiful, life is great and splendid, we had only to lift up our eyes and see. Think of the glories through which we have been driving, like a herd of swine in a garden place. The color in life—the sounds—the shapes! We have had our jealousies, our quarrels, our ticklish rights, our invincible prejudices, our vulgar enterprise and sluggish timidities, we have chattered and pecked one another and fouled the world—like daws in the temple, like unclean birds in the holy place of God. All my life has been foolishness and pettiness, gross pleasures and mean discretions—all. I am a meager dark thing in this morning's glow, a penitence, a shame! And, but for God's mercy, I might have died this night—like that poor lad there—amidst the squalor of my sins! No more of this! No more of this!—whether the whole world has changed or no, matters nothing. *We two have seen this dawn!...*"

He paused.

"I will arise and go unto my Father," he began presently, "and will say unto Him—"

His voice died away in an inaudible whisper. His hand tightened painfully on my shoulder and he rose....

Chapter 2

The Awakening

1

So the great Day came to me.

And even as I had awakened so in that same dawn the whole world awoke.

For the whole world of living things had been overtaken by the same tide of insensibility; in an hour, at the touch of this new gas in the comet, the shiver of catalytic change had passed about the globe. They say it was the nitrogen of the air, the old *azote*, that in the twinkling of an eye was changed out of itself, and in an hour or so became a respirable gas, differing indeed from oxygen, but helping and sustaining its action, a bath of strength and healing for nerve and brain. I do not know the precise changes that occurred, nor the names our chemists give them, my work has carried me away from such things, only this I know—I and all men were renewed.

I picture to myself this thing happening in space, a planetary moment, the faint smudge, the slender whirl of meteor, drawing nearer to this planet—this planet like a ball, like a shaded rounded ball, floating in the void, with its little, nearly impalpable coat of cloud and air, with its dark pools of ocean, its gleaming ridges of land. And as that midge from the void touches it, the transparent gaseous outer shell clouds in an instant green and then slowly clears again....

Thereafter, for three hours or more—we know the minimum time for the Change was almost exactly three hours because all the clocks and watches kept going—everywhere, no man, nor beast, nor bird, nor any living thing that breathes the air stirred at all but lay still....

Everywhere on earth that day, in the ears of everyone who breathed, there had been the same humming in the air, the same rush of green vapors, the crepitation, the streaming down of shooting stars. The Hindu had stayed his morning's work in the fields to stare and marvel and fall, the blue-clothed Chinaman fell head foremost athwart his midday bowl of rice, the Japanese merchant came out from some chaffering in his office amazed and presently lay there before his door, the evening gazers by the Golden Gates were overtaken as they waited for the rising of the great star. This had happened in every city of the world, in every lonely valley, in every home and house and shelter and every open place. On the high seas, the crowding steamship passengers, eager for any wonder, gaped and marveled, and were suddenly terror-stricken, and struggled for the gangways and were overcome, the captain staggered on the bridge and fell, the stoker fell headlong among his coals, the engines throbbed upon their way untended, the fishing craft drove by without a hail, with swaying rudder, heeling and dipping....

The great voice of material Fate cried Halt! And in the midst of the play the actors staggered, dropped, and were still. The figure runs from my pen. In New York that very thing occurred. Most of the theatrical audiences dispersed, but in two crowded houses the company, fearing a panic, went on playing amidst the gloom, and the people, trained by many a previous disaster, stuck to their seats. There they sat, the back rows only moving a little, and there, in disciplined lines, they drooped and failed, nodded, and fell forward or slid down upon the floor. I am told by Parload—though indeed I know nothing of the reasoning on which his confidence rests—that within an hour of the great moment of impact the first green modification of nitrogen had dissolved and passed away, leaving the air as translucent as ever. The rest of that wonderful interlude was clear, had any had eyes to see its clearness. In London it was night, but in New York, for example, people were in the full bustle of the evening's enjoyment, in Chicago they were sitting down to dinner, the whole world was abroad. The moonlight must have illuminated streets and squares littered with crumpled figures, through which such electric cars as had no automatic brakes had plowed on their way until they were stopped by the fallen bodies. People lay in their dress clothes, in dining rooms, restaurants, on staircases, in halls, everywhere just as they had been overcome. Men gambling, men drinking, thieves lurking in hidden places, sinful couples, were caught, to arise with awakened mind and conscience amidst the disorder of their sin. America the comet reached in the full tide of evening life, but Britain lay asleep. But as I have told, Britain did not slumber so deeply but that she was in the full tide of what may have been battle and a great victory. Up and down the North Sea her warships swept together like a net about their foes. On land, too, that night was to have decided great issues. The German camps were under arms from Redingen to Markirch, their infantry columns were lying in swathes like mown hay, in arrested night march on every track between Longnyon and Thiancourt, and between Avricourt and Donen. The hills beyond Spincourt were dusted thick with hidden French riflemen; the thin lash of the French skirmishers sprawled out amidst spades and unfinished rifle pits in coils that wrapped about the heads of the German columns, thence along the Vosges watershed and out across the frontier near Belfort nearly to the Rhine....

The Hungarian, the Italian peasant, yawned and thought the morning dark, and turned over to fall into a dreamless sleep; the Mohammedan world spread its carpet and was taken in prayer. And in Sydney, in Melbourne, in New Zealand, the thing was a fog in the afternoon, that scattered the crowd on racecourses and cricket-fields, and stopped the unloading of shipping and brought men out from their afternoon rest to stagger and litter the streets....

2

My thoughts go into the woods and wildernesses and jungles of the world, to the wildlife that shared man's suspension, and I think of a thousand feral acts interrupted and truncated—as it were frozen, like the frozen words Pantagruel met at sea. Not only men it was that were quieted, all living creatures that breathe the air became insensible, impassive things. Motionless brutes and birds lay amidst the drooping trees and herbage in the universal twilight, the tiger sprawled beside his fresh-struck victim, who bled to death in a dreamless sleep. The very flies came sailing down the air with wings outspread; the spider hung crumpled in his loaded net; like some gaily painted snowflake the butterfly drifted to earth and grounded, and was still. And as a queer contrast one gathers that the fishes in the sea suffered not at all....

Speaking of the fishes reminds me of a queer little inset upon that great world-dreaming. The odd fate of the crew of the submarine vessel B 94 has always seemed memorable to me. So far as I know, they were the only men alive who never saw that veil of green drawn across the world. All the while that the stillness held above, they were working into the mouth of the Elbe, past the booms and the mines, very slowly and carefully, a sinister crustacean of steel, explosive crammed, along the muddy bottom. They trailed a long clue that was to guide their fellows from the mother ship floating awash outside. Then in the long channel beyond the forts they came up at last to mark down their victims and get air. That must have been before the twilight of dawn, for they tell of the brightness of the stars. They were amazed to find themselves not three hundred yards from an ironclad that had run ashore in the mud, and heeled over with the falling tide. It was afire amidships, but no one heeded that—no one in all that strange clear silence heeded that—and not only this wrecked vessel, but all the dark ships lying about them, it seemed to their perplexed and startled minds must be full of dead men!

Theirs I think must have been one of the strangest of all experiences; they were never insensible; at once, and, I am told, with a sudden catch of laughter, they began to breathe the new air. None of them has proved a writer; we have no picture of their wonder, no description of what was said. But we know these men were active and awake for an hour and a half at least before the general awakening came, and when at last the Germans stirred and sat up they found these strangers in possession of their battleship, the submarine carelessly adrift, and the Englishmen, begrimed and weary, but with a sort of furious exultation, still busy, in the bright dawn, rescuing insensible enemies from the sinking conflagration....

But the thought of certain stokers the sailors of the submarine failed altogether to save brings me back to the thread of grotesque horror that runs through all this event, the thread I cannot overlook for all the splendors of human well-being that have come from it. I cannot forget the unguided ships that drove ashore, that went down in disaster with all their sleeping hands, nor how, inland, motorcars rushed to destruction upon the roads, and trains upon the railways kept on in spite of signals, to be found at last by their amazed, reviving drivers standing on unfamiliar lines, their fires exhausted, or, less lucky, to be discovered by astonished peasants or awakening porters smashed and crumpled up into heaps of smoking, crackling ruin. The foundry fires of the Four Towns still blazed, the smoke of our burning still defiled the sky. Fires burned indeed the brighter for the Change—and spread....

3

Picture to yourself what happened between the printing and composing of the copy of the *New Paper* that lies before me now. It was the first newspaper that was printed upon earth after the Great Change. It was pocket-worn and browned, made of a paper no man ever intended for preservation. I found it on the arbor table in the inn garden while I was waiting for Nettie and Verrall, before that last conversation of which I have presently to tell. As I look at it all that scene comes back to me, and Nettie stands in her white raiment against a blue-green background of sunlit garden, scrutinizing my face as I read....

It is so frayed that the sheet cracks along the folds and comes to pieces in my hands. It lies upon my desk, a dead souvenir of the dead ages of the world, of the ancient passions of my heart. I know we discussed its news, but for the life of me I cannot recall what we said, only I remember that Nettie said very little, and that Verrall for a time read it over my shoulder. And I did not like him to read over my shoulder....

The document before me must have helped us through the first awkwardness of that meeting.

But of all that we said and did then I must tell in a later chapter....

It is easy to see the *New Paper* had been set up overnight, and then large pieces of the stereo plates replaced subsequently. I do not know enough of the old methods of printing to know precisely what happened. The thing gives one an impression of large pieces of type having been cut away and replaced by fresh blocks. There is something very rough and ready about it all, and the new portions print darker and more smudgily than the old, except toward the left, where they have missed ink and indented. A friend of mine, who knows something of the old typography, has suggested to me that the machinery actually in use for the *New Paper* was damaged that night, and that on the morning of the Change Banghurst borrowed a neighboring office—perhaps in financial dependence upon him—to print in.

The outer pages belong entirely to the old period, the only parts of the paper that had undergone alteration are the two middle leaves. Here we found set forth in a curious little four-column oblong of print, WHAT HAS HAPPENED. This cut across a column with scare headings beginning, "Great Naval Battle Now in Progress. The Fate of Two Empires in the Balance. Reported Loss of Two More—"

These things, one gathered, were beneath notice now. Probably it was guesswork, and fabricated news in the first instance.

It is curious to piece together the worn and frayed fragments, and reread this discolored first intelligence of the new epoch.

The simple clear statements in the replaced portion of the paper impressed me at the time, I remember, as bald and strange, in that framework of shouting bad English. Now they seem like the voice of a sane man amidst a vast faded violence. But they witness to the prompt recovery of London from the gas; the new, swift energy of rebound in that huge population. I am surprised now, as I reread, to note how much research, experiment, and induction must have been accomplished in the day that elapsed before the paper was printed....But that is by the way. As I sit and muse over this partly carbonized sheet, that same curious remote vision comes again to me that quickened in my mind that morning, a vision of those newspaper offices I have already described to you going through the crisis.

The catalytic wave must have caught the place in full

swing, in its nocturnal high fever, indeed in a quite exceptional state of fever, what with the comet and the war, and more particularly with the war. Very probably the Change crept into the office imperceptibly, amidst the noise and shouting, and the glare of electric light that made the night atmosphere in that place; even the green flashes may have passed unobserved there, the preliminary descending trails of green vapor seemed no more than unseasonable drifting wisps of London fog. (In those days London even in summer was not safe against dark fogs.) And then at the last the Change poured in and overtook them.

If there was any warning at all for them, it must have been a sudden universal tumult in the street, and then a much more universal quiet. They could have had no other intimation.

There was no time to stop the presses before the main development of green vapor had overwhelmed everyone. It must have folded about them, tumbled them to the earth, masked and stilled them. My imagination is always curiously stirred by the thought of that, because I suppose it is the first picture I succeeded in making for myself of what had happened in the towns. It has never quite lost its strangeness for me that when the Change came, machinery went on working. I don't precisely know why that should have seemed so strange to me, but it did, and still to a certain extent does. One is so accustomed, I suppose, to regard machinery as an extension of human personality that the extent of its autonomy the Change displayed came as a shock to me. The electric lights, for example, hazy green-haloed nebulae, must have gone on burning at least for a time; amidst the thickening darkness the huge presses must have roared on, printing, folding, throwing aside copy after copy of that fabricated battle report with its quarter column of scare headlines, and all the place must have still quivered and throbbed with the familiar roar of the engines. And this though no men ruled there at all anymore! Here and there beneath that thickening fog the crumpled or outstretched forms of men lay still.

A wonderful thing that must have seemed, had any man had by chance the power of resistance to the vapor, and could he have walked amidst it.

And soon the machines must have exhausted their feed of ink and paper, and thumped and banged and rattled emptily amidst the general quiet. Then I suppose the furnaces failed for want of stoking, the steam pressure fell in the pistons, the machinery slackened, the lights burned dim, and came and went with the ebb of energy from the power station. Who can tell precisely the sequence of these things now?

And then, you know, amidst the weakening and terminating noises of men, the green vapor cleared and vanished, in an hour indeed it had gone, and it may be a breeze stirred and blew and went about the earth.

The noises of life were all dying away, but some there were that abated nothing, that sounded triumphantly amidst the universal ebb. To a heedless world the church towers tolled out two and then three. Clocks ticked and chimed everywhere about the earth to deafened ears....

And then came the first flush of morning, the first rustlings of the revival. Perhaps in that office the filaments of the lamps were still glowing, the machinery was still pulsing weakly, when the crumpled, booted heaps of cloth became men again and began to stir and stare. The chapel of the printers was, no doubt, shocked to find itself asleep. Amidst that dazzling dawn the *New Paper* woke to wonder, stood up and blinked at its amazing self....

The clocks of the city churches, one pursuing another, struck four. The staffs, crumpled and disheveled, but with a strange refreshment in their veins, stood about the damaged machinery, marveling and questioning; the editor read his overnight headlines with incredulous laughter. There was much involuntary laughter that morning. Outside, the mailmen patted the necks and rubbed the knees of their awakening horses....

Then, you know, slowly and with much conversation and doubt, they set about to produce the paper.

Imagine those bemused, perplexed people, carried on by the inertia of their old occupations and doing their best with an enterprise that had suddenly become altogether extraordinary and irrational. They worked amidst questionings, and yet lightheartedly. At every stage there must have been interruptions for discussion. The paper only got down to Menton five days late.

4

Then let me give you a vivid little impression I received of a certain prosaic person, a grocer, named Wiggins, and how he passed through the Change. I heard this man's story in the post office at Menton, when, in the afternoon of the First Day, I bethought me to telegraph to my mother. The place was also a grocer's shop, and I found him and the proprietor talking as I went in. They were trade competitors, and Wiggins had just come across the street to break the hostile silence of a score of years. The sparkle of the Change was in their eyes; their slightly flushed cheeks, their more elastic gestures, spoke of new physical influences that had invaded their beings.

"It did us no good, all our hatred," Mr. Wiggins said to me, explaining the emotion of their encounter; "it did our customers no good. I've come to tell him that. You bear that in mind, young man, if ever you come to have a shop of your own. It was a sort of stupid bitterness possessed us, and I can't make out we didn't see it before in that light. Not so much downright wickedness it wasn't as stupidity. A stupid jealousy! Think of it!—two human beings within a stone's throw, who have not spoken for twenty years, hardening our hearts against each other!"

"I can't think how we came to such a state, Mr. Wiggins," said the other, packing tea into pound packets out of mere habit as he spoke. "It was wicked pride and obstinacy. We *knew* it was foolish all the time."

I stood affixing the adhesive stamp to my telegram.

"Only the other morning," he went on to me, "I was cutting French eggs. Selling at a loss to do it. He'd marked down with a great staring ticket to ninepence a dozen—I saw it as I went past. Here's my answer!" He indicated a ticket, "'Eight pence a dozen—same as sold elsewhere for ninepence.' A whole penny down, bang off! Just a touch above cost—if that—and even then—" He leaned over the counter to say impressively, *"Not the same eggs!"*

"Now, what people in their senses would do things like that?" said Mr. Wiggins.

I sent my telegram—the proprietor dispatched it for me, and while he did so I fell to exchanging experiences with Mr. Wiggins. He knew no more than I did then the nature of the change that had come over things. He had been alarmed by the green flashes, he said, so much so that after watching for a time from behind his bedroom window blind, he had got up and hastily dressed and made his family get up also, so that they might be ready for the end. He made them put on their Sunday clothes. They all went out into the garden together, their minds divided between admiration at the gloriousness of the spectacle and a great growing awe. They were Dissenters, and very religious people out of business hours, and it seemed to them in those last magnificent moments that, after all, science must be wrong and the fanatics right. With the green vapors came conviction, and they prepared to meet their God....

This man, you must understand, was a common-looking man, in his shirt-sleeves and with an apron about his paunch, and he told his story in an Anglian accent that sounded mean and clipped to my Staffordshire ears; he told his story without a thought of pride, and as it were incidentally, and yet he gave me a vision of something heroic.

These people did not run hither and thither as many people did. These four simple, common people stood beyond their back door in their garden pathway between the gooseberry bushes, with the terrors of their God and His Judgments closing in upon them, swiftly and wonderfully —and there they began to sing. There they stood, father and mother and two daughters, chanting out stoutly, but no doubt a little flatly after the manner of their kind—

"In Zion's Hope abiding,
My soul in Triumph sings—"

until one by one they fell, and lay still.

The postmaster had heard them in the gathering darkness, "In Zion's Hope abiding...."

It was the most extraordinary thing in the world to hear this flushed and happy-eyed man telling that story of his recent death. It did not seem at all possible to have happened in the last twelve hours. It was minute and remote, these people who went singing through the darkling to their God. It was like a scene shown to me, very small and very distinctly painted, in a locket.

But that effect was not confined to this particular thing. A vast number of things that had happened before the coming of the comet had undergone the same transfiguring reduction. Other people, too, I have learned since, had the same illusion, a sense of enlargement. It seems to me even now that the little dark creature who had stormed across England in pursuit of Nettie and her lover must have been about an inch high, that all that previous life of ours had been an ill-lit marionette show, acted in the twilight....

5

The figure of my mother comes always into my conception of the Change.

I remember how one day she confessed herself.

She had been very sleepless that night, she said, and took the reports of the falling stars for shooting; there had been rioting in Clayton and through Swathinglea all day, and so she got out of bed to look. She had a dim sense that I was in all such troubles.

But she was not looking when the Change came.

"When I saw the stars a-raining down, dear," she said, "and thought of you out in it, I thought there'd be no harm in saying a prayer for you, dear? I thought you wouldn't mind that."

And so I got another of my pictures—the green vapors come and go, and there by her patched coverlet that dear old woman kneels and droops, still clasping her poor gnarled hands in the attitude of prayer—prayer to IT—for me!

Through the meager curtains and blinds of the flawed refracting window I see the stars above the chimneys fade, the pale light of dawn creeps into the sky, and her candle flares and dies....

That also went with me through the stillness—that silent kneeling figure, that frozen prayer to God to shield me, silent in a silent world, rushing through the emptiness of space....

6

With the dawn that awakening went about the earth. I have told how it came to me, and how I walked in wonder through the transfigured cornfields of Shaphambury. It came to everyone. Near me, and, for the time, clear forgotten by me, Verrall and Nettie woke—woke near one another, each heard before all other sounds the other's voice amidst the stillness, and the light. And the scattered people who had run to and fro, and fallen on the beach of Bungalow village, awoke; the sleeping villagers of Menton started, and sat up in that unwonted freshness and newness; the contorted figures in the garden, with the hymn still upon their lips, stirred amidst the flowers and touched each other timidly , and thought of Paradise. My mother found herself crouched against the bed, and rose—rose with a glad invincible conviction of accepted prayer....

Already, when it came to us, the soldiers, crowded between the lines of dusty poplars along the road to Allarmont, were chatting and sharing coffee with the French riflemen, who had hailed them from their carefully hidden pits among the vineyards up the slopes of Beauville. A certain perplexity had come to these marksmen, who had dropped asleep tensely ready for the rocket that should wake the whirr and rattle of their magazines. At the sight and sound of the stir and human confusion in the roadway below, it had come to each man individually that he could not shoot. One conscript, at least, has told his story of his awakening, and how curious he thought the rifle there beside him in his pit, how he took it on his knees to examine. Then, as his memory of its purpose grew clearer, he dropped the thing, and stood up with a kind of joyful horror at the crime escaped, to look more closely at the men he was to have assassinated. *Brave types,* he thought, they looked for such a fate. The summoning rocket never flew. Below, the men did not fall into ranks again, but sat by the roadside, or stood in groups talking, discussing with a novel incredulity the ostensible causes of the war. "The Emperor!" said they; and "Oh, nonsense! We're civilized men. Get someone else for this job...Where's the coffee?"

The officers held their own horses, and talked to the men frankly, regardless of discipline. Some Frenchmen out of the rifle pits came sauntering down the hill. Others stood doubtfully, rifles still in hand. Curious faces scanned these latter. Little arguments sprang as: "Shoot at us! Nonsense! They're respectable French citizens." There is a picture of it all, very bright and detailed in the morning light, in the battle gallery amidst the ruins at old Nancy, and one sees the old-world uniform of the "soldier," the odd caps and belts and boots, the ammunition belt, the water bottle, the sort of tourist's pack the men carried, a queer elaborate equipment. The soldiers had awakened one by one, first one and then another. I wonder sometimes whether, perhaps, if the two armies had come awake in an instant, the battle, by mere habit and inertia, might not have begun. But the men who waked first, sat up, looked about them in astonishment, had time to think a little....

7

Everywhere there was laughter, everywhere tears.

Men and women in the common life, finding themselves suddenly lit and exalted, capable of doing what had hitherto been impossible, incapable of doing what had hitherto been irresistible, happy, hopeful, unselfishly energetic, rejected altogether the supposition that this was merely a change in the blood and material texture of life. They denied the bodies God had given them, at once the Upper Nile savages struck out their canine teeth, because these made them like the beasts. They declared that this was the coming of a spirit, and nothing else would satisfy their need for explanations. And in a sense the spirit came. The Great Revival sprang directly from the Change—the last, the deepest, widest, and most enduring of all the vast inundations of religious emotion that go by that name.

But indeed it differed essentially from its innumerable predecessors. The former revivals were a phase of fever, this was the first movement of health, it was altogether quieter, more intellectual, more private, more religious than any of those others. In the old time, and more especially in the Protestant countries where the things of religion were outspoken, and the absence of confession and well-trained priests made religious states of emotion explosive and contagious, revivalism upon various scales was a normal phase in the religious life, revivals were always going on—now a little disturbance of consciences in a village, now an evening of emotion in a Mission Room, now a great storm that swept a continent, and now an organized effort that came to town with bands and banners and handbills and motorcars for the saving of souls. Never at any time did I take part in nor was I attracted by any of these movements. My nature, although passionate, was too critical (or skeptical if you like, for it amounts to the same thing) and shy to be drawn into these whirls; but on several occasions Parload and I sat scoffing, but nevertheless disturbed, in the back seats of revivalist meetings.

I saw enough of them to understand their nature, and I am not surprised to learn now that before the comet came, all about the world, even among savages, even among cannibals, these same, or at any rate closely similar, periodic upheavals went on. The world was stifling; it was in a fever, and those phenomena were neither more nor less than the instinctive struggle of the organism against the ebb of its powers, the clogging of its veins, the limitation of its life. Invariably these revivals followed periods of sordid and restricted living. Men obeyed their base immediate motives until the world grew unendurably bitter. Some disappointment, some thwarting, lit up for them—darkly indeed, but yet enough for indistinct vision—the crowded squalor, the dark enclosure of life. A sudden disgust with the insensate smallness of the old-world way of living, a realization of sin, a sense of the unworthiness of all individual things, a desire for something comprehensive, sustaining, something greater, for wider communions and less habitual things, filled them. Their souls, which were shaped for wider issues, cried out suddenly amidst the petty interests, the narrow prohibitions, of life, "Not this! not this!" A great passion to escape from the jealous prison of themselves, an inarticulate, stammering, weeping passion shook them....

I have seen— I remember how once in Clayton Calvinistic Methodist chapel I saw—his spotty fat face strangely distorted under the flickering gas-flares—old Pallet the ironmonger repent. He went to the form of repentance, a bench reserved for such exhibitions, and slobbered out his sorrow and disgust for some sexual indelicacy—he was a widower—and I can see now how his loose fat body quivered and swayed with his grief. He poured it out to five hundred people, from whom in common times he hid his every thought and purpose. And it is a fact, it shows where reality lay, that we two youngsters laughed not at all at that blubbering grotesque, we did not even think the distant shadow of a smile. We two sat grave and intent—perhaps wondering.

Only afterward and with an effort did we scoff....

Those old-time revivals were, I say, the convulsive movements of a body that suffocates. They are the clearest manifestations from before the Change of a sense in all men that things were not right. But they were too often but momentary illuminations. Their force spent itself in incoordinated shouting, gesticulations, tears. They were but flashes of outlook. Disgust of the narrow life, of all baseness, took shape in narrowness and baseness. The quickened soul ended the night a hypocrite; prophets disputed for precedence; seductions, it is altogether indisputable, were frequent among penitents! and Ananias went home converted and returned with a falsified gift. And it was almost universal that the converted should be impatient and immoderate, scornful of reason and a choice of expedients, opposed to balance, skill, and knowledge. Incontinently full of grace, like thin old wineskins overfilled, they felt they must burst if once they came into contact with hard fact and sane direction.

So the former revivals spent themselves, but the Great Revival did not spend itself, but grew to be, for the majority of Christendom at least, the permanent expression of the Change. For many it has taken the shape of an outright declaration that this was the Second Advent—it is not for me to discuss the validity of that suggestion; for nearly all, it has amounted to an enduring broadening of all the issues of life....

8

One irrelevant memory comes back to me, irrelevant, and yet by some subtle trick of quality it summarizes the Change for me. It is the memory of a woman's very beautiful face, a woman with a flushed face and tear-bright eyes who went by me without speaking, rapt in some secret purpose. I passed her when in the afternoon of the first day, struck by a sudden remorse, I went down to Menton to send a telegram to my mother telling her all was well with me. Whither this woman went I do not know, nor whence she came; I never saw her again, and only her face, glowing with that new and luminous resolve, stands out for me....

But that expression was the world's.

Chapter 3

The Cabinet Council

1

And what a strange unprecedented thing was that cabinet council at which I was present, the council that was held two days later in Melmount's bungalow, and which convened the conference to frame the constitution of the World State. I was there because it was convenient for me to stay with Melmount. I had nowhere to go particularly, and there was no one at his bungalow, to which his broken ankle confined him, but a secretary and a valet to help him to begin his share of the enormous labors that evidently lay before the rulers of the world. I wrote shorthand, and as there was not even a phonograph available, I went in so soon as his ankle had been dressed, and sat at his desk to write at his dictation. It is characteristic of the odd slackness that went with the spasmodic violence of the old epoch, that the secretary could not use shorthand and that there was no telephone whatever in the place. Every message had to be taken to the village post office in that grocer's shop at Menton, half a mile away....So I sat in the back of

Melmount's room, his desk had been thrust aside, and made such memoranda as were needed. At that time his room seemed to me the most beautifully furnished in the world, and I could identify now the vivid cheerfulness of the chintz of the sofa on which the great statesman lay just in front of me, the fine rich paper, the red sealing wax, the silver equipage of the desk I used. I know now that my presence in that room was a strange and remarkable thing, the open door, even the coming and going of Parker the secretary, innovations. In the old days a cabinet council was a secret conclave, secrecy and furtiveness were in the texture of all public life. In the old days everybody was always keeping something back from somebody, being wary and cunning, prevaricating, misleading—for the most part for no reason at all. Almost unnoticed, that secrecy had dropped out of life.

I close my eyes and see those men again, hear their deliberating voices. First I see them a little diffusely in the cold explicitness of daylight, and then concentrated and drawn together amidst the shadow and mystery about shaded lamps. Integral to this and very clear is the memory of biscuit crumbs and a drop of spilled water, that at first stood shining upon and then sank into the green tablecloth....

I remember particularly the figure of Lord Adisham. He came to the bungalow a day before the others, because he was Melmount's personal friend. Let me describe this statesman to you, this one of the fifteen men who made the last war. He was the youngest member of the Government, and an altogether pleasant and sunny man of forty. He had a clear profile to his clean gray face, a smiling eye, a friendly, careful voice upon his thin, clean-shaven lips, an easy disabusing manner. He had the perfect quality of a man who had fallen easily into a place prepared for him. He had the temperament of what we used to call a philosopher —an indifferent, that is to say. The change had caught him at his weekend recreation, fly-fishing; and, indeed, he said,

I remember, that he recovered to find himself with his head within a yard of the water's brim. In times of crisis Lord Adisham invariably went fly-fishing at the weekend to keep his mind in tone, and when there was no crisis then there was nothing he liked so much to do as fly-fishing, and so, of course, as there was nothing to prevent it, he fished. He came resolved, among other things, to give up fly-fishing altogether. I was present when he came to Melmount, and heard him say as much; and by a more naive route it was evident that he had arrived at the same scheme or intention as my master. I left them to talk, but afterward I came back to take down their long telegrams to their coming colleagues. He was, do doubt, as profoundly affected as Melmount by the Change, but his tricks of civility and irony and acceptable humor had survived the Change, and he expressed his altered attitude, his expanded emotions, in a quaint modification of the old-time man-of-the-world style, with excessive moderation, with a trained horror of the enthusiasm that swayed him.

These fifteen men who ruled the British Empire were curiously unlike anything I had expected, and I watched them intently whenever my services were not in request. They made a peculiar class at that time, these English politicians and statesmen, a class that has now completely passed away. In some respects they were unlike the statesmen of any other region of the world, and I do not find that any really adequate account remains of them.... Perhaps you are a reader of the old books. If so, you will find them rendered with a note of hostile exaggeration by Dickens in *Bleak House,* with a mingling of gross flattery and keen ridicule by Disraeli, who ruled among them accidentally by misunderstanding them and pleasing the court, and all their assumptions are set forth, portentously, perhaps, but truthfully, so far as people of the "permanent official" class saw them, in the novels of Mrs. Humphry Ward. All these books are still in this world and at the disposal of the curious, and in addition the philosopher

Bagehot and the picturesque historian Macaulay give something of their method of thinking, the novelist Thackeray skirts the seamy side of their social life, and there are some good passages of irony, personal descriptions, and reminiscence to be found in the *Twentieth Century Garner* from the pens of such writers, for example, as Sidney Low. But a picture of them as a whole is wanting. Then they were too near and too great; now, very rapidly, they have become incomprehensible.

We common people of the old time based our conception of our statesmen almost entirely on the caricatures that formed the most powerful weapon in political controversy. Like almost every main feature of the old condition of things these caricatures were an unanticipated development, they were a sort of parasitic outgrowth from, which had finally altogether replaced, the thin and vague aspirations of the original democratic ideals. They presented not only the personalities who led our public life, but the most sacred structural conceptions of that life, in ludicrous, vulgar, and dishonorable aspects that in the end came near to destroying entirely all grave and honorable emotion or motive toward the State. The state of Britain was represented nearly always by a red-faced, purse-proud farmer with an enormous belly; that fine dream of freedom, the United States, by a cunning, lean-faced rascal in striped trousers and a blue coat. The chief ministers of state were pickpockets, washerwomen, clowns, whales, asses, elephants, and what not, and issues that affected the welfare of millions of men were dressed and judged like a rally in some idiotic pantomime. A tragic war in South Africa, that wrecked many thousand homes, impoverished two whole lands, and brought death and disablement to fifty thousand men, was presented as a quite comical quarrel between a violent queer being named Chamberlain, with an eyeglass, an orchid, and a short temper, and "old Kroojer," an obstinate and very cunning old man in a shocking bad hat. The conflict was carried through in a mood sometimes of brutish irritability and sometimes of lax slovenliness, the merry embezzler plied his trade congenially in that asinine squabble, and behind these fooleries and masked by them, marched Fate—until at last behind the clowning, the curtains of the booth opened and revealed—hunger and suffering, brands burning and swords and shame.... These men had come to fame and power in that atmosphere, and to me that day there was the oddest suggestion in them of actors who have suddenly laid aside grotesque and foolish parts; the paint was washed from their faces, the posing put aside.

Even when the presentation was not frankly grotesque and degrading it was entirely misleading. When I read of Laycock, for example, there arises a picture of a large, active, if a little wrong-headed, intelligence in a compact heroic body, emitting that "Goliath" speech of his that did so much to precipitate hostilities; it tallies not at all with the stammering, high-pitched, slightly bald, and very conscience-stricken personage I saw, nor with Melmount's contemptuous first description of him. I doubt if the world at large will ever get a proper vision of those men as they were before the Change. Each year they pass more and more incredibly beyond our intellectual sympathy. Our estrangement cannot, indeed, rob them of their portion in the past, but it will rob them of any effect of reality. The whole of their history becomes more and more foreign, more and more like some queer barbaric drama played in a forgotten tongue. There they strut through their weird metamorphoses of caricature, those premiers and presidents, their height preposterously exaggerated by political buskins, their faces covered by great resonant inhuman masks, their voices couched in the foolish idiom of public utterance, disguised beyond any semblance to sane humanity, roaring and squeaking through the public press. There it stands, this incomprehensible faded show, a thing left on one side, and now still and deserted by any interest, its many emptinesses as inexplicable now as the cruelties of medieval Venice, the theology of old Byzantium. And they ruled and influenced the lives of nearly a quarter of mankind, these politicians, their clownish conflicts swayed the world, made mirth perhaps, made excitement, and permitted—infinite misery.

I saw these men quickened indeed by the Change, but still wearing the queer clothing of the old time, the manners and conventions of the old time; if they had disengaged themselves from the outlook of the old time they still had to refer back to it constantly as a common starting point. My refreshed intelligence was equal to that, so that I think I did indeed see them. There was Gorrell-Browning, the Chancellor of the Duchy; I remember him as a big round-faced man, the essential vanity and foolishness of whose expression, whose habit of voluminous platitudinous speech, triumphed absurdly once or twice over the roused spirit within. He struggled with it, he burlesqued himself, and laughed. Suddenly he said simply, intensely—it was a moment for everyone of clean, clear pain, "I have been a vain and self-indulgent and presumptuous old man. I am of little use here. I have given myself to politics and intrigues, and life is gone from me." Then for a long time he sat still. There was Carton, the Lord Chancellor, a white-faced man with understanding, he had a heavy, shaven face that might have stood among the busts of the Caesars, a slow, elaborating voice, with self-indulgent, slightly oblique, and triumphant lips, and a momentary, voluntary, humorous twinkle. "We have to forgive," he said. "We have to forgive—even ourselves."

These two were at the top corner of the table, so that I saw their faces well. Madgett, the Home Secretary, a smaller man with wrinkled eyebrows and a frozen smile on his thin wry mouth, came next to Carton; he contributed little to the discussion save intelligent comments, and when the electric lights above glowed out, the shadows deepened queerly in his eye sockets and gave him the quizzical expression of an ironical goblin. Next to him was that great peer, the Earl of Richover, whose self-indulgent indolence had accepted the role of a twentieth-century British Roman patrician of culture, who had divided his time almost equally between his jockeys, politics, and the composition of literary studies in the key of his role. "We have done nothing worth doing," he said. "As for me, I have cut a figure!" He reflected—no doubt on his ample patrician years, on the fine great houses that had been his setting, the teeming racecourses that had roared his name, the enthusiastic meetings he had fed with fine hopes, the futile Olympian beginnings...."I have been a fool," he said compactly. They heard him in a sympathetic and respectful silence.

Gurker, the Chancellor of the Exchequer, was partially obscured, so far as I was concerned, by the back of Lord Adisham. Ever and again Gurker protruded into the discussion, swaying forward, a deep throaty voice, a big nose, a coarse mouth with a drooping everted lower lip, eyes peering amidst folds and wrinkles. He made his confession. "I," he said, "have gone through the system of this world, creating nothing, consolidating many things, destroying much. My self-conceit has been monstrous. I seem to have used my ample coarse intellectuality for no other purpose than to develop and master and maintain the convention of property, to turn life into a sort of mercantile chess and spend my winnings grossly....I have had no sense of service to mankind. Beauty which is godhead—I made it a possession."

These men and these sayings particularly remain in my memory. Perhaps, indeed, I wrote them down at the time, but that I do not now remember. How Sir Digby Privet, Revel, Marheimer, and the others sat I do not now recall; they came in as voices, interruptions, imperfectly assigned comments....

One got a queer impression that except perhaps for Gurker or Revel these men had not particularly wanted the power they held; had desired to do nothing very much in the positions they had secured. They had found themselves in the cabinet, and until this moment of illumination they had not been ashamed; but they had made no ungentlemanly fuss about the matter. Eight of that fifteen came from the same school, had gone through an entirely parallel education; some Greek linguistics, some elementary mathematics, some emasculated "science," a little history, a little reading in the silent or timidly orthodox English literature of the seventeenth, eighteenth, and nineteenth centuries, all eight had imbibed the same dull gentlemanly tradition of behavior; essentially boyish, unimaginative—with neither keen swords nor art in it, a tradition apt to slobber into sentiment at a crisis and make a great virtue of a simple duty rather clumsily done. None of these eight had made any real experiments with life, they had lived in blinkers, they had been passed from nurse to governess, from governess to preparatory school, from Eton to Oxford, from Oxford to the politico-social routine. Even their vices and lapses had been according to certain conceptions of good form. They had all gone to the races surreptitiously from Eton, had all cut up to town from Oxford to see life—music-hall life—had all come to heel again. Now suddenly they discovered their limitations....

"What are we to do?" asked Melmount. "We have awakened; this empire in our hands...." I know this will seem the most fabulous of all the things I have to tell of the old order, but, indeed, I saw it with my eyes, I heard it with my ears. It is a fact that this group of men who constituted the Government of one-fifth of the habitable land of the earth, who ruled over a million of armed men, who had such navies as mankind had never seen before, whose empire of nations, tongues, peoples still dazzles in these greater days, had no common idea whatever of what they meant to do with the world. They had been a Government for three long years, and before the Change came to them it had never even occurred to them that it was necessary to have a common idea. There was no common idea at all. That great empire was no more than a thing adrift, an aimless thing that ate and drank and slept and bore arms, and was inordinately proud of itself because it had chanced to happen. It had no plan, no intention; it meant nothing at all. And the other great empires adrift, perilously adrift like marine mines, were in the selfsame case. Absurd as a British cabinet council must seem to you now, it was no whit more absurd than the controlling ganglion, autocratic council, president's committee, or whatnot, of each of its blind rivals....

2

I remember as one thing that struck me very forcibly at the time, the absence of any discussion, any difference of opinion, about the broad principles of our present state. These men had lived hitherto in a system of conventions and acquired motives, loyalty to a party, loyalty to various secret agreements and understandings, loyalty to the Crown; they had all been capable of the keenest attention to precedence, all capable of the most complete suppression of subversive doubts and inquiries, all had their religious emotions under perfect control. They had seemed protected by invisible but impenetrable barriers from all the heady and destructive speculations, the socialistic, republican, and communistic theories that one may still trace through the literature of the last days of the comet. But now it was as if at the very moment of the awakening those barriers and defenses had vanished, as if the green vapors had washed through their minds and dissolved and swept away a hundred once rigid boundaries and obstacles. They had admitted and assimilated at once all that was good in the ill-dressed propagandas that had clamored so vehemently and vainly at the doors of their minds in the former days. It was exactly like the awakening from an absurd and limiting dream. They had come out together naturally and inevitably upon the broad daylight platform of obvious and reasonable agreement upon which we and all the order of our world now stand.

Let me try to give the chief things that had vanished from their minds. There was, first, the ancient system of "ownership" that made such an extraordinary tangle of our administration of the land upon which we lived. In the old time no one believed in that as either just or ideally convenient, but everyone accepted it. The community which lived upon the land was supposed to have waived its necessary connection with the land, except in certain limited instances of highway and common. All the rest of the land was cut up in the maddest way into patches and oblongs and triangles of various sizes between a hundred square miles and a few acres, and placed under the nearly absolute government of a series of administrators called landowners. They owned the land almost as a man now owns his hat; they bought it and sold it, and cut it up like cheese or ham; they were free to ruin it, or leave it waste, or erect upon it horrible and devastating eyesores. If the community needed a road or a tramway, if it wanted a town or a village in any position, nay, even if it wanted to go to and fro, it had to do so by exorbitant treaties with each of the monarchs whose territory was involved. No man could find foothold on the face of the earth until he had paid toll and homage to one of them. They had practically no relations with and no duties to the nominal, municipal, or national Government amidst whose larger areas their own dominions lay.... This sounds, I know, like a lunatic's dream, but mankind was that lunatic; and not only in the old countries of Europe and Asia, where this sytem had arisen out of the rational delegation of local control to territorial magnates, who had in the universal baseness of those times at last altogether evaded and escaped their duties, did it obtain, but the "new countries," as we called them then—the United States of America, the Cape Colony, Australia, and New Zealand—spent much of the nineteenth century in the frantic giving away of land forever to any casual person who would take it. Was there coal, was there petroleum or gold, was there rich soil or harborage, or the site for a fine city, these obsessed and witless Governments cried out for scramblers, and a stream of shabby, tricky, and violent adventurers set out to found a new section of the landed aristocracy of the world. After a brief century of hope and pride, the great republic of the United States of America, the hope as it was deemed of mankind, became for the most part a drifting crowd of landless men; landlords and railway lords, food lords (for the land is food) and mineral lords ruled its life, gave it Universities as one gave coins to a mendicant, and spent its resources upon such vain, tawdry, and foolish luxuries as the world had never seen before. Here was a thing none of these statesmen before the Change would have regarded as anything but the natural order of the world, which not one of them now regarded as anything but the mad and vanished illusion of a period of dementia.

And as it was with the question of the land, so was it also with a hundred other systems and institutions and complicated and disingenuous factors in the life of man. They spoke of trade, and I realized for the first time there could be buying and selling that was no loss to any man; they spoke of industrial organization, and one saw it under captains who sought no base advantages. The haze of old associations, of personal entanglements and habitual recognitions had been dispelled from every stage and process of the social training of men. Things long hidden appeared discovered with an amazing clearness and nakedness. These men who had awakened laughed dissolvent laughs, and the old muddle of schools and colleges, books and traditions, the old fumbling, half-figurative, half-formal teaching of the Churches, the complex of weakening and confusing suggestions and hints, amidst which the pride and honor of adolescence doubted and stumbled and fell, became nothing but a curious and pleasantly faded memory. "There must be a common training of the young," said Richover; "a frank initiation. We have not so much educated them as hidden things from them, and set traps. And it might have been so easy—can all be done so easily."

That hangs in my memory as the refrain of that council, "It can all be done so easily," but when they said it then, it came to my ears with a quality of enormous refreshment and power. It can all be done so easily, given frankness, given courage. Time was when these platitudes had the freshness and wonder of a gospel.

In this enlarged outlook the war with the Germans—that mythical, heroic, armed female, Germany, had vanished from men's imaginations—was a mere exhausted episode. A truce had already been arranged by Melmount, and these ministers, after some marveling reminiscences, set aside the matter of peace as a mere question of particular arrangements....The whole scheme of the world's government had become fluid and provisional in their minds, in small details as in great, the unanalyzable tangle of wards and vestries, districts and municipalities, counties, states, boards, and nations, the interlacing, overlapping, and conflicting authorities, the felt of little interests and claims, in which an innumerable and insatiable multitude of lawyers, agents, managers, bosses, organizers lived like fleas in a dirty old coat, the web of the conflicts, jealousies, heated patchings up and jobbings apart, of the old order—they flung it all on one side.

"What are the new needs?" said Melmount. "This muddle is too rotten to handle. We're beginning again. Well, let us begin afresh."

3

"Let us begin afresh!" This piece of obvious common sense seemed then to me instinct with courage, the noblest of words. My heart went out to him as he spoke. It was, indeed, that day as vague as it was valiant; we did not at all see the forms of what we were thus beginning. All that we saw was the clear inevitableness that the old order should end....

And then in a little space of time mankind in halting but effectual brotherhood was moving out to make its world anew. Those early years, those first and second decades of the new epoch, were in their daily detail a time of rejoicing toil; one saw chiefly one's own share in that, and little of the whole. It is only now that I look back at it all from these ripe years, from this high tower, that I see the dramatic sequence of its changes, see the cruel old confusions of the ancient time become clarified, simplified, and dissolve and vanish away. Where is that old world now? Where is London, that somber city of smoke and drifting darkness, full of the deep roar and haunting music of disorder, with its oily, shining, mud-rimmed, barge-crowded river, its black pinnacles and blackened dome, its sad wildernesses of smut-grayed houses, its myriads of draggled prostitutes, its millions of hurrying clerks? The very leaves upon its trees were foul with greasy black defilements. Where is lime-white Paris, with its green and disciplined foliage, its hard unflinching tastefulness, its smartly organized viciousness, and the myriads of workers, noisily shod, streaming over the bridges in the gray cold light of dawn? Where is New York, the high city of clangor and infuriated energy, wind swept and competition swept, its huge buildings jostling one another and straining ever upward for a place in the sky, the fallen pitilessly overshadowed? Where are its lurking corners of heavy and costly luxury, the shameful bludgeoning bribing vice of its ill-ruled underways, and all the gaunt extravagant ugliness of its strenuous life? And where now is Philadelphia, with its innumerable small and isolated homes, and Chicago with its interminable blood-stained stockyards, its polyglot underworld of furious discontent?

All these vast cities have given way and gone, even as my native Potteries and the Black Country have gone, and the lives that were caught, crippled, starved, and maimed amidst their labyrinths, their forgotten and neglected maladjustments, and their vast, inhuman, ill-conceived industrial machinery have escaped—to life. Those cities of growth and accident are altogether none, never a chimney smokes about our world today, and the sound of the weeping of children who toiled and hungered, the dull despair of overburdened women, the noise of brute quarrels in alleys, all shameful pleasures and all the ugly grossness of wealthy pride have gone with them, with the utter change in our lives. As I look back into the past I see a vast exultant dust of house-breaking and removal rise up into the clear air that followed the hour of the green vapors, I live again the Year of Tents, the Year of Scaffolding, and like the triumph of a new theme in a piece of music—the great cities of our new days arise. Come Caerlyon and Armedon, the twin cities of lower England, with the winding summer city of the Thames between, and I see the gaunt dirt of old Edinburgh die to rise again white and tall beneath the shadow of her ancient hill; and Dublin too, reshaped, returning enriched, fair, spacious, the city of rich laughter and warm hearts, gleaming gaily in a shaft of sunlight through the warm rain. I see the great cities America has planned and made; the Golden City, with ever-ripening fruit along its broad warm ways, and the bell-glad City of a Thousand Spires. I see again as I have seen, the city of theaters and meeting places, the City of the Sunlight Bight, and the new city that is still called Utah; and dominated by its observatory dome and the plain and dignified lines of the university facade upon the cliff, Martenabar the great white winter city of the upland snows. And the lesser places, too, the townships, the quiet resting places, villages half-forest with a brawl of streams down their streets, villages laced with avenues of cedar, villages of garden, of roses and wonderful flowers and the perpetual humming of bees. And through all the world go our children, our sons the old world would have made into servile clerks and shopmen, plow drudges and servants; our daughters who were formerly anemic drudges, prostitutes, sluts, anxiety-racked mothers or sere, repining failures; they go about this world glad and brave, learning, living, doing, happy and rejoicing, brave and free. I think of them wandering in the clear quiet of the ruins of Rome, among the tombs of Egypt or the temples of Athens, of their coming to Mainington and its strange happiness, to Orba and the wonder of its white and slender tower.... But who can tell of the fullness and the pleasure of life, who can number all our new cities in the world?—cities made by the loving hands of men for living men, cities men weep to enter, so fair they are, so gracious and so kind....

Some vision surely of these things must have been vouchsafed me as I sat there behind Melmount's couch, but now my knowledge of accomplished things has mingled with and effaced my expectations. Something indeed I must have foreseen—or else why was my heart so glad?

BOOK 3 *THE NEW WORLD*

Chapter 1

Love After the Change

1

So far I have said nothing of Nettie. I have departed widely from my individual story. I have tried to give you the effect of the change in relation to the general framework of human life, its effect of swift, magnificent dawn, of an overpowering letting in and inundation of light, and the spirit of living. In my memory all my life before the Change has the quality of a dark passage, with the dimmest side gleams of beauty that come and go. The rest is dull pain and darkness. Then suddenly the walls, the bitter confines, are smitten and vanish, and I walk, blinded, perplexed, and yet rejoicing, in this sweet, beautiful world, in its fair incessant variety, its satisfaction, its opportunities, exultant in this glorious gift of life. Had I the power of music I would make a worldwide motif swell and amplify, gather to itself this theme and that, and rise at last to sheer ecstasy of triumph and rejoicing. It should be all sound, all pride, all the hope of outsetting in the morning brightness, all the glee of unexpected happenings, all the gladness of painful effort suddenly come to its reward; it should be like blossoms new opened and the happy play of children, like tearful, happy mothers holding their first-born, like cities building to the sound of music, and great ships, all hung with flags and wine bespattered, gliding down through cheering multitudes to their first meeting with the sea. Through it all should march Hope, confident Hope, radiant and invincible, until at last it would be the triumph march of Hope the conqueror, coming with trumpetings and banners through the wide-flung gates of the world.

And then out of that luminous haze of gladness comes Nettie, transfigured.

So she came again to me—amazing, a thing incredibly forgotten.

She comes back, and Verrall is in her company. She comes back into my memories now, just as she came back then, rather quaintly at first—at first not seen very clearly, a little distorted by intervening things, seen with a doubt, as I saw her through the slightly discolored panes of crinkled glass in the window of the Menton post office and grocer's shop. It was on the second day after the Change, and I had been sending telegrams for Melmount, who was making arrangements for his departure for Downing Street. I saw the two of them at first as small, flawed figures. The glass made them seemed curved, and it enhanced and altered their gestures and paces. I felt it became me to say "Peace" to them, and I went out, to the jangling of the doorbell. At the sight of me they stopped short, and Verrall cried with the note of one who has sought, "Here he is!" And Nettie cried, "Willie!"

I went toward them, and all the perspectives of my reconstructed universe altered as I did so.

I seemed to see these two for the first time; how fine they were, how graceful and human. It was as though I had never really looked at them before, and, indeed, always before I had beheld them through a mist of selfish passion. They had shared the universal darkness and dwarfing of the former time; they shared the universal exaltation of the new. Now suddenly Nettie, and the love of Nettie, a great passion for Nettie, lived again in me. This change which had enlarged men's hearts had made no end to love. Indeed, it had enormously enlarged and glorified love. She stepped into the center of that dream of world reconstruction that filled my mind and took possession of it all. A little wisp of hair had blown across her cheek, her lips fell apart in that sweet smile of hers; her eyes were full of wonder, of a welcoming scrutiny, of an infinitely courageous friendliness.

I took her outstretched hand, and wonder overwhelmed me. "I wanted to kill you," I said simply, trying to grasp that idea. It seemed now like stabbing the stars, or murdering the sunlight.

"Afterward we looked for you," said Verrall; "and we could not find you.... We heard another shot."

I turned my eyes to him, and Nettie's hand fell from me. It was then I thought of how they had fallen together, and what it must have been to have awakened in that dawn with Nettie by one's side. I had a vision of them as I had glimpsed them last amidst the thickening vapors, close together, hand in hand. The green hawks of the Change spread their darkling wings above their last stumbling paces. So they fell. And awoke—lovers together in the morning of Paradise. Who can tell how bright the sunshine was to them, how fair the flowers, how sweet the singing of the birds?...

This was the thought of my heart. But my lips were saying, "When I awoke I threw my pistol away." Sheer blankness kept my thoughts silent for a little while; I said empty things. "I am very glad I did not kill you—that you are here, so fair and well....

"I am going away back to Clayton on the day after tomorrow," I said, breaking away to explanations. "I have been writing shorthand here for Melmount, but that is almost over now...."

Neither of them said a word, and though all facts had suddenly ceased to matter anything, I went on informatively, "He is to be taken to Downing Street where there is a proper staff, so that there will be no need of me....Of course, you're a little perplexed at my being with Melmount. You see I met him—by accident—directly I recovered. I found him with a broken ankle—in that lane....I am to go now to the Four Towns to help prepare a report. So that I am glad to see you both again"—I found a catch in my voice—"to say good-bye to you, and wish you well."

This was after the quality of what had come into my mind when first I saw them through the grocer's window, but it was not what I felt and thought as I said it. I went on saying it because otherwise there would have been a gap. It had come to me that it was going to be hard to part from Nettie. My words sounded with an effect of unreality. I stopped, and we stood for a moment in silence looking at one another.

It was I, I think, who was discovering most. I was realizing for the first time how little the Change had altered in my essential nature. I had forgotten this business of love for a time in a world of wonder. That was all. Nothing was lost from my nature, nothing had gone, only the power of thought and restraint had been wonderfully increased, and new interests had been forced upon me. The Green Vapors had passed, our minds were swept and garnished, but we were ourselves still, though living in a new and finer air. My affinities were unchanged; Nettie's personal charm for me was only quickened by the enhancement of my perceptions. In her presence, meeting her eyes, instantly my desire, no longer frantic but sane, was awake again.

It was just like going to Checkshill in the old time, after writing about socialism....

I relinquished her hand. It was absurd to part in these terms.

So we all felt it. We hung awkwardly over our sense of

that. It was Verrall, I think, who shaped the thought for me, and said that tomorrow then we must meet and say goodbye, and so turned our encounter into a transitory making of arrangements. We settled we would come to the inn at Menton, all three of us, and take our midday meal together....

Yes, it was clear that was all we had to say now....

We parted a little awkwardly. I went on down the village street, not looking back, surprised at myself, and infinitely perplexed. It was as if I had discovered something overlooked that disarranged all my plans, something entirely disconcerting. For the first time I went back preoccupied and without eagerness to Melmount's work. I wanted to go on thinking about Nettie; my mind had suddenly become voluminously productive concerning her and Verrall.

2

The talk we three had together in the dawn of the new time is very strongly impressed upon my memory. There was something fresh and simple about it, something young and flushed and exalted. We took up, we handled with a certain naive timidity, the most difficult questions the Change had raised for men to solve. I recall we made little of them. All the old scheme of human life had dissolved and passed away, the narrow competitiveness, the greed and base aggression, the jealous aloofness of soul from soul. Where had it left us? That was what we and a thousand million others were discussing....

It chances that this last meeting with Nettie is inseparably associated—I don't know why—with the landlady of the Menton inn.

The Menton inn was one of the rare pleasant corners of the old order; it was an inn of an unusual prosperity, much frequented by visitors from Shaphambury, and given to the serving of lunches and teas. It had a broad mossy bowling green, and round about it were creeper-covered arbors amidst beds of snapdragon, and hollyhock, and blue delphinium, and many such tall familiar summer flowers. These stood out against a background of laurels and holly, and above these again rose the gables of the inn and its signpost—a white-horsed George slaying the dragon—against copper beeches under the sky.

While I waited for Nettie and Verrall in this agreeable trysting place, I talked to the landlady—a broad-shouldered, smiling, freckled woman—about the morning of the Change. That motherly, abundant, red-haired figure of health was buoyantly sure that everything in the world was now to be changed for the better. That confidence, and something in her voice, made me love her as I talked to her. "Now we're awake," she said, "all sorts of things will be put right that hadn't any sense in them. Why? Oh! I'm sure of it."

Her kind blue eyes met mine in an infinitude of friendliness. Her lips in her pauses shaped in a pretty faint smile.

Old tradition was strong in us; all English inns in those days charged the unexpected, and I asked what our lunch was to cost.

"Pay or not," she said, "and what you like. It's holiday these days. I suppose we'll still have paying and charging, however we manage it, but it won't be the worry it has been—that I feel sure. It's the part I never had no fancy for. Many a time I peeped through the bushes worrying to think what was just and right to me and mine, and what would send 'em away satisfied. It isn't the money I care for. There'll be mighty changes, be sure of that; but here I'll stay, and make people happy—them that go by on the roads. It's a pleasant place here when people are merry; it's only when they're jealous, or mean, or tired, or eat up beyond any stomach's digesting, or when they got the drink in 'em that Satan comes into this garden. Many's the happy face I've seen here, and many that come again like friends, but nothing to equal what's going to be, now things are being set right."

She smiled, that bounteous woman, with the joy of life and hope. "You shall have an omelet," she said, "you and your friends; such an omelet—like they'll have 'em in heaven! I feel there's cooking in me these days like I've never cooked before. I'm rejoiced to have it to do...."

It was just then that Nettie and Verrall appeared under a rustic archway of crimson roses that led out from the inn. Nettie wore white and a sun hat, and Verrall was a figure of gray. "Here are my friends," I said; but for all the magic of the Change, something passed athwart the sunlight in my soul like the passing of the shadow of a cloud. "A pretty couple," said the landlady, as they crossed the velvet green toward us....

They were inded a pretty couple, but that did not greatly gladden me. No—I winced a little at that.

3

This old newspaper, this first reissue of the *New Paper,* desiccated last relic of a vanished age, is like the little piece of identification the superstitious of the old days—those queer religionists who brought a certain black-clad Mrs. Piper to the help of Christ—used to put into the hand of a clairvoyant. At the crisp touch of it I look across a gulf of fifty years and see again the three of us sitting about that table in the arbor, and I smell again the smell of the sweetbriar that filled the air about us, and hear in our long pauses the abundant murmuring of bees among the heliotrope of the borders.

It is the dawn of the new time, but we bear, all three of us, the marks and liveries of the old.

I see myself, a dark, ill-dressed youth, with the bruise Lord Redcar gave me still blue and yellow beneath my jaw; and young Verrall sits cornerwise to me, better grown, better dressed, fair and quiet, two years my senior indeed, but looking no older than I because of his light complexion;

and opposite me is Nettie, with dark eyes upon my face, graver and more beautiful than I had ever seen her in the former time. Her dress is still that white one she had worn when I came upon her in the park, and still about her dainty neck she wears her string of pearls and that little coin of gold. She is so much the same, she is so changed; a girl then and now a woman—and all my agony and all the marvel of the Change between! Over the end of the green table about which we sit, a spotless cloth is spread, it bears a pleasant lunch spread out with a simple equipage. Behind me is the liberal sunshine of the green and various garden. I see it all. Again I sit there, eating awkwardly, this paper lies upon the table and Verrall talks of the Change.

"You can't imagine," he says in his sure, fine accents, "how much the Change has destroyed of me. I still don't feel awake. Men of my sort are so tremendously *made*; I never suspected it before."

He leans over the table toward me with an evident desire to make himself perfectly understood. "I find myself like some creature that is taken out of its shell—soft and new. I was trained to dress in a certain way, to behave in a certain way, to think a certain way; I see now it's all wrong and narrow—most of it anyhow—a system of class shibboleths. We were decent to each other in order to be a gang to the rest of the world. Gentlemen indeed! But it's perplexing—"

I can hear his voice saying that now, and see the lift of his eyebrows and his pleasant smile.

He paused. He had wanted to say that, but it was not the thing we had to say.

I leaned forward a little and took hold of my glass very tightly. "You two," I said, "will marry?"

They looked at one another.

Nettie spoke very softly. "I did not mean to marry when I came away," she said.

"I know," I answered. I looked up with a sense of effort and met Verrall's eyes.

He answered me. "I think we two have joined our lives.

...But the thing that took us was a sort of madness."

I nodded. "All passion," I said, "is madness." Then I fell into a doubting of those words.

"Why did we do these things?" he said, turning to her suddenly.

Her hands were clasped under her chin, her eyes downcast.

"We *had* to," she said, with her old trick of inadequate expression.

Then she seemed to open out suddenly.

"Willie," she cried with a sudden directness, with her eyes appealing to me, "I didn't mean to treat you badly—indeed I didn't. I kept thinking of you—and of Father and Mother, all the time. Only it didn't seem to move me. It didn't move me not one bit from the way I had chosen."

"Chosen!" I said.

"Something seemed to have hold of me," she admitted. "It's all so unaccountable...."

She gave a little gesture of despair.

Verrall's fingers played on the cloth for a space. Then he turned his face to me again.

"Something said 'Take her.' Everything. It was a raging desire—for her. I don't know. Everything contributed to that—or counted for nothing. You—"

"Go on," said I.

"When I knew of you—"

I looked at Nettie. "You never told him about me?" I said, feeling, as it were, a sting out of the old time.

Verrall answered for her. "No. But things dropped; I saw you that night, my instincts were all awake. I knew it was you."

"You triumphed over me?...If I could I would have triumphed over you," I said. "But go on!"

"Everything conspired to make it the finest thing in life. It had an air of generous recklessness. It meant mischief, it might mean failure in that life of politics and affairs, for which I was trained, which it was my honor to follow. That made it all the finer. It meant ruin or misery for Nettie. That made it all the finer. No sane or decent man would have approved of what we did. That made it more splendid than ever. I had all the advantages of position and used them basely. That mattered not at all."

"Yes," I said; "it is true. And the same dark wave that lifted you, swept me on to follow. With that revolver—and blubbering with hate. And the word to you, Nettie, what was it? 'Give?' Hurl yourself down the steep?"

Nettie's hands fell upon the table. "I can't tell what it was," she said, speaking bare-hearted straight to me. "Girls aren't trained as men are trained to look into their minds. I can't see it yet. All sorts of mean little motives were there—over and above the 'must.' Mean motives. I kept thinking of his clothes." She smiled—a flash of brightness at Verrall. "I kept thinking of being like a lady and sitting in an hotel—with men like butlers waiting. It's the dreadful truth, Willie. Things as mean as that! Things meaner than that!"

I can see her now pleading with me, speaking with a frankness as bright and amazing as the dawn of the first great morning.

"It wasn't all mean," I said slowly, after a pause.

"No!" they spoke together.

"But a woman chooses more than a man does," Nettie added. "I saw it all in little bright pictures. Do you know—that jacket—there's something— You won't mind my telling you? But you won't now!"

I nodded, "No."

She spoke as if she spoke to my soul, very quietly and very earnestly, seeking to give the truth. "Something cottony in that cloth of yours," she said. "I know there's something horrible in being swung round by things like that, but they did swing me round. In the old time—to have confessed that! And I hated Clayton—and the grime of it. That kitchen! Your mother's dreadful kitchen! And besides,

Willie, I was afraid of you. I didn't understand you and I did him. It's different now—but then I knew what he meant. And there was his voice."

"Yes," I said to Verrall, making these discoveries quietly, "yes, Verrall, you have a good voice. Queer I never thought of that before!"

We sat silently for a time before our vivisected passions.

"Gods!" I cried, "and there was our poor little top-hamper of intelligence on all these waves of instinct and wordless desire, these foaming things of touch and sight and feeling, like—like a coop of hens washed overboard and clucking amidst the seas."

Verrall laughed approval of the image I had struck out. "A week ago," he said, trying it further, "we were clinging to our chicken coops and going with the heave and pour. That was true enough a week ago. But today—?"

"Today," I said, "the wind has fallen. The world storm is over. And each chicken coop has changed by a miracle to a vessel that makes head against the sea."

4

"What are we to do?" asked Verrall.

Nettie drew a deep crimson carnation from the bowl before us, and began very neatly and deliberately to turn down the sepals of its calyx and remove, one by one, its petals. I remember that went on through all our talk. She put those ragged crimson shreds in a long row and adjusted them and readjusted them. When at last I was alone with these vestiges the pattern was still incomplete.

"Well," said I, "the matter seems fairly simple. You two"—I swallowed it—"love one another."

I paused. They answered me by silence, by a thoughtful silence.

"You belong to each other. I have thought it over and looked at it from many points of view. I happened to want—

impossible things....I behaved badly. I had no right to pursue you." I turned to Verrall. "You hold yourself bound to her?"

He nodded assent.

"No social influence, no fading out of all this generous clearness in the air—for that might happen—will change you back...?"

He answered me with honest eyes meeting mine, "No, Leadford, no!"

"I did not know you," I said. "I thought of you as something very different from this."

"I was," he interpolated.

"Now," I said, "it is all changed."

Then I halted—for my thread had slipped away from me.

"As for me," I went on, and glanced at Nettie's downcast face, and then sat forward with my eyes upon the flowers between us, "since I am swayed and shall be swayed by an affection for Nettie, since that affection is rich with the seeds of desire, since to see her yours and wholly yours is not to be endured by me—I must turn about and go from you; you must avoid me and I you....We must divide the world like Jacob and Esau....I must direct myself with all the will I have to other things. After all—this passion is not life! It is perhaps for brutes and savages, but for men. No! We must part and I must forget. What else is there but that?"

I did not look up, I sat very tense with the red petals printing an indelible memory in my brain, but I felt the assent of Verrall's pose. There were some moments of silence. Then Nettie spoke. "But—" she said, and ceased.

I waited for a little while. I sighed and leaned back in my chair. "It is perfectly simple," I smiled, "now that we have cool heads."

"But *is* it simple?" asked Nettie, and slashed my discourse out of being.

I looked up and found her with her eyes on Verrall. "You see," she said, "I like Willie. It's hard to say what one feels—but I don't want him to go away like that."

"But then," objected Verrall, "how—?"

"No," said Nettie, and swept her half-arranged carnation petals back into a heap of confusion. She began to arrange them very quickly into one long straight line.

"It's so difficult— I've never before in all my life tried to get to the bottom of my mind. For one thing, I've not treated Willie properly. He—he counted on me. I know he did. I was his hope. I was a promised delight—something, something to crown life—better than anything he had ever had. And a secret pride....He lived upon me. I knew—when we two began to meet together, you and I— It was a sort of treachery to him—"

"Treachery!" I said. "You were only feeling your way through all these perplexities."

"You thought it treachery."

"I don't now."

"I did. In a sense I think so still. For you had need of me."

I made a slight protest at this doctrine and fell thinking.

"And even when he was trying to kill us," she said to her lover, "I felt for him down in the bottom of my mind. I can understand all the horrible things, the humiliation—the humiliation! he went through."

"Yes." I said, "but I don't see—"

"*I* don't see. I'm only trying to see. But you know, Willie, you are a part of my life. I have known you longer than I have known Edward. I know you better. Indeed I know you with all my heart. You think all your talk was thrown away upon me, that I never understood that side of you, or your ambitions or anything. I did. More than I thought at the time. Now—now it is all clear to me. What I had to understand in you was something deeper than Edward brought me. I have it now.... You are a part of my life, and I don't want to cut all that off from me now I have comprehended it, and throw it away."

"But you love Verrall."

"Love is such a queer thing!...Is there one love? I mean,

only one love?'' She turned to Verrall. ''I know I love you. I can speak out about that now. Before yesterday morning I couldn't have done. It's just as though my mind had got out of a scented prison. But what is it, this love for you? It's a mass of fancies—things about you—ways you look, ways you have. It's the senses—and the senses of certain beauties. Flattery too, things you said, hopes and deceptions for myself. And all that had rolled up together and taken to itself the wild help of those deep emotions that slumbered in my body; it seemed everything. But it wasn't. How can I describe it? It was like having a very bright lamp with a thick shade—everything else in the room was hidden. But you take the shade off and there they are—it is the same light—still there! Only it lights everyone!''

Her voice ceased. For awhile no one spoke, and Nettie, with a quick movement, swept the petals into the shape of a pyramid.

Figures of speech always distract me, and it ran through my mind like some puzzling refrain. ''It is still the same light....''

''No woman believes these things,'' she asserted abruptly.

''What things?''

''No woman ever has believed them.''

''You have to choose a man,'' said Verrall, apprehending her before I did.

''We're brought up to that. We're told—it's in books, in stories, in the way people look, in the way they behave—one day there will come a man. He will be everything, no one else will be anything. Leave everything else; live in him.''

''And a man, too, is taught that of some woman,'' said Verrall.

''Only men don't believe it! They have more obstinate minds....Men have never behaved as though they believed it. One need not be old to know that. By nature they don't believe it. But a woman believes nothing by nature. She goes into a mold hiding her secret thoughts almost from herself.''

"She used to," I said.

"You haven't," said Verrall, "anyhow."

"I've come out. It's this comet. And Willie. And because I never really believed in the mold at all—even if I thought I did. It's stupid to send Willie off—shamed, cast out, never to see him again—when I like him as much as I do. It is cruel, it is wicked and ugly, to prance over him as if he was a defeated enemy, and pretend I'm going to be happy just the same. There's no sense in a rule of life that prescribes that. It's selfish. It's brutish. It's like something that has no sense. I—" there was a sob in her voice: "Willie! I *won't*."

I sat lowering, I mused with my eyes upon her quick fingers.

"It *is* brutish," I said at last, with a careful unemotional deliberation. "Nevertheless—it is in the nature of things.... No!... You see, after all, we are still half brutes, Nettie. And men, as you say, are more obstinate than women. The comet hasn't altered that; it's only made it clearer. We have come into being through a tumult of blind forces.... I come back to what I said just now; we have found our poor reasonable minds, our wills to live well, ourselves, adrift on a wash of instincts, passions, instinctive prejudices, half-animal stupidities.... Here we are like people clinging to something—like people awakening—upon a raft."

"We come back at last to my question," said Verrall, softly; "what are we to do?"

"Part," I said. "You see, Nettie, these bodies of ours are not the bodies of angels. They are the same bodies— I have read somewhere that in our bodies you can find evidence of the lowliest ancestry; that about our inward ears—I think it is—and about our teeth, there remains still something of the fish, that there are bones that recall little—what is it?—marsupial forebears—and a hundred traces of the ape. Even your beautiful body, Nettie, carries this taint. No! Hear me out." I leaned forward earnestly. "Our emotions, our passions, our desires, the substance of them, like the substance of our bodies, is an animal, a competing thing, as well as a desiring thing. You speak to us now a mind to minds—one can do that when one has had exercise and when one has eaten, when one is not doing anything—but when one turns to live, one turns again to matter."

"Yes," said Nettie, slowly following me, "But you control it."

"Only through a measure of obedience. There is no magic in the business—to conquer matter, we must divide the enemy, and take matter as an ally. Nowadays it is indeed true, by faith a man can remove mountains; he can say to a mountain, Be thou removed and be thou cast into the sea; but he does it because he helps and trusts his brother men, because he has the wit and patience and courage to win over to his side iron, steel, obedience, dynamite, cranes, trucks, the money of other people.... To conquer my desire for you, I must not perpetually thwart it by your presence; I must go away so that I may not see you, I must take up other interests, thrust myself into struggles and discussions—"

"And forget?" said Nettie.

"Not forget," I said; "but anyhow—cease to brood upon you."

She hung on that for some moments.

"No," she said, demolished her last pattern and looked up at Verrall as he stirred.

Verrall leaned forward on the table, elbows upon it, and the fingers of his two hands intertwined.

"You know," he said, "I haven't thought much of these things. At school and the university, one doesnt.... It was part of the system to prevent it. They'll alter all that, no doubt. We seem"—he thought—"to be skating about over questions that one came to at last in Greek—with variorum readings—in Plato, but which it never occurred to anyone to translate out of a dead language into living realities...." He halted and answered some unspoken question from his own mind with, "No. I think with Leadford, Nettie, that, as he put it, it is in the nature of things for men to be exclusive.... Minds are free things and go about the world, but only one man can possess a woman. You must dismiss rivals. We are made for the struggle for existence—we *are* the struggle for existence incarnate—and that works out that the men struggle for their mates; for each woman one prevails. The others go away."

"Like animals," said Nettie.

"Yes...."

"There are many things in life," I said, "but that is the rough universal truth."

"But," said Nettie, "you don't struggle. That has been altered because men have minds."

"You choose," I said.

"If I don't choose to choose?"

"You have chosen."

She gave a little impatient "Oh! Why are women always the slaves of sex? Is this great age of Reason and Light that has come to alter nothing of that? And men too! I think it is all—stupid. I do not believe this is the right solution of the thing, or anything but the bad habits of the time that was... Instinct! You don't let your instincts rule you in a lot of other things. Here am I between you. Here is Edward. I—love him because he is gay and pleasant, and because—because I *like* him! Here is Willie—a part of me—my first secret, my oldest friend! Why must I not have both? Am I not a mind that you must think of me as nothing but a woman? Imagine me always as a thing to struggle for?" She paused; then she made her distressful proposition to me. "Let us three keep together," she said. "Let us not part. To part is hate, Willie. Why should we not anyhow keep friends? Meet and talk?"

"Talk?" I said. "About this sort of thing?"

I looked across at Verrall and met his eyes, and we studied one another. It was the clean, straight scrutiny of honest antagonism. "No," I decided. "Between us, nothing of that sort can be."

"Ever?" said Nettie.

"Never," I said, convinced.

I made an effort within myself. "We cannot tamper with the law and customs of these things," I said; "these passions are too close to one's essential self. Better surgery than a lingering disease! From Nettie my love—asks all. A man's love is not devotion—it is a demand, a challenge. And besides"—and here I forced my theme—"I have given myself now to a new mistress—and it is I, Nettie, who am unfaithful. Behind you and above you rises the coming City of the World, and I am in that building. Dear heart! you are only happiness—and that— Indeed that calls! If it is only that my life blood shall christen the foundation stones—I could almost hope that should be my part. Nettie—I will join myself in that." I threw all the conviction I could into these words...."No conflict of passion," I added a little lamely, "must distract me."

There was a pause.

"Then we must part," said Nettie, with the eyes of a woman one strikes in the face.

I nodded assent....

There was a little pause, and then I stood up. We stood up, all three. We parted almost sullenly, with no more memorable words, and I was left presently in the arbor alone.

I do not think I watched them go. I only remember myself left there somehow—horribly empty and alone. I sat down again and fell into a deep shapeless musing.

5

Suddenly I looked up. Nettie had come back and stood looking down at me.

"Since we talked I have been thinking," she said. "Edward has let me come to you alone. And I feel perhaps I can talk better to you alone."

I said nothing and that embarrassed her.

"I don't think we ought to part," she said.

"No—I don't think we ought to part," she repeated.

"One lives," she said, "in different ways. I wonder if you will understand what I am saying, Willie. It is hard to say what I feel. But I want it said. If we are to part forever I want it said—very plainly. Always before I have had the woman's instinct and the woman's training which makes one hide. But—Edward is not all of me. Think of what I am saying—Edward is not all of me.... I wish I could tell you better how I see it. I am not all of myself. You, at any rate, are a part of me and I cannot bear to leave you. And I cannot see why I should leave you. There is a sort of blood link between us, Willie. We grew together. We are in one another's bones. I understand you. Now indeed I understand. In some way I have come to an understanding at a stride. Indeed I understand you and your dream. I want to help you. Edward—Edward has no dreams.... It is dreadful to me, Willie, to think we two are to part."

"But we have settled that—part we must."

"But *why*?"

"I love you."

"Well, and why should I hide it, Willie?—I love you...." Our eyes met. She flushed, she went on resolutely: "You are stupid. The whole thing is stupid. I love you both."

I said, "You do not understand what you say. No!"

"You mean that I must go."

"Yes, yes. Go!"

For a moment we looked at one another, mute, as though deep down in the unfathomable darkness below the surface and present reality of things dumb meanings strove to be. She made to speak and desisted.

"But *must* I go?" she said at last, with quivering lips, and the tears in her eyes were stars. Then she began, "Willie—"

"Go!" I interrupted her.... "Yes."

Then again we were still.

She stood there, a tearful figure of pity, longing for me, pitying me. Something of that wider love, that will carry our descendants at last out of all the limits, the hard, clear obligations of our personal life, moved us, like the first breath of a coming wind out of heaven that stirs and passes away. I had an impulse to take her hand and kiss it, and then a trembling came to me, and I knew that if I touched her, my strength would all pass from me....

And so standing at a distance one from the other, we parted, and Nettie went, reluctant and looking back, with the man she had chosen, to the lot she had chosen, out of my life—like the sunlight out of my life....

Then, you know, I suppose I folded up this newspaper and put it in my pocket. But my memory of that meeting ends with the face of Nettie turning to go.

6

I remember all that very distinctly to this day. I could almost vouch for the words I have put into our several mouths. Then comes a blank. I have a dim memory of being back in the house near the Links and the bustle of Melmount's departure, of finding Parker's energy distasteful, and of going away down the road with a strong desire to say good-bye to Melmount alone.

Perhaps I was already doubting my decision to part forever from Nettie, for I think I had it in mind to tell him all that had been said and done....

I don't think I had a word with him or anything but a hurried hand clasp. I am not sure. It has gone out of my mind. But I have a very clear and certain memory of my phase of bleak desolation as I watched his car recede and climb and vanish over Mapleborough Hill, and that I got there my first full and definite intimation that, after all, this great Change and my new wide aims in life, were not to mean indiscriminate happiness for me. I had a sense of protest, as against extreme unfairness, as I saw him go. "It is too soon," I said to myself, "to leave me alone."

I felt I had sacrificed too much, that after I had said good-bye to the hot immediate life of passion, to Nettie and desire, to physical and personal rivalry, to all that was most intensely myself, it was wrong to leave me alone and sore hearted, to go on at once with these steely cold duties of the wider life. I felt newborn, and naked, and at a loss.

"Work!" I said with an effort at the heroic, and turned about with a sigh, and I was glad that the way I had to go would at least take me to my mother....

But, curiously enough, I remember myself as being fairly cheerful in the town of Birmingham that night, I recall an active and interested mood. I spent the night in Birmingham because the train service was disarranged, and I could not get on. I went to listen to a band that was playing its brassy old-world music in the public park, and I fell into conversation with a man who said he had been a reporter upon one of their minor local papers. He was full and keen upon all the plans of reconstruction that were now shaping over the lives of humanity, and I know that something of that noble dream came back to me with his words and phrases. We walked up to a place called Bourneville by moonlight, and talked of the new social groupings that must replace the old isolated homes, and how the people would be housed.

This Bourneville was germane to that matter. It had been an attempt on the part of a private firm of manufacturers to improve the housing of their workers. To our ideas today it would seem the feeblest of benevolent efforts, but at the time it was extraordinary and famous, and people came long journeys to see its trim cottages with baths sunk under the kitchen floors (of all conceivable places), and other brilliant inventions. No one seemed to see the danger to liberty in that aggressive age, that might arise through making work-people tenants and debtors of their employer, though an Act called the Truck Act had long ago intervened to prevent minor developments in the same direction....But I and my chance acquaintance seemed that night always to have been aware of that possibility, and we had no doubt in our minds of the public nature of the housing duty. Our interest lay rather in the possibility of common nurseries and kitchens and public rooms that should economize toil and give people space and freedom.

It was very interesting, but still a little cheerless, and when I lay in bed that night I thought of Nettie and the queer modifications of preference she had made, and among other things and in a way, I prayed. I prayed that night, let me confess it, to an image I had set up in my heart, an image that still serves with me as a symbol for things inconceivable, to a Master Artificer, the unseen captain of all who go about the building of the world, the making of mankind.

But before and after I prayed I imagined I was talking and reasoning and meeting again with Nettie....She never came into the temple of that worshiping with me.

Chapter 2

My Mother's Last Days

1

Next day I came home to Clayton.

The new strange brightness of the world was all the brighter there, for the host of dark distressful memories, of darkened childhood, toilsome youth, embittered adolescence that wove about the place for me. It seemed to me that I saw morning there for the first time. No chimneys smoked that day, no furnaces were burning, the people were busy with other things. The clear strong sun, the sparkle in the dustless air, made a strange gaiety in the narrow streets. I passed a number of smiling people coming home from the public breakfasts that were given in the Town Hall until better things could be arranged, and happened on Parload among them. "You were right about that comet," I sang out at the sight of him; and he came toward me and clasped my hand.

"What are people doing here?" said I.

"They're sending us food from outside," he said, "and we're going to level all these slums—and shift into tents on to the moors;" and he began to tell me of many things that were being arranged; the Midland land committees had got to work with remarkable celerity and directness of purpose, and the redistribution of population was already in its broad outlines planned. He was working at an improvised college of engineering. Until schemes of work were made out, almost everyone was going to school again to get as much technical training as they could against the demands of the huge enterprise of reconstruction that was now beginning.

He walked with me to my door, and there I met old Pettigrew coming down the steps. He looked dusty and tired, but his eye was brighter than it used to be, and he carried, in a rather unaccustomed manner, a workman's tool basket.

"How's the rheumatism, Mr. Pettigrew?" I asked.

"Dietary," said old Pettigrew, "can work wonders...." He looked me in the eye. "These houses," he said, "will have to come down, I suppose, and our notions of property must undergo very considerable revision—in the light of reason; but meanwhile I've been doing something to patch that disgraceful roof of mine! To think that I could have dodged and evaded—"

He raised a deprecatory hand, drew down the loose corners of his ample mouth, and shook his old head.

"The past is past, Mr. Pettigrew."

"Your poor dear mother! So good and honest a woman! So simple and kind and forgiving! To think of it! My dear young man!"—he said it manfully—"I'm ashamed."

"The whole world blushed at dawn the other day, Mr. Pettigrew," I said, "and did it very prettily. That's over now. God knows, who is *not* ashamed of all that came before last Tuesday."

I held out a forgiving hand, naively forgetful that in this place I was a thief, and he took it and went his way, shaking his head and repeating he was ashamed, but I think a little comforted.

The door opened and my poor old mother's face,

marvelously cleaned, appeared. "Ah, Willie, boy! *You.* You!"

I ran up the steps to her, for I feared she might fall.

How she clung to me in the passage, the dear woman!...

But first she shut the front door. The old habit of respect for my unaccountable temper still swayed her. "Ah deary!" she said, "ah deary! But you were sorely tried," and kept her face close to my shoulder, lest she should offend me by the sight of the tears that welled within her.

She made a sort of gulping noise and was quiet for a while, holding me very tightly to her heart with her worn, long hands....

She thanked me presently for my telegram, and I put my arm about her and drew her into the living room.

"It's all well with me, Mother dear," I said, "and the dark times are over—are done with forever, Mother."

Whereupon she had courage and gave way and sobbed aloud, none chiding her.

She had not let me know she could still weep for five grimy years....

2

Dear heart! There remained for her but a very brief while in this world that had been renewed. I did not know how short that time would be, but the little I could do—perhaps after all it was not little to her—to atone for the harshness of my days of wrath and rebellion, I did. I took care to be constantly with her, for I perceived now her curious need of me. It was not that we had ideas to exchange or pleasures to share, but she liked to see me at table, to watch me working, to have me go to and fro. There was no toil for her anymore in the world, but only such light services as are easy and pleasant for a worn and weary old woman to do, and I think she was happy even at her end.

She kept to her queer old eighteenth-century version of

religion, too, without a change. She had worn this particular amulet so long it was a part of her. Yet the Change was evident even in that persistence. I said to her one day, "But do you still believe in that hell of flame, dear Mother? You—with your tender heart!"

She vowed she did.

Some theological intricacy made it necessary to her, but still—

She looked thoughtfully at a bank of primulas before her for a time, and then laid her tremulous hand impressively on my arm. "You know, Willie, dear," she said, as though she was clearing up a childish misunderstanding of mine, "I don't think anyone will *go* there. I never *did* think that...."

3

That talk stands out in my memory because of that agreeable theological decision of hers, but it was only one of a great number of talks. It used to be pleasant in the afternoon, after the day's work was done and before one went on with the evening's study—how odd it would have seemed in the old time for a young man of the industrial class to be doing post-graduate work in sociology, and how much a matter of course it seems now!—to walk out into the gardens of Lowchester House, and smoke a cigarette or so and let her talk ramblingly of the things that interested her....Physically the Great Change did not do so very much to reinvigorate her—she had lived in that dismal underground kitchen in Clayton too long for any material rejuvenescence—she glowed out indeed as a dying spark among the ashes might glow under a draft of fresh air—and assuredly it hastened her end. But those closing days were very tranquil, full of an effortless contentment. With her, life was like a rainy, windy day that clears only to show the sunset afterglow. The light had passed. She acquired no new habits amid the comforts of the new life, did no new things, but only found a happier light upon the old.

She lived with a number of other old ladies belonging to our commune in the upper rooms of Lowchester House. Those upper appartments were simple and ample, fine and well done in the Georgian style, and they had been organized to give the maximum of comfort and conveniences and to economize the need of skilled attendance. We had taken over the various "great houses," as they used to be called, to make communal dining rooms and so forth—their kitchens were conveniently large—and pleasant places for the old people of over sixty whose time of ease had come, and for suchlike public uses. We had done this not only with Lord Redcar's house, but also with Checkshill House—where old Mrs. Verrall made a dignified and capable hostess—and indeed with most of the fine residences in the beautiful wide country between the Four Towns district and the Welsh mountains. About these great houses there had usually been good outbuildings, laundries, married servants' quarters, stabling, dairies, and the like, suitably masked by trees; we turned these into homes, and to them we added first tents and wood chalets and afterward quadrangular residential buildings. In order to be near my mother I had two small rooms in the new collegiate buildings which our commune was almost the first to possess, and they were very convenient for the station of the high-speed electric railway that took me down to our daily conferences and my secretarial and statistical work in Clayton.

Ours had been one of the first modern communes to get in order; we were greatly helped by the energy of Lord Redcar, who had a fine feeling for the picturesque associations of his ancestral home—the detour that took our line through the beeches and bracken and bluebells of the West Wood and saved the pleasant open wildness of the park was one of his suggestions; and we had many reasons to be proud of our surroundings. Nearly all the other communes that sprang up all over the pleasant parkland round the industrial valley of the Four Towns, as the workers moved out, came to us to study the architecture of the residential squares and quadrangles with which we had replaced the back streets between the great houses and the ecclesiastical residences about the cathedral, and the way in which we had adapted all these buildings to our new social needs. Some claimed to have improved on us. But they could not emulate the rhododendron garden out beyond our shrubberies; that was a thing altogether our own in our part of England, because of its ripeness and of the rarity of good peat free from lime.

These gardens had been planned under the third Lord Redcar, fifty years ago and more; they abounded in rhododendra and azaleas, and were in places so well sheltered and sunny that great magnolias flourished and flowered. There were tall trees smothered in crimson and yellow climbing roses, and an endless variety of flowering shrubs and fine conifers, and such pampas grass as no other garden can show. And barred by the broad shadows of these, were glades and broad spaces of emerald turf, and here and there banks of pegged roses, and flowerbeds, and banks given over some to spring bulbs, and some to primroses and primulas and polyanthuses. My mother loved these latter banks and the little round staring eyes of their innumerable yellow, ruddy brown, and purple corollas, more than anything else the gardens could show, and in the spring of the Year of Scaffolding she would go with me day after day to the seat that showed them in the greatest multitude.

It gave her, I think, among other agreeable impressions, a sense of gentle opulence. In the old time she had never known what it was to have more than enough of anything agreeable in the world at all.

We would sit and think, or talk—there was a curious effect of complete understanding between us whether we talked or were still.

"Heaven," she said to me one day, "Heaven is a garden."

I was moved to tease her a little. "There's jewels, you know, walls and gates of jewels—and singing."

"For such as like them," said my mother firmly, and thought for a while. "There'll be things for all of us, o' course. But for me it couldn't be Heaven, dear, unless it was a garden—a nice sunny garden....And feeling such as we're fond of, are close and handy by."

You of your happier generation cannot realize the wonderfulness of those early days in the new epoch, the sense of security, the extraordinary effects of contrast. In the morning, except in high summer, I was up before dawn, and breakfasted upon the swift, smooth train, and perhaps saw the sunrise as I rushed out of the little tunnel that pierced Clayton Crest, and so to work like a man. Now that we had got all the homes and schools and all the softness of life away from our coal and iron ore and clay, now that a thousand obstructive "rights" and timidities had been swept aside, we could let ourselves go, we merged this enterprise with that, cut across this or that anciently obstructive piece of private land, joined and separated, effected gigantic consolidations and gigantic economies, and the valley, no longer a pit of squalid human tragedies and meanly conflicting industries, grew into a sort of beauty of its own, a savage inhuman beauty of force and machinery and flames. One was a Titan in that Etna. Then back one came at midday to bathe and change in the train, and so to the leisurely gossiping lunch in the club dining room in Lowchester House, and the refreshment of these green and sunlit afternoon tranquilities.

Sometimes in her profounder moments my mother doubted whether all this last phase of her life was not a dream.

"A dream," I used to say, "a dream indeed—but a dream that is one step nearer awakening than that nightmare of the former days."

She found great comfort and assurance in my altered clothes—she liked the new fashions of dress, she alleged. It was not simply altered clothes. I did grow two inches, broaden some inches round my chest, and increase in weight three stones before I was twenty-three. I wore a soft brown cloth and she would caress my sleeve and admire it greatly—she had the woman's sense of texture very strong in her.

Sometimes she would muse upon the past, rubbing together her poor rough hands—they never got softened —one over the other. She told me much I had not heard before about my father, and her own early life. It was like finding flat and faded flowers in a book still faintly sweet, to realize that once my mother had been loved with passion; that my remote father had once shed hot tears of tenderness in her arms. And she would sometimes even speak tentatively in those narrow, old-world phrases that her lips could rob of all their bitter narrowness, of Nettie.

"She wasn't worthy of you, dear," she would say abruptly, leaving me to guess the person she intended.

"No man is worthy of a woman's love," I answered. "No woman is worthy of a man's. I love her, dear Mother, and that you cannot alter."

"There's others," she would muse.

"Not for me," I said. "No! I didn't fire a shot that time; I burned my magazine. I can't begin again, Mother, not from the beginning."

She sighed and said no more then.

At another time she said—I think her words were: "You'll be lonely when I'm gone, dear."

"You'll not think of going, then," I said.

"Eh, dear! but man and maid should come together."

I said nothing to that.

"You brood overmuch on Nettie, dear. If I could see you married to some sweet girl of a woman, some good, *kind* girl—"

"Dear Mother, I'm married enough. Perhaps some day— Who knows? I can wait."

"But to have nothing to do with women!"

"I have my friends. Don't you trouble, Mother. There's plentiful work for a man in this world though the heart of love is cast out from him. Nettie was life and beauty for me—is—will be. Don't think I've lost too much, Mother."

(Because in my heart I told myself the end had still to come.)

And once she sprang a question on me suddenly that surprised me.

"Where are they now?" she asked.

"Who?"

"Nettie and—him."

She had pierced to the marrow of my thoughts. "I don't know," I said shortly.

Her shriveled hand just fluttered into touch of mine.

"It's better so," she said, as if pleading. "Indeed...it is better so."

There was something in her quivering old voice that for a moment took me back across an epoch, to the protests of the former time, to those counsels of submission, those appeals not to offend It, that had always stirred an angry spirit of rebellion within me.

"That is the thing I doubt," I said, and abruptly I felt I could talk no more to her of Nettie. I got up and walked away from her, and came back after a while, to speak of other things, with a bunch of daffodils for her in my hand.

But I did not always spend my afternoons with her. There were days when my crushed hunger for Nettie rose again, and then I had to be alone; I walked, or bicycled, and presently I found a new interest and relief in learning to ride. For the horse was already very swiftly reaping the benefit of the Change. Hardly anywhere was the inhumanity of horse traction to be found after the first year of the new epoch, everywhere lugging and dragging and straining was done by machines, and the horse had become a beautiful instrument for the pleasure and carriage of youth. I rode both in the saddle and, what is finer, naked and bareback. I found violent exercises were good for the states of enormous melancholy that came upon me, and when at last horse riding palled, I went and joined the aviators who practiced soaring upon airplanes beyond Horsemarden Hill.... But at least every alternate day I spent with my mother, and altogether I think I gave her two-thirds of my afternoons.

4

When presently that illness, that fading weakness that made an euthanasia for so many of the older people in the beginning of the new time, took hold upon my mother, there came Anna Reeves to daughter her—after our new custom. She chose to come. She was already known to us a little from chance meetings and chance services she had done my mother in the garden; she sought to give her help. She seemed then just one of those plainly good girls the world at its worst has never failed to produce, who were indeed in the dark old times the hidden antiseptic of all our hustling, hating, faithless lives. They made their secret voiceless worship, they did their steadfast, uninspired, unthanked, unselfish work as helpful daughters, as nurses, as faithful servants, as the humble providences of homes. She was almost exactly three years older than I. At first I found no beauty in her; she was short but rather sturdy and ruddy, with red-tinged hair, and fair hairy brows and red-brown eyes. But her freckled hands, I found, were full of apt help, her voice carried good cheer....

At first she was no more than a blue-clad, white-aproned benevolence, that moved in the shadows behind the bed on which my old mother lay and sank restfully to death. She would come forward to anticipate some little need, to proffer some simple comfort, and always then my mother smiled on her. In a little while I discovered the beauty of that helpful poise of her woman's body, I discovered the grace of untiring goodness, the sweetness of a tender pity, and the great riches of her voice, of her few reassuring words and phrases. I noted and remembered very clearly how once my mother's lean old hand patted the firm gold-flecked strength of hers, as it went by upon its duties with the coverlet.

"She is a good girl to me," said my mother one day. "A good girl. Like a daughter should be....I never had a daughter—really." She mused peacefully for a space. "Your little sister died," she said.

I had never heard of that little sister.

"November the tenth," said my mother. "Twenty-nine months and three days....I cried. I cried. That was before you came, dear. So long ago—and I can see it now. I was a young wife then, and your father was very kind. But I can see its hands, its dear little quiet hands....Dear, they say that now—now they will not let the little children die."

"No, dear Mother," I said. "We shall do better now."

"The club doctor could not come. Your father went twice. There was someone else, someone who paid. So your father went on into Swathinglea, and that man wouldn't come unless he had his fee. And your father had changed his clothes to look more respectful and he hadn't any money, not even his tram fare home. It seemed cruel to be waiting there with my baby thing in pain....And I can't help thinking perhaps we might have saved her....But it was like that with the poor always in the bad old times—always. When the doctor came at last he was angry. 'Why wasn't I called before?' he said, and he took no pains. He was angry because someone hadn't explained. I begged him—but it was too late."

She said these things very quietly with drooping eyelids, like one who describes a dream. "We are going to manage all these things better now," I said, feeling a strange resentment at this pitiful story her faded, matter-of-fact voice was telling me.

"She talked," my mother went on. "She talked for her age wonderfully....Hippopotamus."

"Eh?" I said.

"Hippopotamus, dear—quite plainly one day, when her father was showing her pictures....And her little prayers. 'Now I lay me...down to sleep.'...I made her little socks. Knitted they was, dear, and the heel most difficult."

Her eyes were closed now. She spoke no longer to me but to herself. She whispered other vague things, little sentences, ghosts of long-dead moments....Her words grew less distinct.

Presently she was asleep and I got up and went out of the room, but my mind was queerly obsessed by the thought of that little life that had been glad and hopeful only to pass so inexplicably out of hope again into nonentity, this sister of whom I had never heard before....

And presently I was in a black rage at all the irrecoverable sorrows of the past, of that great ocean of avoidable suffering of which this was but one luminous and quivering red drop. I walked in the garden and the garden was too small for me; I went out to wander on the moors. "The past is past," I cried, and all the while across the gulf of five and twenty years I could hear my poor mother's heart-wrung weeping for that daughter baby who had suffered and died. Indeed that old spirit of rebellion has not altogether died in me, for all the transformation of the new time....I quieted down at last to a thin and austere comfort in thinking that the whole is not told to us, that it cannot perhaps be told to such minds as ours; and anyhow, what was far more sustaining, that now we have strength and courage and this new gift of wise love, whatever cruel and sad things marred the past; none of these sorrowful things that made the very warp and woof of the old life, need now go on happening. We could foresee, we could prevent and save. "The past is past," I said, between sighing and resolve, as I came into view again on my homeward way of the hundred sunset-lit windows of old Lowchester House. "Those sorrows are sorrows no more."

But I could not altogether cheat that common sadness of the new time, that memory and insoluble riddle of the countless lives that had stumbled and failed in pain and darkness before our air grew clear....

Chapter 3

Beltane and New Year's Eve

1

In the end my mother died rather suddenly, and her death came as a shock to me. Diagnosis was still very inadequate at that time. The doctors were, of course, fully alive to the incredible defects of their common training and were doing all they could to supply its deficiencies, but they were still extraordinarily ignorant. Some unintelligently observed factor of her illness came into play with her, and she became feverish and sank and died very quickly. I do not know what remedial measures were attempted. I hardly knew what was happening until the whole thing was over.

At that time my attention was much engaged by the stir of the great Beltane festival that was held on May Day in the Year of Scaffolding. It was the first of the ten great rubbish burnings that opened the new age. Young people nowadays can scarcely hope to imagine the enormous quantities of pure litter and useless accumulation with which we had to deal; had we not set aside a special day and season, the whole world would have been an incessant reek of small fires; and it was, I think, a happy idea to revive this ancient festival of the May and November burnings. It was inevitable that the old idea of purification should revive with the name, it was felt to be a burning of other than material encumbrances, innumerable quasi-spiritual things, deeds, documents, debts, vindictive records, went up on those great flares. People passed praying between the fires, and it was a fine symbol of the new and wiser tolerance that had come to men, that those who still found their comfort in the orthodox faiths came hither unpersuaded, to pray that all hate might be burned out of their professions. For even in the fires of Baal, now that men have done with base hatred, one may find the living God.

Endless were the things we had to destroy in those great purgings. First, there were nearly all the houses and buildings of the old time. In the end we did not save in England one building in five thousand that was standing when the comet came. Year by year, as we made our homes afresh in accordance with the saner needs of our new social families, we swept away more and more of those horrible structures, the ancient residential houses, hastily built, without imagination, without beauty, without common honesty, without even comfort or convenience, in which the early twentieth century had sheltered until scarcely one remained; we saved nothing but what was beautiful or interesting out of all their gaunt and melancholy abundance. The actual houses, of course, we could not drag to our fires, but we brought all their ill-fitting deal doors, their dreadful window sashes, their servant-tormenting staircases, their dank, dark cupboards, the verminous papers from their scaly walls, their dust- and dirt- sodden carpets, their ill-designed and yet pretentious tables and chairs, sideboards and chests of drawers, the old dirt-saturated books, their ornaments—their dirty, decayed, and altogether painful ornaments—amidst which I remember there were sometimes even *stuffed dead birds!*—we burned them all. The paint-plastered woodwork, with coat above coat of nasty paint, that in particular blazed finely. I have already tried to give you an impression of old-world furniture, of Parload's bedroom, my mother's room, Mr. Gabbitas's sitting room, but, thank Heaven! there is nothing in life now to convey the peculiar dinginess of it all. For one thing, there is no more imperfect combustion of coal going on everywhere, and no roadways like grassless open scars along the earth from which dust pours out perpetually. We burned and destroyed most of our private buildings and all the woodwork, all our furniture, except a few score thousand pieces of distinct and intentional beauty, from which our present forms have developed, nearly all our hangings and carpets, and also we destroyed almost every scrap of old-world clothing. Only a few carefully disinfected types and vestiges of that remain now in our museums.

One writes now with a peculiar horror of the dress of the old world. The men's clothes were worn without any cleansing process at all, except an occasional superficial brushing, for periods of a year or so; they were made of dark obscurely mixed patterns to conceal the stage of defilement they had reached, and they were of a felted and porous texture admirably calculated to accumulate drifting matter. Many women wore skirts of similar substances, and of so long and inconvenient a form that they inevitably trailed among all the abomination of our horse-frequented roads. It was our boast in England that the whole of our population was booted—their feet were for the most part ugly enough to need it—but it becomes now inconceivable how they could have imprisoned their feet in the amazing cases of leather and imitations of leather they used. I have heard it said that a large part of the physical decline that was apparent in our people during the closing years of the nineteenth century, though no doubt due in part to the miscellaneous badness of the food they ate, was in the main attributable to the vileness of the common footwear. They shirked open-air exercise altogether because their boots wore out ruinously and pinched and hurt them if they took it. I have mentioned, I think, the part my own boots played in the squalid drama of my adolescence. I had a sense of unholy triumph over a fallen enemy when at last I found myself steering truck after truck of cheap boots and shoes (unsold stock from Swathinglea) to the run-off by the top of the Glanville blast furnaces.

"Plup!" they would drop into the cone when Beltane came, and the roar of their burning would fill the air. Never a cold would come from the saturation of their brown paper soles, never a corn from their foolish shapes, never a nail in them get home at last in suffering flesh....

Most of our public buildings we destroyed and burned as we reshaped our plan of habitation, our theater sheds, our banks, and inconvenient business warrens, our factories (these in the first year of all), and all the "unmeaning repetition" of silly little sham Gothic churches and meeting houses, mean looking shells of stone and mortar without love, invention, or any beauty at all in them, that men had thrust into the face of their sweated God, even as they thrust cheap food into the mouths of their sweated workers; all these we also swept away in the course of that first decade. Then we had the whole of the superseded steam-railway system to scrap and get rid of, stations, signals, fences, rolling stock; a plant of ill-planned, smoke-distributing nuisance apparatus, that would, under former conditions, have maintained an offensive dwindling obstructive life for perhaps half a century. Then also there was a great harvest of fences, notice boards, billboards, ugly sheds, all the corrugated iron in the world, and everything that was smeared with tar, all our gas works and petroleum stores, all our horse vehicles and vans and lorries had to be erased.... But I have said enough now perhaps to give some idea of the bulk and quality of our great bonfires, our burnings up, our meltings down, our toil of sheer wreckage, over and above the constructive effort, in those early years.

But these were the coarse material bases of the Phoenix

fires of the world. These were but the outward and visible signs of the innumerable claims, rights, adhesions, debts, bills, deeds, and charters that were cast upon the fires; a vast accumulation of insignia and uniforms neither curious enough nor beautiful enough to preserve, went to swell the blaze, and all (saving a few truly glorious trophies and memories) of our symbols, our apparatus and material of war. Then innumerable triumphs of our old, bastard, half-commercial, fine art were presently condemned, great oil paintings, done to please the half-educated middle class, glared for a moment and were gone, Academy marbles crumbled to useful lime, a gross multitude of silly statuettes and decorative crockery, and hangings, and embroideries, and bad music, and musical instruments shared this fate. And books, countless books, too, and bales of newspapers went also to these pyres. From the private houses in Swathinglea alone—which I had deemed, perhaps not injustly, altogether illiterate—we gathered a whole dust cart full of cheap ill-printed editions of the minor English classics—for the most part very dull stuff indeed and still clean—and about a truckload of thumbed and dog-eared penny fiction, watery base stuff, the dropsy of our nation's mind.... And it seemed to me that when we gathered those books and papers together, we gathered together something more than print and paper, we gathered warped and crippled ideas and contagious base suggestions, the formulae of dull tolerances and stupid impatiences, the mean defensive ingenuities of sluggish habits of thinking and timid and indolent evasions. There was more than a touch of malignant satisfaction for me in helping gather it all together.

I was so busy, I say, with my share in this dustman's work that I did not notice, as I should otherwise have done, the little indications of change in my mother's state. Indeed, I thought her a little stronger; she was slightly flushed, slightly more talkative....

On Beltane Eve, and our Lowchester rummage being

finished, I went along the valley to the far end of Swathinglea to help sort the stock of the detached group of pot-banks there—their chief output had been mantel ornaments in imitation of marble, and there was very little sorting, I found, to be done—and there it was nurse Anna found me at last by telephone, and told me my mother had died in the morning suddenly and very shortly after my departure.

For a while I did not seem to believe it; this obviously imminent event stunned me when it came, as though I had never had an anticipatory moment. For a while I went on working, and then almost apathetically, in a mood of half-reluctant curiosity, I started for Lowchester.

When I got there the last offices were over, and I was shown my old mother's peaceful white face, very still, but a little cold and stern to me, a little unfamiliar, lying among white flowers.

I went in alone to her, into that quiet room, and stood for a long time by her bedside. I sat down then and thought....

Then at last, strangely hushed, and with the deeps of my loneliness opening beneath me, I came out of that room and down into the world again, a bright-eyed, active world, very noisy, happy, and busy with its last preparations for the mighty cremation of past and superseded things.

2

I remember that first Beltane festival as the most terribly lonely night in my life. It stands in my mind in fragments, fragments of intense feeling with forgotten gaps between.

I recall very distinctly being upon the great staircase of Lowchester House (though I don't remember getting there from the room in which my mother lay), and how upon the landing I met Anna ascending as I came down. She had but just heard of my return, and she was hurrying upstairs to me. She stopped and so did I, and we stood and clasped hands, and she scrutinized my face in the way women sometimes do. So we remained for a second or so. I could say nothing to her at all, but I could feel the wave of her emotion. I halted, answered the earnest pressure of her hand, relinquished it, and after a queer second of hesitation went on down, returning to my own preoccupations. It did not occur to me at all then to ask myself what she might be thinking or feeling.

I remember the corridor full of mellow evening light, and how I went mechanically some paces toward the dining room. Then at the sight of the little tables, and a gusty outburst of talking voices as someone in front of me swung the door open and to, I remembered that I did not want to eat.... After that comes an impression of myself walking across the open grass in front of the house, and the purpose I had of getting alone upon the moors, and how somebody passing me said something about a hat. I had come out without my hat.

A fragment of thought has linked itself with an effect of long shadows upon turf golden with the light of the sinking sun. The world was singularly empty, I thought, without either Nettie or my mother. There wasn't any sense in it any more. Nettie was already back in my mind then....

Then I am out on the moors. I avoided the crests where the bonfires were being piled, and sought the lonely places....

I rememeber very clearly sitting on a gate beyond the park, in a fold just below the crest, that hid the Beacon Hill bonfire and its crowd, and I was looking at and admiring the sunset. The golden earth and sky seemed like a little bubble that floated in the globe of human futility....Then in the twilight I walked along an unknown, bat-haunted road between high hedges.

I did not sleep under a roof that night. But I hungered and ate. I ate near midnight at a little inn over toward Birmingham, and miles away from my home. Instinctively I had avoided the crests where the bonfire crowds gathered, but here there were many people, and I had to share a table with a man who had some useless mortgage deeds to burn. I talked to him about them—but my soul stood at a great distance behind my lips.

Soon each hilltop bore a little tulip-shaped flame flower. Little black figures clustered round and dotted the base of its petals, and as for the rest of the multitude abroad, the kindly night swallowed them up. By leaving the roads and clear paths and wandering in the fields I contrived to keep alone, though the confused noise of voices and the roaring and crackling of great fires was always near me.

I wandered into a lonely meadow, and presently in a hollow of deep shadows I lay down to stare at the stars. I lay hidden in the darkness, and ever and again the sough and uproar of the Beltane fires that were burning up the withered follies of a vanished age, and the shouting of the people passing through the fires and praying to be delivered from the prison of themselves, reached my ears....

And I thought of my mother, and then of my new loneliness and the hunger of my heart for Nettie.

I thought of many things that night, but chiefly of the overflowing personal love and tenderness that had come to me in the wake of the Change, of the greater need, the unsatisfied need in which I stood, for this one person who could fulfill all my desires. So long as my mother had lived, she had in a measure held my heart, given me a food these emotions could live upon, and mitigated that emptiness of spirit, but now suddenly that one possible comfort had left me. There had been many at the season of the Change who had thought that this great enlargement of mankind would abolish personal love; but indeed it had only made it finer, fuller, more vitally necessary. They had thought that, seeing men now were all full of the joyful passion to make and do, and glad and loving and of willing service to all their fellows, there would be no need of the one intimate trusting communion that had been the finest thing of the former life. And indeed, so far as this was a matter of advantage and the struggle for existence, they were right. But so far as it was a matter of the spirit and the fine perceptions of life, it was altogether wrong.

We had indeed not eliminated personal love, we had but stripped it of its base wrappings, of its pride, its suspicions, its mercenary and competitive elements, until at last it stood up in our minds stark, shining and invincible. Through all the fine, divaricating ways of the new life, it grew ever more evident, there were for everyone certain persons, mysteriously and indescribably in the key of one's self, whose mere presence gave pleasure, whose mere existence was interest, whose idiosyncrasy blended with accident to make a completing and predominant harmony for their predestined lovers. They were the essential thing in life. Without them the fine brave show of the rejuvenated world was a caparisoned steed without a rider, a bowl without a flower, a theater without a play.... And to me that night of Beltane, it was as clear as white flames that Nettie, and Nettie alone, roused those harmonies in me. And she had gone! I had sent her from me; I knew not whither she had gone. I had in my first virtuous foolishness cut her out of my life forever!

So I saw it then, and I lay unseen in the darkness and called upon Nettie, and wept for her, lay upon my face and wept for her, while the glad people went to and fro, and the smoke streamed thick across the distant stars, and the red reflections, the shadows and the fluctuating glares, danced over the face of the world.

No! the Change had freed us from our baser passions indeed, from habitual and mechanical concupiscence and mean issues and coarse imaginings, but from the passions of love it had not freed us. It had but brought the lord of life, Eros, to his own. All through the long sorrow of that night I, who had rejected him, confessed his sway with tears and unappeasable regrets....

I cannot give the remotest guess of when I rose up, nor of my tortuous wanderings in the valleys between the midnight fires, nor how I evaded the laughing and rejoicing multitudes who went streaming home between three and four, to resume their lives, swept and garnished, stripped and clean. But at dawn, when the ashes of the world's gladness were ceasing to glow—it was a bleak dawn that made me shiver in my thin summer clothes—I came across a field to a little copse full of dim blue hyacinths. A queer sense of familiarity arrested my steps, and I stood puzzled. Then I was moved to go a dozen paces from the path, and at once a singularly misshapen tree hitched itself into a notch in my memory. This was the place! Here I had stood, there I had placed my old kite, and shot with my revolver, learning to use it, against the day when I should encounter Verrall.

Kite and revolver had gone now, and all my hot and narrow past, its last vestiges had shriveled and vanished in the whirling gusts of the Beltane fires. So I walked through a world of gray ashes at last, back to the great house in which the dead, deserted image of my dear lost mother lay.

3

I came back to Lowchester House very tired, very wretched; exhausted by my fruitless longing for Nettie. I had no thought of what lay before me.

A miserable attraction drew me into the great house to look again on the stillness that had been my mother's face, and as I came into that room, Anna, who had been sitting by the open window, rose to meet me. She had the air of one who waits. She, too, was pale with watching; all night she had watched between the dead within and the Beltane fires abroad, and longed for my coming. I stood mute between her and the bedside....

"Willie," she whispered, and eyes and body seemed incarnate pity.

An unseen presence drew us together. My mother's face

became resolute, commanding. I turned to Anna as a child may turn to its nurse. I put my hands about her strong shoulders, she folded me to her, and my heart gave way. I buried my face in her breast and clung to her weakly, and burst into a passion of weeping....

She held me with hungry arms. She whispered to me, "There, there!" as one whispers comfort to a child.... Suddenly she was kissing me. She kissed me with a hungry intensity of passion, on my cheeks, on my lips. She kissed me on my lips with lips that were salt with tears. And I returned her kisses....

Then abruptly we desisted and stood apart—looking at one another.

4

It seems to me as if the intense memory of Nettie vanished utterly out of my mind at the touch of Anna's lips. I loved Anna.

We went to the council of our group—commune it was then called—and she was given me in marriage, and within a year she had borne me a son. We saw much of one another, and talked ourselves very close together. My faithful friend she became and has been always, and for a time we were passionate lovers. Always she has loved me and kept my soul full of tender gratitude and love for her; always when we met our hands and eyes clasped in friendly greeting, all through our lives from that hour we have been each other's secure help and refuge, each other's ungrudging fastness of help and sweetly frank and open speech....And after a little while my love and desire for Nettie returned as though it had never faded away.

No one will have a difficulty now in understanding how that could be, but in the evil days of the world malaria, that would have been held to be the most impossible thing. I should have had to crush that second love out of my thoughts, to have kept it secret from Anna, to have lied about it to all the world. The old-world theory was there was only one love—we who float upon a sea of love find that hard to understand. The whole nature of a man was supposed to go out to the one girl or woman who possessed him, her whole nature to go out to him. Nothing was left over—it was a discreditable thing to have any overplus at all. They formed a secret secluded system of two, two and such children as she bore him. All other women he was held bound to find no beauty in, no sweetness, no interest; and she likewise, in no other man. The old-time men and women went apart in couples, into defensive little houses, like beasts into little pits, and in these "homes" they sat down purposing to love, but really coming very soon to jealous watching of this extravagant mutual proprietorship. All freshness passed very speedily out of their love, out of their conversation, all pride out of their common life. To permit each other freedom was blank dishonor. That I and Anna should love, and after our love-journey together, go about our separate lives and dine at the public tables, until the advent of her motherhood, would have seemed a terrible strain upon our unmitigable loyalty. And that I should have it in me to go on loving Nettie—who loved in different manner both Verrall and me—would have outraged the very quintessence of the old convention.

In the old days love was a cruel proprietary thing. But now Anna could let Nettie live in the world of my mind, as freely as a rose will suffer the presence of white lilies. If I could hear notes that were not in her compass, she was glad, because she loved me, that I should listen to other music than hers. And she, too, could see the beauty of Nettie. Life is so rich and generous now, giving friendship, and a thousand tender interests and helps and comforts, that no one stints another of the full realization of all possibilities of beauty. For me from the beginning Nettie was the figure of beauty, the shape and color of the divine principle that lights the world. For everyone there are certain types, certain faces and forms, gestures, voices and intonations that have that inexplicable unanalyzable quality. These come through the crowd of kindly friendly fellow men and women—one's own. These touch one mysteriously, stir deeps that must otherwise slumber, pierce and interpret the world. To refuse this interpretation is to refuse the sun, to darken and deaden all life....I loved Nettie, I loved all who were like her, in the measure that they were like her, in voice, or eyes, or form, or smile. And between my wife and me there was no bitterness that the great goddess, the life-giver, Aphrodite, Queen of the Living Seas, came to my imagination so. It qualified our mutual love not at all, since now in our changed world love is unstinted; it is a golden net about our globe that nets all humanity together.

I thought of Nettie much, and always movingly beautiful things restored me to her, all fine music, all pure deep color, all tender and solemn things. The stars were hers, and the mystery of moonlight; the sun she wore in her hair, powdered finely, beaten into gleams and threads of sunlight in the wisps and strands of her hair....Then suddenly one day a letter came to me from her, in her unaltered clear handwriting, but in a new language of expression, telling me many things. She had learned of my mother's death, and the thought of me had grown so strong as to pierce the silence I had imposed on her. We wrote to one another—like common friends with a certain restraint between us at first, and with a great longing to see her once more arising in my heart. For a time I left that hunger unexpressed, and then I was moved to tell it to her. And so on New Year's Day in the Year Four, she came to Lowchester and me. How I remember that coming, across the gulf of fifty years! I went out across the park to meet her, so that we should meet alone. The windless morning was clear and cold, the ground new carpeted with snow, and all the trees motionless lace and glitter of frosty crystals. The rising sun had touched the white with a spirit of gold, and my heart beat and sang within me. I remember now the snowy shoulder of the down, sunlit against the bright blue sky. And presently I saw the woman I loved coming through the white still trees....

I had made a goddess of Nettie, and behold she was a fellow creature! She came, warm-wrapped tremulous, to me, with the tender promise of tears in her eyes, with her hands outstretched and that dear smile quivering upon her lips. She stepped out of the dream I had made of her, a thing of needs and regrets and human kindliness. Her hands as I took them were a little cold. The goddess shone through her indeed, glowed in all her body, she was a worshipful temple of love for me—yes. But I could feel, like a thing new discovered, the texture and sinews of her living, her dear personal and mortal hands....

Epilogue

The Window of the Tower

This was as much as this pleasant-looking, gray-haired man had written. I had been lost in his story throughout the earlier portions of it, forgetful of the writer and his gracious room, and the high tower in which he was sitting. But gradually, as I drew near the end, the sense of strangeness returned to me. It was more and more evident to me that this was a different humanity from any I had known, unreal, having different customs, different beliefs, different interpretations, different emotions. It was no mere change in conditions and institutions the comet had wrought. It had made a change of heart and mind. In a manner it had dehumanized the world, robbed it of its spites, its little intense jealousies, its inconsistencies, its humor. At the end, and particularly after the death of his mother, I felt his story had slipped away from my sympathies altogether. Those Beltane fires had burned something in him that worked living still and unsubdued in me, that rebelled in particular at that return of Nettie. I became a little inattentive. I no longer felt with him, nor gathered a sense of complete understanding from his phrases. His Lord Eros indeed! He and these transfigured people—they were beautiful and noble people, like the people one sees in great pictures, like the gods of noble sculpture, but they had no nearer fellowship than these to men. As the Change was realized, with every stage of realization the gulf widened and it was harder to follow his words.

I put down the last fascicle of all, and met his friendly eyes. It was hard to dislike him.

I felt a subtle embarrassment in putting the question that perplexed me. And yet it seemed so material to me I had to put it. "And did you—?" I asked. "Were you— lovers?"

His eyebrows rose. "Of course."

"But your wife—?"

It was manifest he did not understand me.

I hesitated still more. I was perplexed by a conviction of baseness. "But—" I began. "You remained lovers?"

"Yes." I have grave doubts if I understood him. Or he me.

I made a still more courageous attempt. "And had Nettie no other lovers?"

"A beautiful woman like that! I know not how many loved beauty in her, nor what she found in others. But we four from that time were very close, you understand, we were friends, helpers, personal lovers in a world of lovers."

"Four?"

"There was Verrall.'

Then suddenly it came to me that the thoughts that stirred in my mind were sinister and base, that the queer suspicions, the coarseness and coarse jealousies of my old world were over and done with for these more finely living souls. "You made," I said, trying to be liberal minded, "a home together."

"A home!" He looked at me, and, I know not why, I glanced down at my feet. What a clumsy, ill-made thing a boot is, and how hard and colorless seemed my clothing! How harshly I stood out amidst these fine, perfect things. I had a moment of rebellious detestation. I wanted to get out of all this. After all, it wasn't my style. I wanted intensely to say something that would bring him down a peg, make sure, as it were, of my suspicions by launching an offensive accusation. I looked up and he was standing.

"I forgot," he said. "You are pretending the old world is still going on. A home!"

He put out his hand, and quite noiselessly the great window widened down to us, and the splendid nearer prospect of that dreamland city was before me. There for one clear moment I saw it; its galleries and open spaces, its tres of golden fruit and crystal waters, its music and rejoicing, love and beauty without ceasing flowing through its varied and intricate streets. And the nearer people I saw now directly and plainly, and no longer in the distorted mirror that hung overhead. They really did not justify my suspicions, and yet—! They were such people as one sees on earth—save that they were changed. How can I express that change? As a woman is changed in the eyes of her lover, as a woman is changed by the love of a lover. They were exalted....

I stood up beside him and looked out. I was a little flushed, my ears a little reddened, by the inconvenience of my curiosity, and by my uneasy sense of profound moral differences. He was taller than I....

"This is our home," he said smiling, and with thoughtful eyes on me.

About the author:

H. G. Wells

Herbert George Wells was the son of a poor British tradesman. Through a scholarship, Wells was able to attend the Royal School of Science in London, where he studied biology.

H.G. Wells aspired to become a journalist or a teacher, but with the successful publication of THE TIME MACHINE in 1895, he turned his attention to literature. The author of over 100 books, he is best known for his science-fiction stories, including THE INVISIBLE MAN and THE WAR OF THE WORLDS. In the latter, he describes a Martian invasion of Earth. In 1938, a dramatic reading of the radio adaptation of this novel brought panic to thousands of listeners in the U.S. Wells died at the age of 80 in 1946.